Sabotage

A Christine Lane Mystery #4

Dianne Scott

Danforth Press

BOOKS IN THE CHRISTINE LANE MYSTERY
SERIES

FINAL LOOK: *A Christine Lane Mystery Book 1*
MISSING: *A Christine Lane Mystery Book 2*
LOST AND FOUND: *A Christine Lane Mystery Book 3*
SABOTAGE:*A Christine Lane Mystery Book 4*

These books are standalone mysteries and can be read independently
or in order.

Praise for the Christine Lane Mystery series

"I've just devoured *Final Look*. I especially enjoyed the historical and
political insights, the nostalgic trip back to Toronto's hippie-dippy
days, Scott's loving, detailed description of the Toronto Islands and
the chase scene!" *-Pearle Gemyndig*

"Original and entrancing." *-Maureen Jennings*, author of the *Murdoch Mysteries*

"This was one of the best 'Who dunnits' I have read in a while.
This was an exciting page turner. Keeps you guessing all the way.
I was so enthralled that I read this book straight through. Highly
recommended by this bookworm."   *—Roseanne Doiron*

"Take a boat trip out to the Toronto Islands, circa the 1960s, when
skirt-wearing cop Christine Lane takes on bad guys and the male
local constabulary in Scott's debut novel. A fun romp! *-Robert
Rotenberg*, best-selling author of *City Hall*

Chapter 1

July 1969

Policewoman Christine Lane glided on her bike, careful that the chain grease didn't smear her nylons or uniform skirt. The shriek of children's voices carried across the lagoon from the amusement park. It was mid-July, and Centreville was filled with the cotton-candy-smeared faces of children lining up for bumper cars and roller coasters.

She pumped her legs as the path ascended, following the meandering lagoon, the summer heat muted by the shade of the overhanging willows. After her four-month undercover assignment in Yorkville, she was content to return to sandy beaches, cooling breezes, lapping water and friendly locals.

One thing marring her return was that she and her patrol partner were on the outs. PC Geoffrey Fillingham was currently on the other end of the Island, patrolling alone. Christine shook her head. Fillingham would come around.

As she rounded a turn, the Algonquin Island Bridge came into view, baskets of potted flowers dotting its arched frame like a colorful necklace. It led to a community of a hundred families trying to keep their tenuous hold on their homes. The local government was evicting residents as their leases expired, with the goal of turning the Island into a large public park.

She would check in with Algonquin Island residents later, visit the marina and bike to Seneca Avenue with its spectacular view of downtown Toronto across the Inner Harbor.

For now, the blueberry scones Mrs. Polotov had baked for her return were waiting. Christine would go on her dinner break when she arrived at her friend's house on Ward's Island. They would drink iced tea as they caught up on the last months of Island news.

The radio on Christine's belt squawked. "25-01. Citizen reporting vandalism at…" the dispatcher's voice paused, "68 Lakeshore. Request a response."

Christine braked and pulled the radio from her belt. "Dispatch, 25-01, PW Lane. I'm in the vicinity. Responding to complainant at 68 Lakeshore."

"Confirmed, 10-4."

Christine pedaled hard along the pathway, the gravel stones now parallel slabs of concrete. She took a sharp right turn toward the boardwalk that lined the southeastern edge of the Island. In a few seconds, a vista opened in between the trees like a box window featuring cobalt skies over the twinkling waters of Lake Ontario.

Her tires bumped rhythmically over the wooden slats as she headed east along the boardwalk. The waves slapped the seawall beside her, white spray pluming the air, spotting the cedar boards.

Stray brown hairs whipped across her face. Christine smiled. How she had missed this feeling of exhilaration, of wind and sun and the elements that were the bane and the balm of Island patrol.

Her bike slowed as the easterly wind pressed her, and she pondered which house had been vandalized. Patches of overgrown grass on her left were the remnants of the front yards of grand houses that had lined the southern part of the Island, occupied by businesspeople, yacht club members and Toronto's elite. Over the past twenty years, the houses had been bulldozed, reclaimed by a government intent on replacing the residential neighborhoods with parkland.

A string of modest houses still stood along the end of Lakeshore Avenue. Sixty-eight Lakeshore must be one of those. Through petitions, protests and court battles, these residents had held on to their homes. Christine wondered if the vandalism call pertained to an empty house. Sometimes tenants left, and the abandoned house remained until the city boated over an excavator. Within a couple of hours, the home would be reduced to a pile of bricks, snapped timbers and broken windows.

Biking past the first group of houses, Christine spotted bathing suits and towels pegged on laundry lines and hung over porch rails. Gardens were crowded with irises competing for space with roses, with just enough room for a table and chairs for outdoor dining. Houses were painted in pastel hues of green, blue and yellow. Abstract metal sculptures adorned one front lawn, reflecting the artistic streak of Islanders who painted, sculpted, wove, sang and composed. Mind you, there were also businesspeople, housewives, veterinarians, plumbers and politicians calling the Island their home, all attracted by the natural beauty and sense of community.

Number 72. Then an empty lot. Sixty-eight Lakeshore was next.
Christine angled her handlebars and rode onto the vacant lot.
Oh, my goodness.
She had expected a broken window or an expletive spray-painted on a shed. *But this.*
The front lawn was a lumpy mess. Grass was pockmarked with holes dug two feet deep, roots lacing the openings. The garden looked like it had been tilled of its plants, the brown earth dotted with divots and littered with errant green leaves and snapped flower heads. Roots and broken branches lay across the grass as if the plants had been hacked out of their homes and kidnapped. White, pink and

purple flower petals sprinkled the ground like confetti. A party gone awry.

"You're here," a female voice said, followed by the sound of a screen door banging.

Christine walked up the center path of the yard, regarding the well-dressed woman on the porch. Females on Ward's Island usually wore shorts, t-shirts or beach dresses in the summer, sometimes thrown over bathing suits. This woman looked attired for a luncheon at the Royal Canadian Yacht Club: white linen dress, low heels, brown hair pulled high into a beehive, tasteful gold necklace, watch and earrings.

"Are you the police?"

"Yes, ma'am," Christine responded. "PW Lane. Toronto Island Police." She opened the flap of her police-issue purse and grabbed her memo book.

The woman shook her head. "Of course, they wouldn't send a *real* officer."

Christine frowned as she pulled a pen out of her front uniform pocket. She had heard this line before, how a policewoman was inferior to a policeman. Less gravitas. Less authority. "I'm a police officer, ma'am." Christine pointed to the metal badge on her hat brim engraved with her number, W16. "I've been on Island patrol for over a year."

The woman harrumphed and then gestured to a pair of white rattan chairs with floral cushions. They sat beside each other, a circular rattan table between them. Black cast-iron urns bracketed the porch, devoid of flowers, soil scattered around the bases.

Christine poised her pen over her memo book. "Your name, ma'am."

"Mrs. Douglas Martin. Barbara Martin. You must know my husband," she added.

Christine knew quite a few families on Ward's Island, but not all of them. She shook her head.

Mrs. Martin's brown eyes widened as if Christine was a dolt. "My husband is the new superintendent of Parks and Recreation." Her tone made the occupation sound akin to being prime minister.

Parks and Recreation was a city-funded department that supervised the city's parks, lawns, gardens, outdoor sports facilities, beaches, washrooms and change rooms. The superintendent had influence on Metro Council and was given a home on Toronto Island to reside.

Mrs. Martin retrieved a package of Virginia Slims from the bottom shelf of the side table. After lighting a cigarette with the silver lighter that had been tucked in the package, she gestured to the front lawn. "We've been pillaged."

Christine's gaze turned to the overturned yard.

"The back is the same," Mrs. Martin remarked, then took a drag on her cigarette, her peach lipstick coloring the tip.

"Any other vandalism, aside from the gardens?"

Mrs. Martin's upper lip curled. "Isn't that enough?"

"Was the house broken into? Any items missing?"

"The inside is a dumpy mess. Doors are scratched, the floors worn and the furniture sags. The wallpaper is fifty-years old." She sighed. "But that's not vandalism. Just the poor taste of the previous owner."

Christine raised her eyebrows. "So, no concerns inside the house?"

"Correct." Her tone was clipped. "My husband secured the house for us this past Monday. It was given to us by the city commissioner. Do you know who that is?"

Christine frowned. Commissioner Harry Westmore was a leading voice in the city's urban policy planning. He was in the news regularly.

"Yes," Christine responded. The woman liked to name-drop. And was condescending to boot. She wouldn't make too many friends this way on the Island, especially if the Martins were friends of the commissioner, who was bent on making the Island parkland.

Mrs. Martin said, "I arrived this afternoon to take measurements for curtains and rugs. Record the room sizes. Meet with the phone company for installation of our new line. Our move-in date is next week."

"Was the lawn like this before?"

"No!" Mrs. Martin cried. "That's why I called the police. We were here Monday. The gardens were lovely. One of the nicest on Ward's Island. Roses, hydrangeas, lilies, irises. A Japanese maple out front. A vegetable garden in the back." She took a long drag on her cigarette and exhaled. "It's the reason we picked this house in the first place."

"When you were here three days ago on July 14th, the lawns were fine?" Christine asked.

"Yes, the outside gardens were intact." She paused. "The inside was another story. It was crammed with boxes and furniture and...people."

Christine looked up from her notebook. "People?"

Mrs. Martin shivered with disgust. "Yes, the tenants were still here."

"Who were they?"

"The Merriweathers."

Christine nodded. Of course. Now she remembered this house...seeing Carol Merriweather watering the garden, her three children racing to the beach, the grandmother following behind with a bag full of snacks. "Any scheduled services to the house between Monday and today?"

Mrs. Martin glanced up as she thought. "The family left by end of day Monday. I requested a housekeeper to clean on Tuesday."

"Were the plants here then?"

"I assume so. The housekeeper didn't mention anything other than saying furniture and boxes had been left behind. I had them removed."

"Who is the housekeeper?"

"Judith..." Mrs. Martin waved her hand through the cigarette smoke, "something or other. She's a local."

Christine made a mental note to find out Judith's last name. "Where did you send the house contents?"

"To the dump."

Christine blinked. "Was there no forwarding address?"

Mrs. Martin shrugged.

"Can I see the backyard?"

Mrs. Martin crushed her cigarette in an ashtray and led Christine along the side of the house to the backyard.

The garden on the left was dug out and overturned, root tendrils dangling in brown clods of soil. The grass in the middle was flattened, as if tromped on by many shoes, with parallel lines crisscrossing the yard from the wheels of a wagon or dolly. A brown rectangle in the back corner had been the vegetable garden, Popsicle sticks inked with labels such as carrots, peppers, leeks and potatoes angled in the soil.

Christine scribbled her observations in her notebook.

Mrs. Martin surveyed the yard, arms crossed.

Christine flipped her notebook closed and placed it in her purse. "Thank you for the information. I'll check with the neighbors, see if they noticed any suspicious behaviors so we can pinpoint a time window for the vandalism."

"Ha!" Mrs. Martin said. Her right arm gestured east toward the Ward Island community. "They're in on it."

"Who?" Christine asked.

Mrs. Martin's eyebrows rose. "My neighbors."

"Who, specifically?"

"All the Islanders."

Christine frowned. "It could be teenagers. Or drunk college students pulling a prank. A mainlander."

"Were you born yesterday, Miss...Miss... What was your name again?"

"PW Lane."

"PW Lane. No one wants us here. On the Island. In this house." She gestured with her arm toward the adjacent houses. "They want to continue squatting illegally. Keep the Island to themselves. And my husband and Metro Council are trying to remedy that."

They walked in silence to the front of the house.

"I'd start with the Merriweathers," Mrs. Martin suggested.

"Did they leave voluntarily?"

"A legal eviction. They were squatting on city property. Their lease had expired."

Isabel Merriweather, the grandmother, had lived in the house most of her life. The Merriweather family must have been on Ward's Island for over fifty years.

Christine jotted a few notes. "Thank you for your time. We will follow up after we've had a chance to investigate."

Mrs. Martin said, "My husband will be speaking to your sergeant about this violation. And the chief of police."

Great. Christine grabbed her bike and rolled it onto the boardwalk. Just what she needed, the brass breathing down her neck. And she was still on the outs with her partner. Her first day back on Island patrol was off to an outstanding start.

Chapter 2

Christine rolled her bike across the boardwalk and leaned it against a lamppost. She scanned the nine houses east of the Martins' that ended at Withrow Street.

The adjacent neighbor was George Mackey, a long-time fireman on the Island. He opened the door in shorts and sandals, gray hair tousled as if he had been lying down. When Christine asked him about the missing vegetation, he laughed uproariously.

"Serves 'em right for kicking out the Merriweathers. Isabel spent years on her gardens. Guess the Martins don't get to benefit from her green thumb."

"Did you see or hear anything?" she persisted as she stood on his front porch.

He shook his head. "I've been doing twelve-hour shifts all week. My wife's in Scarborough with the grandkids. When I've come home, I eat and collapse. Just woke up from a nap now. I haven't heard a peep outside. But I wouldn't have noticed an airplane landing next door if I was sleeping."

Christine interviewed four more neighbors. All seemed surprised at the vandalism, hands going to their mouths in shock, followed by laughter. And none had seen or heard anything untoward in the past week. Four houses didn't answer Christine's knock. The families were likely on the beach or the children in camp. She'd return later.

It was hard to tell if the neighbors knew about the vandalism. They seemed genuinely surprised. But the removal of flowers, bushes, potted plants and a vegetable garden was not a clandestine activity. Someone would have seen the spades, wheelbarrows and wagons. Since it was a car-free island, with only emergency services, Parks and Recreation and hydro vehicles allowed, Christine wondered how they had removed the small tree.

Mrs. Martin had been right about one thing: if Douglas Martin supported Metro Council's policy to evict Islanders, he would be public enemy number one. The locals would not welcome the family, especially if they had supplanted the Merriweathers.

Christine navigated around a family of beachgoers coming off the sand. She should patrol the beach on her way to Mrs. Polotov, check if any of the sunbathing locals had noticed activity at 68 Lakeshore. And check that beachgoers were having clean fun—no alcohol or bonfires.

Ward's Island Beach was not usually a problem. It was filled with local families, kids from the Island's supervision camp and mainlanders attracted to its quiet ambiance compared with Centre Island's boisterous Manitou Beach.

Leaving her bike against a tree trunk, Christine beelined to the shoreline, sand trickling into the heels of her Oxfords. She smiled anyway, happy to see the tossed beach balls, sandcastle making and splashing children in the shallows.

She wandered amongst the beachcombers, saying hello to families she recognized, asking them casually if they had noticed any activity amongst their neighbors. None had. Moving on, she admired a shell handed to her by a toddler in a sandy bathing suit and reminded tourists that the last ferry was at eleven o'clock.

She angled off the beach to follow a path through the sandy grass. She should quickly check the Eastern Gap, a thoroughfare for boats between Toronto Island and the portlands. Its narrow width meant the waves crashed against its concrete walls at all angles, making it a dangerous place to swim. The choppy waters were a magnet for local kids who liked to jump in the wavy current, despite signs prohibiting swimming and denoting a dangerous undertow.

The dirt pathway toward the Eastern Gap was surrounded by overarching trees; it felt like she was walking through a lush botanical tunnel. Suddenly, the trail opened up. The sun was bright and yolk hot as she stood on the deserted concrete pier. To her right was a hill of boulders that marked the eastern boundary of Ward's Island Beach. Across the Gap were docking facilities for cruise and cargo ships. Walking north along the ten-foot-wide pavement, Christine spied a freighter at the Redpath factory on the mainland, sitting low in the water with its containers of raw sugar cane.

All clear. Christine smiled, even though she was hot in her dark wool uniform. Time for her dinner break. In less than five minutes, she would be sipping lemonade, pastry in hand, with Mrs. Polotov.

What is that? Floating in the water?

Christine ran over to the edge of the pier.

It was a person, bobbing in the waves, auburn hair floating in a starburst around the submerged head.

Christine kneeled at the edge, the water a six-foot drop.

He could be swimming, holding his breath in a dead man's float. Christine stared at the back of the white t-shirt, willing him to turn over.

She counted to ten.

Darn it! Darn it! Darn it!

"Sir, can you hear me?" she shouted. "Come up for air! Raise your head!" A few more seconds ticked away. She stood up, scanning left and right for a safety pole or ring. Nothing.

She slid her purse off her shoulder to the ground, then unpinned her hat and tossed it on the concrete. Next was her belt, shoes and jacket in quick succession.

She grabbed her radio from her discarded belt. "Dispatch, 25-01. PW Lane; 10-32. I repeat, 10-32. The Eastern Gap. Attempting rescue."

She wasn't the best swimmer. Backup better arrive soon.

She sat on the concrete edge then pushed herself off, slicing into the water like a knife, the quick coolness shocking her. Thrashing to the top, she forced her panic down. The water was deep, and the waves bounced off the wall and back, splashing her face. Nothing to hold on to. The wall was flat and unscalable.

It's okay. I'm okay.

Dog-paddling over to the man, she tried to recall the life-saving techniques Fillingham had taught her last summer. *Turn the person on their back. Ensure their mouth and nose are out of the water. Curl your arm around their shoulders and under their neck and swim them back to shore.*

She touched the man's shoulder from behind. Suddenly, she was shoved underwater and then punched in the stomach. Her mouth gasped open, and she swallowed water.

Choking, she kicked frantically, her left leg hitting something hard as her arms flailed, pushing her to the surface.

She broke the surface, took an immense breath and then plunged again, pulled by something hooked to her left leg.

Underwater, the auburn-haired man lunged at her. She kicked him in the chest with her right foot.

With tremendous effort, she swooshed herself to the surface but was immediately pulled down by the weight around her leg. She grabbed her ankle, trying to free herself. Something hung around her foot. A wire? A fish trap? It was cutting into her skin.

She was grabbed around the middle and pulled to the surface. The man held her from behind. She elbowed him hard in the gut, and his hold loosened. She began sinking again.

"Stop fighting!" the man roared. "I'm trying to help."

She turned just as she went under, a quick image of a tanned man with dark auburn hair and a beard. *Karl Olsen.* He lived on Ward's Island. Christine had met him and his roommates on a patrol call. They were sunbathing nude on their rooftops, and Christine threatened to charge them with public indecency.

The surrounding water swirled as Karl grabbed her around the waist. This time, she let him. She gasped as they surfaced, feeling her ankle bending, hurting. The cord was sawing into her. Her foot felt wet, as if it were bleeding.

"Hey!"

Karl and Christine looked up. Fillingham held up a safety ring and tossed it to them.

Karl grabbed the orange ring with one hand. "I work for a fisheries project. A wire from our water collection equipment is wrapped around her foot. It's anchored with a twenty-pound weight, so it's pulling her down. I got to unwind it or cut it off."

"Here," Fillingham said. He pulled cutting pliers from a case on his belt. Lying on his stomach, he held them out.

Karl released his hold on Christine to swim over and retrieve them.

Christine took a breath as she slipped underwater again. A metal safety pole appeared beside her, and she grasped the end with the crook. She was pulled up, the pain in her ankle causing her to gasp.

"I got you," Fillingham said.

Christine gritted her teeth as her foot bent painfully underneath her, one arm hooked through the pole as she bobbed in the turbulent water.

"Don't panic," Fillingham said, squatting on the pier. "I'm holding on to you."

"My leg," she said.

"I know. He's going to untie you. Hold on tight to the pole. Can you do that?"

Christine's hands clutched the pole, her arms bent in rigid tension. Staring into her partner's serious blue eyes, she nodded.

"What's going on? Where's Karl?" A short, wiry man with a receding hairline appeared behind Fillingham, a square case in one hand and a knapsack in the other. He dropped both to the ground.

"Who are you?" said Fillingham.

"Phil. Phil Merton. I work with Karl on a fisheries project."

Christine felt fingers on her left ankle, feeling around, loosening the wire.

Karl burst to the surface. "I've almost got it!" He plunged back down.

Christine said through gritted teeth, "I have to go under. It's hurting too much."

Fillingham said, "Hold on to the pole while you go under. Give it a shake when you are ready, and I'll pull you back up."

Christine slid under water, sinking low until the weight on her leg lessened. She could hear the muted burble of voices above her.

Fingers gripped her left heel. Metal pressed against her ankle. Then a release, the wire loosening, and then a second release. Her foot was free.

She yanked on the pole and was pulled to the surface. She held on to the metal crook, her foot throbbing, as she floated on her back, undulating with the waves, her skirt like a dark flag on the lake.

Karl surfaced beside her, snippers in hand.

"Show me her leg," Fillingham said to Karl.

With a nod from Christine, Karl carefully raised Christine's left shin out of the water. Her nylons were shredded. Her foot pulsed an angry red, already swollen, with scratches and deep rings crisscrossing her anklebone. One line oozed blood. None of the cuts looked like they needed stitches.

"I'm okay," Christine said, easing her foot back into the water. "It's not broken."

"What happened here?" Phil said.

Karl said, "Her leg caught on the wire attached to a water sampling jug."

"Geez," Phil said. "Did she break any bottles? Do we have to rerig everything?"

Fillingham frowned. "Let's get her out alive first before we worry about the equipment."

"What was she doing here in the first place?" Phil asked.

Fillingham ignored Phil's query. "Karl, you've been a tremendous help. Let's see if we can lift her out."

Christine pulled up in alarm.

Fillingham continued, "It's a long way up. I'll pull on the hook, and Karl, if you push her from behind, we should be able to get her out."

"No!" Christine yelled. She wasn't going to be hauled out of the water like a prize salmon. She didn't have the strength to hold on to the pole as they lifted her. And she was too heavy. They'd drop her back in the water. In a calmer voice, she added, "I just need a minute. I'll pull myself out."

Fillingham said, "How? The wall is six feet high."

"I'll swim to the beach."

"From here?" Fillingham's tone was incredulous.

She heard the wail of a fire engine. *Great.* She'd soon have the Island firemen in fits of laughter.

"Call the firemen off," she directed Fillingham. "Let Dispatch know it's a false alarm." She let go of the safety pole and started a sloppy front crawl south, head above water, kicking with her good foot.

She heard Fillingham said, "I'll go with her."

"I have to fix the equipment. That's why I was in the water in the first place," said Karl.

Fillingham said, "Phil. Can you watch Karl? Make sure we don't have another drowning. I'll leave the safety ring here."

Phil mumbled his assent.

Christine kept swimming, bobbing in the waves, mouth closed to avoid swallowing water. The men's voices diminished as she swam, her clothes weighing her down. Her breathing grew rapid as she tired in the choppy water, hearing Fillingham's police boots pounding beside her on the concrete pier.

"Lane, grab the pole," Fillingham said.

She could sense the safety pole in the water beside her, pacing her.

"I'm not being pulled out!" she yelled above the smack of the waves against the pier.

"Hold on to the pole," he said. "I'll pull you to the rocks by the beach. You can get out there."

"I don't need your help." But her strokes were getting weaker. She was making slow headway, kicking with one leg, her injured leg dragging behind her.

"Please, Christine."

Christine paused her thrashing and turned to meet Fillingham's concerned glance. In a part of her brain, she registered he was talking to her again. Acting like her partner.

She grabbed the pole, looping her arm through the crook, and let her legs drag behind her as Fillingham walked quickly along the pier parallel to her, pulling her like she was the mechanical rabbit at a greyhound racetrack.

After a minute, she approached the mound of gray and white rocks that capped the eastern edge of the shoreline. She would have to climb the boulders and make her way onto the beach on the other side.

Fillingham swirled her around the end of the concrete wall. "There's a spot there." He pointed at a sandy space between rocks.

Grabbing a boulder with both hands, she lifted her good leg out of the water and pulled. She had just enough momentum to land on the edge of a large, flat rock. She collapsed over it, face down, wishing she could lie there forever and avoid the inevitable humiliation of her rescue.

Chapter 3

"Lane, you okay?" Fillingham's voice.

"Go away," Christine said, her voice muffled against the rock.

"Let me check—"

"Go away. I'm fine." She didn't look up.

"I have to meet the firefighters. They're parked by the beach."

"Tell them to go back to the station. Everything's all right."

After a pause, she heard him scrabble away over the rocks.

She lay there, the late afternoon sun drying the back of her white cotton shirt. She knew she'd have to move soon, make her way over the rocky hill back to her bike.

Something wet touched her thumb. "Ah!" She jerked her hand away.

She looked up and got a lick on her cheek.

A small dog with white, gray and brown hair, a terrier mix, stared at her with alert brown eyes, tail wagging, mouth open in what looked like a smile.

Christine's mouth quirked. She was being rescued by a dog, like the St. Bernards in the movies. She pushed herself up so she was sitting on the rock, avoiding weight on her injured foot. Immediately, the dog jumped into her lap. Christine could she was a female.

Christine was taken aback but automatically curled her arm around the dog's silky chest. A few dry leaves stuck to the fur, and Christine carefully pulled them out.

Growing up, she never had a pet. There hadn't been enough food in the pantry for Christine and her siblings, let alone a dog. This one seemed friendly enough. And it was so light—it must be ten pounds, fifteen at most. She could carry it under her arm.

"Okay, girl." She placed the dog on a rock beside her as she stood up. "Time to face the music."

"Ow!" Christine placed her weight on her left leg and felt a jab of pain. She must have sprained it. Looking down, she observed that only her right leg was sheathed in nylons. She quickly pulled the tattered hosiery off.

She would hobble back to her bike. And take a painkiller at the station.

"Off you go," she said to the dog, gesturing with her arms.

The dog wagged her tail, staying put.

Carefully, Christine climbed over the mound of rocks, taking her time, trying to keep her weight on her good leg, the dog bounding ahead and then back to her.

When Christine made it onto the beach, she paused, teeth gritted against the pain. The dog licked her leg. "It's going to be a slow journey back to the station," she said out loud.

A family of five looked up at the barefoot policewoman standing by the rocks, but most beachcombers were suntanning with eyes closed or cavorting in the water.

Dragging her foot behind her, she walked across the sand, the dog pacing her. She spotted Fillingham jogging along the grassy area parallel to the beach, followed by a firefighter pulling a wheeled gurney. Behind the fireman walked her friend Mrs. Polotov in a sleeveless green blouse and plaid skirt.

Great. A welcoming party.

Christine headed for them, trying to walk without lurching, her mouth closed tight against the pain.

She met the group at the pathway through the grass. "I'm fine."

"Hop on the gurney," the firefighter said. "I'll wheel you to the truck, and we'll check you out."

She put up a hand. "I'll retrieve my bike and head back to the station."

"Christine, love," Mrs. Polotov interjected. "You're hurt."

"I'm okay. Just a little sore. Mostly embarrassed."

The firefighter and Fillingham met glances, their mouths twitching with suppressed laughter.

That was it. She brushed by them and limped along the trail, avoiding the roots and sharp stones, the dog padding behind her.

"Wait!" Fillingham ran in front of her, blocking her way. "Let Jim check you out. You don't have to go back to the truck."

"No."

Fillingham put his hand on his radio. "I'll have to call in a 10-13."

She glared at him. A 10-13. Officer down. Publicize her embarrassment to the entire force and add reams of paperwork to her day. She would have to go to the hospital for sure.

She hated him. Why did she think she had to bend over backward to regain his friendship? He was a horrible partner. A blackmailer.

"She's agreed," Fillingham said over his shoulder to Jim.

Jim pushed the gurney over to Christine and lowered it so that she could sit.

"Jim," Fillingham said, "while you check her out, I'll retrieve her stuff." He took off down the footpath.

"Dear," Mrs. Polotov said, frowning with concern as she looked at Christine's ballooning foot in Jim's hands.

Christine shook her head. Any sympathy from the Islander and she would lose it. Tears prickled at the corners of her eyes.

"Look who wants to be friends," Mrs. Polotov said, smiling. The dog was up on its hind legs, front paws on the gurney. Mrs. Polotov patted the cushion beside Christine. "Up, up," she said.

The dog jumped onto the gurney and sat beside Christine. Mrs. Polotov scratched the dog's neck.

"Whose pet is it?" Christine asked.

"I'm not sure," Mrs. Polotov said. "She's not wearing a collar. She certainly is a friendly pup." The older woman petted the dog's back.

Jim asked Christine to flex and point her foot, then rotate her ankle.

Christine grimaced.

"It's not broken," he said. "Looks like a sprain, with swelling, bruising and abrasions. Nothing that needs a stitch. If I were you, I'd keep off of it for a couple of days and load up on acetaminophen."

"Okay." Christine stood up, weight on one leg.

"Not so fast," Jim said, smiling, his teeth white in his tanned face. "Let me clean the cuts and wrap the ankle to give you stability."

Jim was fastening the stretchy cotton bandage around her ankle when Fillingham returned.

"Where's my stuff?" Christine asked.

Fillingham said, "I found your bike by the beach. I put your belt, purse and shoes in the bike basket and parked your bike in Mrs. P's backyard. We'll wheel you over to her place. I'll pick you up later in the police car."

Mrs. Polotov turned to Fillingham. "I'll get some food into her. Give her a change of clothes."

He nodded, then turned to Christine. "Karl repaired the equipment. He and Phil collect water samples around the Island for a municipal project."

Christine nodded.

"He says he knows you," Fillingham said. "He hope's you're okay."

Christine stood up. "Yes, I almost arrested him." She addressed Jim. "Thank you for the first aid. You guys can head out."

Fillingham said, "But you're going to Mrs. P's."

"I know. That's where I'm heading."

"It's a bit far to walk," Jim said, "on a sprain."

"We'll take you there," Fillingham said. He smacked the cushion bed of the gurney. "Hop on."

She shook her head.

Fillingham ignored her. "Jim, think we can push her to Mrs. P's in four minutes?"

"Third Street?" Jim asked.

Fillingham nodded.

"More like five," he said.

"Bet's on!" Fillingham said. "Winner pays for dinner." He turned to Christine. "Get on. We'll run you there."

Mrs. Polotov said, "I'll head out. Christine, my door's open. Make yourself at home if you get there first."

"For goodness' sake!" Christine said, hands on hips.

Fillingham bowed low over the gurney, gesturing to it with his one hand.

She sat beside the dog.

"Tuck your legs in and swivel onto the bed," Jim advised. He angled the back of the gurney so Christine could sit propped up, then belted her in and raised the side safety bars.

Christine sat on the gurney, legs extended in front, one hand around the dog beside her, the other clutching the side bar.

Fillingham looked at his watch. "On your mark, get set, go!"

The ride to Mrs. Polotov's was as harrowing as her tangle with Karl and his equipment. They bounced along the forest trail, Christine's ankle complaining when the wheels hit a rock, the dog yapping in excitement.

Once the trio reached the concrete slab sidewalk of the Ward's Island community, it was like a track-and-field event. People hopped out of the way as Fillingham called out, "Excuse me! Emergency!" A few onlookers clapped. Christine clutched the bedrail and the dog tightly. If they rolled over, she and the dog would go sprawling.

The two men slowed as they turned onto Third Street.

"Yee-haw!" Fillingham said from his position at the front of the cot. "There it is! Into the backyard!"

Christine and the dog swayed right as the trolley angled onto the path beside Mrs. Polotov's house. They pushed the gurney onto the back patio. Jim put on the brakes.

"Time?" asked Fillingham, panting.

Jim looked at his watch. "Four minutes, twenty seconds."

"I'm the closest," Fillingham said, one hand pressed against his heaving chest. Turning to Jim, he said, "I'll have the gourmet burger at Chapel House, extra pickles, with a side Caesar salad."

Jim shook his head. "I shouldn't bet with a national sailing champion."

"Words of wisdom, Jim," Fillingham said. "Words of wisdom."

Jim lowered the gurney and helped Christine into a patio chair.

The two men shook hands. With a wave to Christine, Jim exited, gurney in tow.

Fillingham said, "I'll be back after dinner with the patrol car. We'll fit your bike in the back." He leaned over and scratched the dog's ear. "See you later, Lifeguard."

Chapter 4

"There you are, dear," Mrs. Polotov said as she exited the back door of her house.

Christine sat in the backyard beside the round glass patio table, the dog in an adjacent chair. Her wet wool skirt emanated a musty smell, even though Christine's cotton blouse was partially dry.

"I've put clothes for you on my bed. We're not the same size, but I did my best. Come on in and I'll get you an iced tea. Then we'll think about rustling up proper food."

Christine stood up, and the dog jumped off the chair, tail wagging.

"What do we do about the dog?" Christine asked.

Mrs. Polotov shrugged. "I'm not sure. She must belong to someone. Clearly, she is good with people. We'll leave her outside and she'll find her way home."

"Fillingham called her Lifeguard," Christine said. "Maybe he knows the owner."

Mrs. Polotov chuckled. "I think it's because the dog dragged you off the rocks and back to life."

Christine gave a little laugh as she bade goodbye to Lifeguard and went inside.

Within a few minutes, Christine was wearing a t-shirt that was too wide and short for her and a pair of elasticized shorts from her friend's wardrobe. Her underwear and bra were still damp, but she'd have to live with that. Mrs. Polotov had hung Christine's uniform blouse and skirt on the laundry line outside to catch the late day wind and sun.

"Here you go." Mrs. Polotov handed Christine a glass of iced tea, slices of lemon floating inside, and the two sat at the square kitchen table. Out of the sun, with the wind breezing through the open windows, the kitchen felt like an oasis.

Christine quickly gulped her tea, and her host refilled her glass.

"Sorry, I'm thirsty," Christine said.

"You've been through a lot today. I have homemade tomato soup warming on the stovetop. And a Cobb salad. And, of course, scones." She pointed to the tray of blueberry scones in front of her.

Christine smiled. "Thanks so much. I could have gone back to the station to change and have dinner."

Mrs. Polotov waved away her protest.

Christine sipped her iced tea. "Well, that's one way to announce my return to the Island. Drown myself."

The Islander leaned forward to pat Christine's bare arm. "You were doing your job, dear. Helping people in distress."

Christine shook her head. "He was floating face-down for the longest time. I was watching him. His lung capacity must be tremendous. He never came up for air. I thought he was dead."

"Karl does a great deal of swimming. Has the lungs of a baleen whale." Mrs. Polotov got up. "It's better to err on the side of caution than to ignore it and have something terrible happen." She went over to the stovetop to stir the soup.

A few minutes later, they sat across from each other, spooning their soup.

"Other than today's misunderstanding, is it nice to be back?" Mrs. Polotov smiled, her brown eyes warm, her hair in variegating shades of gray tucked in a bun at her neck.

Christine nodded, spoon in hand. "I really missed the trees. And the wind. It's so much cooler on the Island than the city. Seeing people biking, picnicking, and swimming. Even the smells: water and fish and flowers."

"Yes, it's so lovely in the summer."

"My first call today was 68 Lakeshore. Do you know the superintendent of Parks and Recreation, Douglas Martin, and his wife Barbara?"

Mrs. Polotov swallowed her last spoonful of soup. "I haven't met them. I heard they were moving into the Merriweather place. And Douglas Martin has been in the paper." She sighed. "He's one of those modern men who wants to clear this old clapboard community out," she swished her hands one way, "to usher in modern apartments." She swished her hands the other way.

Christine speared a forkful of lettuce and bacon from her salad bowl. "I don't understand. Evict people then let new people on the Island?"

Mrs. Polotov shook her head, her beaded earrings swaying. "Land's hard to come by in the city. Real estate prices in Toronto are rising. Someone can make a pretty penny if they make the Island into an exclusive neighborhood."

"But...but...the charm of the Island *is* the community. Its history. The gardens and houses and people."

"Thank you, dear. We think so," Mrs. Polotov said with a smile. "I'm not sure Douglas Martin thinks the same."

Christine swallowed a wedge of egg. "I haven't told you about the call," she said. "Someone removed the Martins' gardens. Every plant, bush, tree and potato."

Mrs. Polotov nodded, chewing on her salad.

"You don't seem surprised," Christine added.

"The Merriweather family did not want to leave. The house has been in the family for generations. They petitioned the government to extend their lease, as they've done for residents like me. But the new superintendent of Parks and Recreation needed a house on the Island. Douglas Martin picked the Merriweather house."

"Do you think the Merriweathers destroyed the gardens before they vacated?"

"Who said the gardens were destroyed?"

Christine frowned. "I saw them. Front and back. Everything gone."

"Gone from 68 Lakeshore," Mrs. Polotov said.

"Did someone take them and put them elsewhere?"

"That's my guess," the older woman said.

Christine shook her head. Island politics. Still frothing and fermenting.

"Do you know where the Merriweathers are staying on the mainland?" Christine asked. She'd try to contact them today.

"No, dear. They are hoping to rent an Island house. I'm not sure if they've been successful."

The phone rang. Mrs. Polotov got up to answer the phone. "Yes, Geoffrey, she's fine. We're finishing dinner." She paused. "Yes, come by. There are scones."

"I don't need a ride," Christine protested, but Mrs. Polotov hung up.

"I want to see Geoffrey. I haven't seen him for months."

Christine nodded. Fillingham liked Mrs. Polotov too.

"How are things between the two of you?" Her calm gaze fixed on Christine.

Christine looked down, sliding her hands on the white linen of her borrowed shorts. "Not so good." She looked up. "He's polite. Civil.

But we haven't made up." She took a deep breath. "He's asked to be removed from future shifts with me."

Mrs. Polotov's head jerked back in surprise. "That doesn't sound like Geoffrey. He's not vindictive."

"When we were undercover for Project Niagara, I had to keep some things secret. He feels I don't trust him."

"You said he broke up with Julie, so he must be hurting. Geoffrey is reasonable. And optimistic. He'll see the light. You two are such good friends. Look at today."

"He helped me because he thought I was going to drown."

"It's more than that, dear."

A few minutes later, there was a cheery "Beep, beep!" from the road. Christine recognized the police car's horn.

Mrs. Polotov greeted Fillingham at the front door, a box of scones in hand. Christine followed her, hobbling, her half-dry uniform over one arm. Back out on the street, Christine waved goodbye to her friend and opened the passenger door of the patrol car. Her bike and belongings had been placed in the back hatch.

Suddenly, the dog appeared and jumped onto the passenger seat.

"Out!" Christine said, pointing to the road.

The dog panted, eyeing her, not moving.

Fillingham got into the driver's side.

"What do we do about the dog?" she asked.

"Let her stay. She'll just follow us to the station." He grabbed the dog and placed her in the back seat.

As Christine got in, he said, "I'm not sure Lifeguard has an owner. People have spotted her wandering around yards and scratching at back doors. Maybe she was left by an Islander whose lease was up and moved away."

"An Islander wouldn't do that," she protested. Islanders created gardens to attract butterflies and left open grasses as sanctuary for nesting bird populations. They wouldn't let a dog starve.

He shrugged. "Could be she was owned by an American boater. Or a mainlander abandoned her on the Island, thinking she would have a place to run." He continued, "We can call the Humane Society, see if someone has reported a missing dog. And ask Grant Young to include a found dog announcement in the *Ward's Island Weekly*."

Lifeguard was cute. A comforting companion. Her presence had made Christine feel better as she sat on the rock, stewing in humiliation.

Christine scratched the dog behind the ear. "All right, Lifeguard. You're in. An honorary member of the Toronto Island police force."

Chapter 5

"I can take care of Donna," Wayne said.

Christine brought her plate of peanut butter toast over to the kitchen table and sat across from her brother. "I don't know, Wayne," she said. "Don't you want to go to Mrs. Simon's?"

Christine's mom, Phyllis, was working day shift at the Toronto Police Records department and wouldn't be home until four. Christine had to leave for her Toronto Island shift at 1:45 p.m. Her siblings would be home for two hours by themselves.

"I'm old enough now," he said, smacking his thin chest. At almost eleven, he was tall and wiry, a baseball player, his brown hair grown shaggy to his shoulders. He refused to cut it, since short hair wasn't cool. Next month, he'd start Grade Six.

"I wouldn't charge you much for babysitting," he said.

Christine raised her eyebrows. "Free babysitting is par for the course for older brothers."

Wayne rolled his eyes but smiled, sensing victory.

Christine took a bite of toast. After a moment, she said, "We'll try it for today. But you can't take off on Donna to throw the ball around or go to the store with your buddies. You can go outside to the school or the park as long as you are together."

Wayne saluted and then spooned the last of his cereal. As he got up, Christine said, "Wash your bowl and spoon."

With an exaggerated sigh, he turned on the kitchen faucet.

Donna and Wayne had been in summer camp for the first two weeks in July. The Boys and Girls Club offered free camps that had weekly themes like arts and crafts, games or science that Donna loved attending. Wayne was getting too old for the community center camps. He wanted to attend sports camps and expensive baseball training camps.

Christine and Phyllis tried to organize their work so that an adult was home when Donna and Wayne were not in camp, but they were only partially successful. Christine had just received her new Island patrol schedule yesterday.

"Do you want tea?" Wayne asked Christine. "I can put the kettle on so you can relax. Put your sore foot up."

Christine looked over her shoulder at her brother at the kitchen counter. "You are a smart, smart boy."

He flashed her a smile, his teeth white in his tanned, freckled face. Wayne spent his summer days outdoors, playing baseball, hanging out with school friends, heading over to the local outdoor pool with a towel slung over his shoulder.

As the water boiled, Christine elevated her sprained ankle on a kitchen chair. It was swollen but not as sore as yesterday. She would take a painkiller before going into work. She didn't want to be limping her entire shift.

After handing her a cup of tea, Wayne left to shoot baskets at the school with his friends. Donna was in her pajamas in bed, stuffed animals crowded around her as she read to them from *Black Beauty*.

The telephone rang. Christine stood on one foot and leaned to pick up the receiver off the wall.

"Christine?" a male voice queried.

"Hawk," Christine whispered, although there was no one else in the room. Hawk Johnson had been her secret love when she first transferred to the Island. Christine couldn't handle the public reaction to her going out with an Anishinabek man. Hawk eventually ended their romance, tired of the subterfuge, and had since married a woman from his reserve, an old childhood friend.

"Is it okay to talk?" he asked.

"Yes, for a few minutes." She sat back down at the kitchen table.

"How are you?"

"I had a week off after the undercover job in Yorkville. I was on Island patrol yesterday."

"Nice to be back?" His deep, warm voice was magnetic. She pictured him, wide, strong shoulders, attentive brown eyes.

"Yes," she said curtly, advising herself not to be drawn in to him again. She cared for him. But he wasn't for her. End of story. "I forgot how beautiful the Island was in the summer. The sunlight bouncing off the lake. How green everything is. The sound of the ferry horn throughout the day."

"I started back at Centreville, but I had to come back to the reserve, and I missed too many shifts. Now I have a job at a downtown garage and a room nearby."

"How's that working out?"

"I'm not there a lot. I try to work in stretches, so I get a few days off in a row. And then I go back up to see Remi."

Christine placed her injured foot on the floor. *Remi.* Hawk's wife.

"How is she doing?" Christine asked. The last time she and Hawk had spoken, Children's Aid had taken Remi's daughter Layla into care after Remi crashed her car while drunk. The girl was subsequently adopted despite his plea to the courts to return Layla home after he married Remi.

"Same. Upset. Holding on. Trying not to drink."

There was a pause. Hawk was phoning her for a reason. Usually, he waylaid her on the way to the ferry or found her after patrol. Calling her was direct. It must be important.

"I...I would like you to do something for me."

"Okay," Christine said.

"For Remi and Layla," he added.

She waited.

"There's a barbeque picnic for families who have adopted children. It's on the August long weekend. Can you go as a policewoman?"

Christine often took extra paid shifts working at dances and community events, since finances were tight at home. Wayne's baseball training was expensive, and Fillingham had loaned her money last year, which she repaid partially every paycheck.

"Why?" she asked. "Do you think Layla will be there?"

"Quite a few Native children who have been taken from their families are adopted in Toronto." He sighed. "It's a long shot. She could be anywhere. But you said before you would help."

"I did," she affirmed, "as long as it's legal. I'll check the overtime job postings and see if the barbeque is listed. That weekend is the Gala Day reunion on the Island, so it's busy. I'll have to work around my patrol schedule."

"The barbeque is Saturday at lunch. You could go and still make an afternoon or overnight shift." He paused. "I'll leave a photo of Layla in your bike basket."

"I remember what she looks like," she said. She had seen Remi, Layla and Hawk at an Island event last year. It had broken her heart. "But the photo will help."

"Thank you. This is important to me. She is like a daughter. She *is* my daughter."

"That's why I'm doing it." She didn't know Hawk's intentions. Was he trying to find Layla to make sure she was okay? Did he intend to get her back somehow? The less she knew, the better. "This is all

I can do. The barbeque picnic. Then I'm out. I don't want to know the rest."

"I understand." He hung up.

Chapter 6

"Hey, it's Lifeguard," Fillingham said as the patrol car drove into the driveway.

The salt-and-pepper mutt sat by the police station door, mouth open, tongue lolling, tail windshield wiping behind her as she watched them exit the car.

"I'm sure she has another name," Christine said.

The officers gave her a pat and went inside. The dog slipped through the open door and trotted into the waiting room furnished with benches for civilian visitors.

"Are we allowed to have a dog in here?" she asked.

He shrugged. "Want some water?" he asked the dog. Lifeguard's ears perked up.

In the kitchen, Fillingham ran the water as Christine placed her dinner in the fridge.

"Do you want me to make coffee?" she asked after he placed the water bowl on the floor. Usually, her partner made the coffee, asserting that the sludge she brewed was undrinkable.

She smiled in anticipation of his joke, but he merely said, "I'll make it." He was back to being civil but cool. Christine remained unforgiven. Sure, he had helped her yesterday, but that was life-and death. They weren't back to being friends.

"I'll check the logbook in case someone called about Lifeguard," she said.

The coffee percolated loudly as Christine stood at the front counter, scanning incident reports. The front doorbell tinkled. Christine looked up from the pile of papers.

A lean woman entered in a sleeveless cotton shirt and navy cotton pants, pail hooked over one elbow, a basket of cleaning products clasped in her other hand. She was tanned, her brown hair pulled into a ponytail. Christine would guess her age to be thirty-five from the few gray strands around her temple.

"I'm here to clean," the woman said.

Christine nodded. "Hi, I'm PW Christine Lane. My sergeant mentioned that someone had been hired for the summer. You look familiar. Have we met?"

"Judith Purnell," she said as she placed the bucket and mop on the floor. "I live on Ward's. You might have seen me. Or heard one of my three screaming children."

Christine said, "There are several screaming children on the Island, so I may not be able to pick yours out of a crowd."

Judith's mouth quirked at the corner. Her expression turned serious. "Sorry I'm late. I was at the Merriweather place, and it took longer than expected."

"No problem. We weren't given a specific time for you. Right now, we're at the beginning of a shift sorting ourselves out, so it's a good time to show up."

Judith pulled a rag out of her bag and a spray bottle. "I'll start here in the waiting room."

"Judith, you came from the Merriweathers'. You mean Superintendent Martin's place?"

"Yes. Right."

"Have you cleaned there before?"

Judith sprayed a window with vinegar water and began wiping it, one knee on the bench below the window. "I was there a couple of days ago. The Martins wanted the inside of the house cleaned before the family moved in. Kitchen, oven and fridge. The bathroom. That type of thing."

"Did you notice anything while you were there?"

Judith paused, arm raised to the window. "Like what?"

"Anything out of the ordinary?"

"The Merriweathers left furniture and boxes. The Martins said to junk it all. I got my neighbor Paul to help me lift things onto the big wagon. A few people took pieces before Paul hauled them away."

"How was the Martins' front yard?"

Judith coughed out a laugh as she headed to the windows on the far side. "Are you asking if it was dug up?"

"Yes, I am," Christine said. "I responded to a theft complaint by Mrs. Martin yesterday."

"The lawns were fine on Tuesday when I was there. Isabel always grew a beautiful garden. Perennials and annuals. Something was always in bloom." Judith bent to retrieve a rag and dampened it with cleaning spray. "That's why I was late today. Mrs. Martin wanted me to fix the garden as well as clean." Judith wiped the wooden frame of the bench. "It was hard work, hauling soil, filling in the holes left by plants and bushes. It took a while." She stood up, pressing a hand to her lower back.

Fillingham came out of the back to introduce himself to Judith and handed both women coffees. He returned to the kitchen.

"What do you think happened?" Christine asked.

Judith didn't meet Christine's glance as she wiped a bench. "Who knows? All I know is that they are paying me to fix their yard and clean their house. Which means I can buy hamburger meat this week at the grocery store."

The telephone rang and Fillingham stepped into the office to answer it.

"What's dead?" he asked.

Christine looked over at him, meeting his glance.

"Ducks. Like in quack, quack?" he said into the phone. After a pause, he asked, "Where in Centreville?... Yes," Fillingham said into the receiver, "call Parks and Recreation too, but don't let anyone touch anything. And cordon off the area. You're by the Swan Ride?" A pause. "Shut it down for the rest of the day. We're on our way."

Christine filed away the incident reports and grabbed a radio from the charging station. "Should we bike or drive?"

"Let's drive. Your foot is injured. And we should bring tape and pylons. Ten ducks are floating dead in the lagoon in Centreville. It's spooking the kids. The staff is worried it'll scare off families. Let's go."

Chapter 7

"It's busy today," Christine remarked to Fillingham as they drove slowly from the police station to Centreville, honking gently to urge people out of their way.

"A Friday afternoon in July," he remarked.

She spotted the Carousel restaurant on their right, anchoring the southwest corner of the amusement park. Its steep metal roof attracted adventurous Island kids who slid down the metal slope when the restaurant was closed, braking before they fell off the eave-strough.

"Where's the Swan Ride?" he asked as the patrol car approached the Centre Island bridge.

"By Olympic Island," Christine said. She knew the rides better than Fillingham, since she had brought her siblings to the park. "Drive past the main entrance and take the back access path along the lagoon. "

Fillingham slowed the car to a crawl, four-way blinkers on as they passed the back of the fire engines and approached the water rides.

Two security officers stood on the path, blocking access, a group of curious people in front of them. Behind the men were four teenage ride employees in their yellow Centreville t-shirts, eyes wide with alarm.

The officers parked the car on the path and introduced themselves to the security guards.

The balding security guard said, "The group of ducks floated in all together. One dad on the Swan Ride noticed that something was wrong. I threw a net over the birds to stop them from floating down the lagoon." He shrugged. "I think they're all dead."

Christine scanned the dock and spotted brown and green feathers under the black cords of netting. They must have tied the net to the dock moorings.

The shorter security guard said, "We shut down the Swan Ride and the Boat Ride."

"Good idea," Christine said. "Can you place pylons on either end of the lagoon path? One person to be posted at the bridge to Olympic Island," she gestured east with one hand, "and the other can stand a hundred feet from the rides the other way. Tell people that the water rides are closed for the day."

The security staff left, and Christine interviewed the Centreville staff and the dad who had discovered the dead birds, jotting information in her memo book. Fillingham examined the net of ducks off the dock.

As Christine spoke with the last of the teenage employees, she spotted Fillingham walking on Olympic Island on the other side of the lagoon that bordered the water rides. She caught his glance. He shook his head. No information gleaned.

The apprehensive teenage employees went on dinner break, advised not to discuss the dead ducks or the closed rides with patrons.

Christine heard a car motor as Fillingham returned to the Swan Ride. A van marked with the Toronto Parks and Recreation logo parked beside the patrol car.

A man with dark hair in a tailored, shiny suit exited the passenger side of the van and approached the officers. He was followed by the van driver, a thin, older man in coveralls with the Parks and Recreation logo above his heart.

"What's going on here?" the suited man said abruptly, glancing from Fillingham to Christine.

"That's what we're trying to find out," Fillingham said pleasantly. He introduced himself and Christine. "And you are?"

The man's chin tucked in as if they should recognize him. "Douglas Martin. Superintendent of Parks and Recreation." He turned to Christine. "Did you meet my wife the other day?"

Christine said, "Yes, I did. I took the call about the vandalized yard."

"Have you apprehended the perpetrator?" Martin asked.

"Ah, no, sir. We interviewed people, but we don't have any witnesses. The investigation is ongoing." None of the Martins' neighbors had seen anything. Sergeant Bard had gotten hold of the Merriweathers this morning. The former tenants said they knew nothing about the destroyed gardens. Mr. Merriweather had been at work that day, and Mrs. Merriweather had gone shopping with her mother and the children. The gardens were intact when the family moved out.

Martin harrumphed. "What happened here?" He gestured toward the water.

Christine glanced at her notes, then met Mr. Martin's green-eyed stare. "At approximately 4:05 p.m. this afternoon, a patron on the Swan Ride, a Mr. Ken Sutton, noticed ten or twelve ducks in the lagoon beside the swan boat he and his daughter occupied. The ducks weren't moving. Two were floating upside down. He flagged the ride operator, who called security. Security netted the ducks, and they are currently tied to the dock. Police were called. We've cordoned off the water ride area on both sides and interviewed staff and security."

Fillingham said, "Mr. Martin, do you have any idea what could have happened to the ducks? Has Parks and Recreation noticed any activity that might explain this?"

"I prefer the honorific superintendent," he said.

Fillingham glanced at Christine.

"Mallory," Martin said, and the van driver came over. Martin turned to the officers. "This is my assistant manager, Oliver Mallory. He says all regular activities were underway today: lawn mowing, flower watering, weed removal, sand raking and garbage removal. We're painting one of the facility sheds. Nothing unusual was noticed in or around the Island."

"Was there a paint spill in the water?" Christine asked Mallory. "Something dumped by accident?"

Mallory shook his head.

"Nothing unusual floated up on any of the beaches or the lagoons?" Fillingham asked.

Mallory shook his head again. "It's been a regular day. Summer is our busiest time." His voice was raspy, as if he were a chain smoker. "None of the workers reported any incidents."

The four walked onto the dock. Martin crouched beside the floating net. Christine examined the ducks as best she could under the black netting—mallards and wood ducks. An orange bill poked through the net opening, and an iridescent teal-green head pressed against the twine.

"Probably a local kid trying out his new BB gun," Martin said.

Christine said, "It's hard to tell, but I don't see any external wounds or bleeding. I don't think kids could kill ten ducks at the same time. They would fly away."

"We need to move this up the chain," Fillingham said to Christine.

Christine nodded. "I'll go into the Centreville office and call the staff sergeant at 52 Division. Get orders from him. I'll phone

Sergeant Bard too." Although her sergeant had gone off shift at three o'clock, he would expect to be notified.

Martin straightened. "You'll do nothing of the sort."

Christine met Fillingham's glance.

"I'm not sure—" Christine began.

"No need to alarm anyone," he said, holding both hands up in the air. "Mallory will call a crew to pick up the ducks, and then everyone can be on their way."

"That's not how it works," Fillingham said.

"That's how it works when I'm in charge," Martin said.

"You're not in charge of Toronto Police," Christine said, trying to keep the annoyed tone out of her voice.

He smiled. "PW Lane. PC Fillingham. I am indebted to your service. Thank you for securing the area, keeping the spectacle to a minimum. I assure you, Parks and Recreation will do our due diligence and sort this out."

"Your job is not investigation," Fillingham said. "Water Management and Wildlife Conservation will be called. As well as Harbor Police." He tilted his head for Christine to leave for the Centreville office.

As Christine turned, a hand clamped her arm. Martin held her in a loose but firm grip.

"Remove your hand," she said.

"You are not calling your sergeant," Martin said.

"Remove your hand or you'll be under arrest for obstruction of justice and interfering with a police officer," she ordered.

"And she'll break your hand," Fillingham added.

Martin looked at Christine, then Fillingham and back to Christine. Abruptly, he released his grip. "You two are making a grave career error. Chief Benson is a friend of mine."

Christine's stomach dropped. Did Martin have that much influence?

Fillingham snorted a laugh. "We're already on Island patrol, *Superintendent.* It doesn't get any lower than this."

The two officers smiled at each other for the first time that shift.

Chapter 8

"Hi, there!" A young woman with freckles and bright brown eyes smiled behind the police station counter. Before Christine and Fillingham could enter the office, she scooted underneath the levered counter and rushed over to take each of their hands in an emphatic shake.

"I'm Cadet Olivia Nelson," the red-haired woman said. She was in a uniform, the shoulder badge on her jacket reflecting her rank. "I've been assigned to Toronto Island for the next two months."

Sergeant Bard had told them that a recruit would be job shadowing them for their shift. To Christine, the young woman looked sixteen. She must be fresh out of high school.

As the three entered the kitchen, Fillingham asked, "Where are you from, Cadet Nelson?"

"A farm in Guelph," she said.

"That so?" Fillingham said, a smile quirking his lips as he put the coffeepot on the burner.

Christine retrieved three mugs from the kitchen cabinet.

As they sat down for their coffee a few minutes later, Nelson said, "I'm so lucky to be here." She grinned at Christine and Fillingham. She had small white teeth, the bottom row slightly crooked. "I applied after I graduated and," she snapped her fingers, "I got an acceptance letter two weeks later. And here I am."

"Lucky you. Lucky us," said Fillingham, smiling.

"I head to the police college at the end of September," Nelson continued. She leaned forward conspiratorially. "I've never been on Toronto Island before."

Nelson continued chattering. She was the oldest of eight children. She hadn't wanted to shovel hay and manure for the rest of her life on the family's dairy farm. Or end up cooking for ten hungry mouths until a local farmer came a-courting.

"Not that anyone's knocking down my door," she added. "The red hair. Puts men off."

Christine laughed. Nelson was a splash of cold water.

"Oh, my goodness!" Nelson exclaimed, scraping back her chair noisily. "I almost forgot. Someone came by for you, PW Lane." Nelson had been on duty since noon, shadowing Sergeant Bard for the first half of her shift, then patrolling with Fillingham and Christine.

Nelson scurried to the office and returned to the kitchen table, note in hand. "He didn't have a shirt on. He was very tanned. He said," she scanned her note, "'tell PW Lane thanks for saving me in the Eastern Gap. And that he hoped you recovered.'" She leaned closer to Christine. "Did you save his life?"

Fillingham guffawed.

"What's wrong?" Nelson asked, looking from one officer to the other.

Christine said, "It's a misunderstanding. I offered help. It wasn't needed. He doesn't need to thank me."

Nelson pressed a hand to her chest. "He seemed very grateful."

Fillingham smirked and got up to wash his coffee cup in the sink. "I'll go check the beaches, make sure everyone's behaving themselves. I'll leave you two to chat. About PW Lane's life-saving techniques." He shrugged. "Or your preferred nail polish color. Whatever you women folk want to discuss."

Christine frowned. "Since when have I worn nail polish?"

Hand on hip, he said, "Don't really know much about you, do I, PW Lane?" He left the station, the doorbells ringing on his way out.

Nelson leaned in from across the table. "What did he mean by that?"

Christine shrugged.

Nelson said, "Sergeant Bard said the two of you have been partners for over a year. Thick as thieves, he said."

Christine tried to keep her tone neutral. "We have been." Changing topics, she said, "Why don't I take you around the two residential communities on the Island? Introduce you to the locals. They're friendly."

Nelson clapped her hands. "Sounds like fun!"

"Do you ride a bike?"

"I can drive," Nelson said. Officers needed to have their driver's license prior to being on the force. "A car, but also a tractor and a combine. A dump truck if need be."

"I'll keep that in mind," Christine said. "Usually, we bike and walk on Island patrol. Or at least Fillingham and I do. There's no vehicle traffic other than emergency and service vehicles, so it's easier to cycle. And it's good exercise."

"I haven't had tons of practice on a bike," Nelson said. "Town was too far away to cycle."

Christine found a woman's bike in the back of the police garage. The station was an informal lost-and-found center, and it usually housed a few bikes visitors had left on the Island.

Nelson was right. She didn't know how to ride a bike well. She wobbled all over the pathway. Christine had to caution her from getting too close to the lagoon.

"I'll lead," Christine said. "Focus on my back, straight ahead of you. Don't look down or to the side."

"All right."

After a few minutes of "Oops" and "Whoa!" from Nelson, they approached the Algonquin Bridge.

Christine pointed to the span connecting the two islands. "This is the Algonquin Island community. About a hundred and ten homes. Three hundred people. It has a marina on one end and a community center on the other. We'll check it out on our way back from dinner break."

As they biked past the arched bridge, Nelson said from behind, "I think that man likes you."

Christine's head swiveled. "Fillingham?"

"No!" Nelson roared. "You're obviously on the outs with him. Although he is good-looking. His eyes are so sparkly."

Oh, for goodness' sake, Christine thought. She was stuck with a boy-crazy adolescent trainee.

"I'm talking about the shirtless man, Karl," Nelson continued. "He was disappointed you weren't at the station. I could tell. He wanted to see you. He wanted to ask you out."

Christine laughed. "You a matchmaker as well as a farmer?"

"Yes," Nelson said, riding up beside Christine. "I'm good at sensing these things. I knew right away when one of my brothers was sweet on a girl. Boys give it away like that." She snapped her fingers, and her handlebars yanked to the right. "Whoa," she said, clamping her hands on the grips. "You know who's also good-looking, like a Hollywood star?"

"Who?" Christine asked.

"Constable Morano," she said. "He looks like Cary Grant."

Christine's smile disappeared. "Don't get fooled by the slick hair and the aftershave. He doesn't like policewomen."

Nelson waved a hand dismissively. "That's not true. He was so charming to me yesterday. I was with him for an entire shift."

"If you're so good at sensing things, then you'll figure out he's someone to avoid." Christine pointed out Willow Avenue to their right and explained it led to a cluster of houses on Ward's Island known as the Annex.

As they continued toward the ferry docks, Christine said, "Turn right at the community center. I'll show you the beach."

Music poured out of the open doors of the community center. A group of adults chatted at the base of the porch steps as teenagers headed inside. Must be youth dance night. The center hosted dances for adolescents and adults, as well as Saturday night events for all ages.

Normally, the teens on the Island dressed in bathing suits or shorts and halter tops, often going barefoot. It was amusing to see the young girls in formal dresses and boys in dress shirts and ironed pants, sporting ties borrowed from their fathers.

A woman in front of the center waved Christine over.

"Mrs. Fairfax. How can I help you?" Christine asked. The Fairfaxes lived on First Street and had four teenage girls.

Mrs. Fairfax glanced at the parents beside her. "We wanted to know about the ducks that were found dead in Centreville. Do you know the cause?"

"Not yet," Christine answered. Water samples had been taken around Centreville, but the lagoon was connected to the inner harbor, so it would be difficult to identify the source of any water toxins.

"Did someone shoot them?" Mrs. Fairfax asked, hand on her throat.

"The investigation is ongoing," Christine answered. "Cause of death hasn't been ascertained. The ducks were sent to a vet for examination."

Music blared from the doorway. The party was underway. Nelson's right shoe tapped to the beat.

Mrs. Fairfax said, "We need to know. We swim and bathe in the water."

"Your concern is understandable."

The man beside her said, "If a ne'er-do-well is shooting wildlife, what's stopping them from targeting our pets?"

The woman beside him said, "I haven't let my cat out since I've heard."

"They'll be an announcement once the cause of death has been determined," Christine said.

"Ma'am," Nelson interrupted, addressing Christine, "should I head inside the center? Introduce myself?"

Christine nodded. Nelson quickly hustled up the stairs and disappeared inside.

"They're trying to kick us off the Island," the man said, crossing his arms. He wore dress pants and white shirt as if he had come from work.

"Make us afraid to live here," Mrs. Fairfax added. All three parents nodded.

Christine frowned. Islanders thought the ducks had been deliberately hurt to create hysteria and make the Island seem unsafe. That seemed far-fetched.

A loud cheer from inside the community center made Christine glance toward the open door. It sounded like the teen dance was in full gear. "I better check on my cadet. I understand your concern. The police will let residents know as soon as the vet's report is completed."

Christine climbed the steps and stopped in the doorway.

Cadet Nelson was swing-dancing with four other couples. Her partner twirled her around twice. Nelson spotted Christine and smiled widely. She crossed hands with her partner, he pulled her through his legs and she sailed through the air, landing slightly crouched on two feet. The onlookers applauded, and Nelson and her partner continued to dance.

"Cadet Nelson," Christine shouted above the music. Waving, she finally caught the trainee's attention and motioned her outside.

Nelson's smile dropped from her face. She let go of her partner's hands and with a shrug of apology to the crowd walked out past Christine.

Christine headed for the bikes, shaking her head. Her first week back on the Island included garden theft, dead ducks, a partner with a grudge and a farm cadet who was boy-crazy and dance-crazy to boot.

Chapter 9

"Wow," Fillingham said, "what a turnout." It was six days since the ducks were found in Centreville, and Islanders were gathering to discuss their concerns. Fillingham, Nelson and Christine walked up the stairs of the Algonquin Island community center. People were standing on both sides of the pathway leading up to the porch, waiting for the residents' meeting to start.

The officers passed through the front foyer of the building into the main room that had been set up with folding chairs on either side of a middle aisle. A podium with a microphone was placed up front.

Christine said, "Cadet Nelson, why don't you take the outdoor area by the playground?" She pointed to a small yard with slides, swings and a sandbox. It had families milling around, parents talking in groups as their children played. "Introduce yourself."

Fillingham tilted his head to the open patio doors between the kitchen and bar that led to a view of the city shoreline. "I'll head out too. You can be our inside man."

Christine greeted Gary Owen, president of the Toronto Island Residents Association. He was passionate about Island history and had deep ties to the community. A bit of a hothead, he was one of the leading voices in the quest to keep Islanders in their homes.

A woman with two long black braids streaked with gray introduced herself to Christine as Rachel Conway, an Islander and the local councilor. She and Owen were leading the meeting tonight.

"I've heard lots about you," Conway said, shaking Christine's hand. "I'm happy to hear that you're back on the Island."

Conway rang a cowbell. Leaning into the microphone, she said, "Please take your seats. We'll be starting the meeting in five minutes."

Leaning against the wall, Christine wiped her forehead with the edge of her hand. The place was warming up, despite the overhead fans and the open doors. There must be two hundred and fifty people scattered in the room and outside. Sergeant Bard had suggested that the police attend because the residents were discussing the duck deaths.

Christine scanned the attendees, focusing on the people she didn't know. Every seat was filled. People were lining the back of the room and up the sides. One man held a notebook—a journalist. Another man had a tape recorder on his lap. Although the meeting was for residents, TIRA welcomed the media to spread the word about Toronto Island concerns.

An engine rumbled. Christine recognized the sound of the police utility vehicle. Two minutes later, Sergeant Bard entered and headed to the front of the room to shake hands with Owen and Conway.

Owen went over to the podium. Bard and Conway sat at the front, facing the audience. Owen surveyed the room and the groups outside on the patio and playground, nodding. "Welcome, everyone, to the Toronto Island Residents Association meeting. I'm Gary Owen, one of the TIRA co-presidents. I want to thank the Algonquin Island community for hosting today," he looked over at Conroy and several other executives up front with him, "and thank you for your attendance. This large turnout reflects our collective concern for the health and longevity of our Island community." He turned to Rachel Conroy. "Our other co-president, Rachel, will say a few words."

Owen stepped aside, and Conroy stood in front of the mike. "Welcome. If you don't know me, I'm Rachel Conroy, a TIRA member and Ward's Island resident. I'm also your local councilor at City Hall for Ward 10. I'll review the agenda for today. As you know, the focus of this emergency meeting is the discovery of ten dead ducks in Centreville. We've invited Sergeant Bard from our local police station for an update. The ecological group Operation Pollution is here to give their expertise. And we have Dr. Rob Hapler," she pointed to a stocky man with shaggy gray hair, "a veterinarian at the Island's Far Enough Farm."

She turned to Bard. "Toronto Police will give an update on the investigation. Welcome, Sergeant Bard."

Bard nodded at Conroy and replaced her at the podium. A breeze blew in from the north doors. Christine was glad it was evening, with a wind that kept the Island several degrees cooler than the mainland.

"As Rachel mentioned," Bard started, "ten ducks were discovered dead last week in the lagoon between Centreville and Olympic Island."

Heads nodded, mouths puckered and serious.

"Did someone shoot them?" A man's voice from the front row.

Bard put up a hand. "Hear me out. Then I will open to questions." He pulled out a folded piece of paper from the inside of his jacket and laid it flat on the podium. "This is the preliminary report by the veterinarian Dr. Hamel, who examined the Centreville ducks. There is no evidence of gunshot or predator wounds." He scanned the report. "No external abrasions, broken bones or other contusions."

"So what killed them?" a woman asked, her tone shrill.

"No evidence of disease," Bard continued, "at least in the preliminary examination. Further tests ordered. At this point, the cause of death is inconclusive."

Murmurs rose around the room.

Again, Bard held up a hand. "Blood and lab test results are pending. That's why the report is preliminary. The vet said that the stomach contents of the ducks were similar: bugs, berries, plants and bread pieces."

"Were they poisoned?" asked a young man with a brown mustache.

Sergeant Bard said, "The stomach contents have been sent to the provincial lab for analysis. That takes time."

"Doc," a man with gray hair addressed the vet, "what do you think happened to the ducks?"

Bard gestured for Rob Hapler to come up to the podium. Hapler said, "As Sergeant Bard said, the lab results will give more information. It's impossible to reach a conclusion without that information."

"Have ducks died before on the Island?" the man with the memo pad asked, pen poised above his notebook.

Hapler thought for a moment. "Ducks and other waterfowl get run over by boats. And tangled in wires or netting. Boat oil or gas spills have killed local birds and fish. Toronto Island wildlife lives in parkland full of tourists. In Far Enough Farm, goats, sheep and hens get sick because people feed them human food: candy floss, pretzels, ice cream."

"Does that kill them?" the reporter asked.

Hapler leaned his head to the side. "Not usually. It makes them sick. These ducks could have eaten rotten food or a toxic chemical. Or contracted a disease. So far as I can tell, the Centreville duck deaths are an isolated incident."

"Are you worried about the farm animals?" Rebecca Conroy asked from behind Hapler.

He shook his head. "No, but we have posted more signs reminding visitors not to feed the animals. Animal feed is locked in a shed, accessible only to farm employees. We can't stop someone from throwing something over a fence, but our staff is being vigilant and watchful."

A man with the words *Operation Pollution* on the back of his yellow t-shirt raised his hand and introduced himself. "Mark Fraser, Operation Pollution. I have a question for Sergeant Bard. Did the city test the water where the ducks were found?"

Bard stood up, facing the crowd. "Toronto's Water Department came in to test. Again, results are not back. We have local fisheries and water management projects currently on the Island. They do regular testing."

"I work for a municipal fisheries management project," a voice said. It was Karl, standing up from his seat at the back of the room. He was wearing a short-sleeved plaid shirt and khaki pants. "We sample water from around the Island. We haven't noticed irregularities in water quality, new contaminants or changes in pH. However, we do not assess all areas of the Island. We don't test that specific area where the ducks were found."

Before sitting down, he looked at Christine and smiled. She gave a quick, perfunctory smile back.

Mark Fraser stood up. "There's a concern that Parks and Recreation are using toxins to control weeds and grubs. And that these toxins are getting into the water supply, poisoning the ducks."

"Who said that?" someone roared.

The crowd turned. It was Superintendent Douglas Martin, in a light gray summer suit and white dress shirt, standing at the base of the aisle.

Gary Owen stepped forward. "You're not on the speakers list, Martin."

Martin scowled at Owen. "I'm the superintendent of Parks and Recreation for Toronto Island. Any meeting that addresses issues related to the welfare of this community, including wildlife, botanicals and water quality, is my business."

"Not if you're the culprit poisoning the wildlife," a man said.

The TIRA executives stood, conceding no space for Martin at the front of the room.

"Ladies and gentlemen," Martin boomed from the back. People swiveled in their chairs to look at him. "We are on the same page. I want the Island to be a park worth visiting, with healthy animals, flora and fauna. Where people want to picnic and swim and bring their families to Centreville."

"But no residents living here!" a woman's voice piped up.

Martin blinked but ignored the comment. "I've checked with my staff, specifically those employed to tend the gardens and lawns. They spray the grass to minimize weeds. They spray the gardens to reduce insect infestations like aphids. We use products that are available from your local hardware store that Torontonians use on their own front lawns. These insecticides and weed killers have been approved by the government. They are no different than the sprays used last year and the year before on the Island. They are no different than the sprays you have in your shed for your gardens."

"We don't believe you," said a man standing in the back.

Martin's eyes grew hard for a second, then softened. He pressed his manicured hand against his chest. "I live on Toronto Island now. We moved in this week. With my wife and two young children, Matilda, who is eleven, and Reginald, who is eight. They play in the grass, on the beach, in the water. I would never expose my family to something harmful."

Mark Fraser said, "Then you support independent agencies drawing water samples from around the Island."

Martin shook his head. "Unnecessary. The municipal government is testing. Any more collection is redundant."

Fraser said, "We don't mind."

"It won't be sanctioned," Martin said, frowning.

Fraser shrugged. "I don't mind."

A man with graying hair in a ponytail stood up. "How about you tell us why you want to evict us from the Island? You can see here," his arm swept around the room, "how much we care."

Martin frowned. "I care too. I want all Torontonians to enjoy it as a park."

A woman with a kerchief over her hair said, "They enjoy it now. Eighty percent of the Island is a park. The residential communities take up less than twenty percent of the land. And we take care of the Island. We have for generations."

People started clapping, a roar of approval. When it died down, Martin put his hand up. "This is a topic to address at Metro Council. It's not the topic for this evening."

The ponytailed man said, "As you well know, we have petitioned Metro Council many times. We have presented to them. We follow all of the council's formal channels of protest, and still we are being evicted."

Martin shook his head. "I can't help with that. It's a legal contract. When your leases are up, you must leave."

The kerchiefed woman said, "Metro Council created these leases. They wouldn't give us permanent leases. That's not our fault. We all want to stay. To have permanent leases. We pay taxes. And all you want to do is get rid of us. The government refuses to let us renovate or improve our property. There are no flood prevention measures, so our streets and houses are regularly underwater every spring. So you know what? We refuse you! We refuse to leave!" She crossed her arms and the room exploded into applause, people standing up to clap.

After the hubbub died, Martin said in a calm voice, "If you refuse to leave when your lease has expired, we'll shut off your electricity."

Angry voices clamored even louder. People stood up, closing in on the superintendent, who stood there, arms crossed, with a small smile on his face. Bard marched down the aisle and gestured for Martin to leave. As Martin turned around, he was jostled by the crowd. Sergeant Bard grabbed Martin by the elbow and plowed him through.

Christine pushed her way through the crowd and grabbed Martin's other elbow.

Martin kept the half-smile on his face, ignoring the crowd, who were yelling insults like, "Go home!" and "Shame!" and "Duck killer!"

As Bard helped Martin into the Parks and Recreation van, Fillingham cleared a pathway for the vehicle, pushing people back with his open arms.

The car left with a roar. Christine looked at Bard. The battle had begun.

Chapter 10

"What's this?" Fillingham asked Christine, pointing to the shovel wedged between the limbs of a towering oak.

The two officers had been leisurely biking eastward along the Island path. Christine had one eye out for her four-legged friend. Lifeguard had shown up after the TIRA meeting, and Fillingham had given her chicken from his dinner. For this afternoon's shift, he had brought in dog treats to store at the station. Nelson had posted found dog signs on telegraph poles, and a notice was placed in local newsletters. So far, no one had claimed the friendly dog.

"It's probably one of the Island teens," Christine said, pointing to the shovel, "mad that their parents asked them to dig weeds."

"Let's see if we can get it," he said. He dismounted and stood in front of the tree, hands on hips.

This was Christine's last week on patrol with Fillingham. After the August long weekend, they wouldn't be regular partners. She still couldn't believe it. At times, her partner seemed like the old Fillingham: good-natured, fun-loving and curious. But Christine felt the cold behind his patina of politeness, the way his smile didn't meet his eyes.

Maybe his anger would cool off. And they could get back to being friends again.

Christine walked her bike over to the tree. "What's the plan, Captain Kirk?"

He smiled at the reference. She knew he liked the show.

"Two options, Mr. Spock," he said. "Either you give me a lift, or I lift you."

She smiled, ready for a joke about her weight.

"Or," he continued, "I could stand on my bike seat and reach up." He angled back to see the entire twenty-foot-tall tree. "I'll do that."

He leaned his bike against the wide tree trunk, placed his foot on a bike pedal and then stepped up onto the seat. The bike rolled, and he hugged the tree.

She ran over and grabbed the bike's handlebars, steadying it.

He placed his feet back on the bike seat, palms braced against the tree. "That's better."

"Do we need to do this?"

Without answering, he stepped onto her shoulder with his right foot and launched himself up into the fork in the tree. He hugged a thick branch to get his balance and then leaned down to pick up the spade.

"Ow," she said belatedly, rubbing her shoulder.

"Here." He lowered the gardening tool to her.

He slithered down the tree trunk without aid. On the ground, he brushed bark off his uniform jacket and pants.

"Should we bring it to the station?" she asked, holding up the shovel. "It's a heavy-duty one."

He shrugged. "The kid will get into more trouble if he comes back to retrieve it and it's not here. Leave it against the trunk."

"All right." She remounted her bike, and they continued.

The line of trees ended, and the riders had a wide view of the Inner Harbor, the soft evening light and waveless water enveloping the scene in tranquility. Twilight was a calm time on the Island, with many of the visitors heading home, the crashing waves reduced to ripples and the community settling for the night.

"More nonsense?" Fillingham said, jolting Christine out of her reverie.

"Is that a rake hanging from the bridge?"

"And a saw and a garden hoe," he added.

As they biked closer to the Algonquin Island bridge, they spotted a man in dark green coveralls leaning over the bridge, pulling on a rope that had a pair of garden shears knotted at the end.

As he pulled the shears over the railing, Christine saw his face. It was the Parks and Recreation employee, Oliver Mallory. He had driven Superintendent Martin over to Centreville after the ducks were found dead.

Christine and Fillingham gained speed before they turned their wheels onto the steep ascent of the bridge. When they reached the apex, they stopped and dismounted.

"Mr. Mallory," Christine said.

He nodded at the two officers and then leaned to pull on another rope. A garden hoe appeared in his hands, and he pulled it over the side.

Fillingham said, "What's going on here?"

"Exactly as you see," he said cryptically. He coughed, pulling a handkerchief from his pocket to wipe his mouth.

Christine said, "Does this equipment belong to Parks and Recreation?"

Mallory picked at the knot around the hoe. "Looks like."

Fillingham said, "Is this an in-house prank?"

Mallory raised his eyebrows. "I have no idea."

"Did someone break into your equipment sheds?" Christine asked.

"Could be," Mallory said dryly, removing the rope from the hoe and dropping it so it landed in a serpentine coil at his feet.

"Where?" she asked.

"Our main equipment shed is by the water treatment plant. We have another by Manitou Beach."

"We didn't see an incident report about a break-in when we came on shift," Fillingham said. "When did this happen?"

Mallory said, "Sometime today. I got on shift at three and was told to round up the equipment."

Fillingham asked, "By whom?"

Mallory shrugged. "My boss."

"Superintendent Martin?" Fillingham said.

"That's him," Mallory said. He leaned over the rail and pulled on another rope.

A family with two teen children walked over the bridge, curiously eyeing the pile of recovered gardening equipment.

"What's missing from the break-in?" Fillingham asked.

Mallory pulled up a rake and set it beside the sheers. "Won't know until I do inventory."

"So nothing big was taken, machinery, lawn mowers or vehicles?"

"My boss was checking the expensive equipment. I was sent out to retrieve the smaller stuff. You need to talk to him."

"Is he at the main facility?" Christine asked.

Mallory checked his watch. "Could be still there. But he usually leaves by five."

"Mr. Mallory," Christine said, "do you know why someone would do this?" She pointed to the roped equipment.

He snorted a laugh. "No idea. Everyone loves Parks and Recreation these days."

"There's a spade by the oak tree down the road," Fillingham told him. "We retrieved it and leaned it against the trunk. It's probably yours."

Mallory nodded and turned back to the bridge.

The officers walked their bikes off the bridge. After they pedaled out of earshot of Mallory, she said, "Given that locals probably removed Martin's plants, does this seem like a similar prank targeting the superintendent? Should we be questioning Gary Owen, the Merriweathers and the TIRA executive about both incidents?"

Fillingham considered her questions as they glided west toward the Hanlan's Point facility. "I don't understand why Martin didn't call in the theft. It's clearly a break-and-enter. For liability reasons, the superintendent would want a copy of a police report."

"Maybe nothing was stolen," she asserted. "The items were taken and placed haphazardly around the Island to be recovered."

Fillingham said, "I bet Martin feels humiliated that someone took his equipment right from under his nose." He shook his head as they headed onto the boardwalk. "Something is rotten in the state of Denmark," he said in a British accent.

"Are you quoting Shakespeare?" she asked as she biked beside him.

"*Hamlet*," he confirmed. "But we probably heard enough of the Bard from your Grizzly friend." Christine and Fillingham had been undercover in Yorkville in the spring, tracking down a gang member who sold drugs and liked to quote Shakespeare.

"Yes," Christine agreed emphatically. They smiled, and for a moment she felt their old kinship.

Fillingham turned away, and the moment was gone.

The officers checked in with the main Parks and Recreation facility on Hanlan's Point, but Mr. Martin had left for the day.

They pedaled back through Centre Island and headed east to Ward's Island. As they turned onto Willow Avenue, they heard shouting from the field ahead.

"Monday night baseball," Fillingham said, pulling ahead. Men in gray jerseys were sitting on the bench beside the baseball diamond, tying their cleats. One man was hammering in the bases. A few black jersey wearers were stretching or practicing their swings.

Several men waved as the officers turned south on Withrow, pedaling parallel to the field. Christine recognized a few of the team members, fathers back from their mainland jobs, their wives and kids setting up folding chairs along the baselines. Bard had told Christine that the Island baseball league was over fifty years old, as was the tennis club. As she got closer, she could read their jersey names. The gray-shirted Osoezes were playing the Dingbats in black.

A Dingbat waved at the officers. Christine and Fillingham waved back. He put two hands in the air, jogging toward them.

They pedaled over the grass to meet him.

Fillingham said, "Hi Ron. Everything okay?"

Ron Hamilton lived with his family on Third Street and worked in an appliance store on the mainland. He shook his head, eyes wide. "No, it is not!"

"What's wrong?" Christine said, looking behind Hamilton to the families and baseball players by the diamond.

"We're short two players," Ron said. "They'll be on the next ferry, but unless we get the minimum seven players in the next two minutes, we have to forfeit."

"How many do you have now?" Fillingham asked.

"Five," Hamilton said. "If Toronto's finest could sub in for half an inning, even if you just stand in the outfield."

"I don't really play—" Christine began.

"We're in," said Fillingham. "We'll have to borrow gloves. Center field." He pointed to Christine. "Left field." He pointed to himself.

Ron clapped his hands. "We got ourselves a game! Come on over and we'll suit you up."

At the bench, the officers slipped off their jackets and pulled a black jersey over their dress shirts. Applause rose from the sidelines from the friends, neighbors and families. Christine had patrolled during Monday night baseball games. The community came out to cheer and good-naturedly heckle the players. Groups sat on blankets with picnic dinners. Coolers were stocked with ice and beer, which the local police ignored.

Christine and Fillingham jogged to the outfield to cheers and hollers.

She said, "I haven't played much baseball. I'm not great at catching. I'm more of a thrower."

Fillingham waved her concern away. "You'll be in center field. Left field gets most of the action. I'll cover you if a ball comes your way."

As they waited for the Osoezes to come up to bat, a dog ran out onto the field.

"Lifeguard!" Christine said, kneeling to give her a pat. The dog wagged her tail ferociously, then headed over to Fillingham for attention.

Fillingham whistled for a spectator to get the dog. A teenager came onto the grass and threw a ball that Lifeguard chased off the field.

The Osoezes had heavy hitters. The first batter hit a double, then stole home when the next batter hit a single. The third batter hit a double, enabling the second run in. The fourth batter struck out.

It was one out, with the Osoezes leading 2–0.

"Back up," Fillingham yelled to Christine from thirty feet away. She walked backward, her eyes on the next batter, who looked like a rugby player.

"Shift toward me," he directed.

Christine just had time to move several steps to her right before the ball cracked off the bat, sailing high, right toward her.

"Go back! Go back!" Fillingham yelled.

She backpedaled, her eyes not leaving the ball. It was too high. It was going to go right over her head.

"Put your glove up," he instructed from behind her.

Still moving, she shoved her glove in the air. As the ball descended, she jumped, tipping it with the bridge of her glove. She fell to the ground on her back with a thud.

Turning, she saw Fillingham kneeling behind her, hand raised with the ball inside the glove.

He had caught it! Right off her glove.

A roar of voices. The runner on second tagged up and was heading toward third base.

"Throw it home, Sixteen," Fillingham said, tossing her the ball.

She scrambled up to standing. She had made it to the city finals three times for javelin. Not the same as a baseball, but she had a good arm.

She centered her eye on the catcher waving his hands at her and took two running strides before flinging the ball in the air.

The runner stomped on third base and was heading home when the catcher fielded Christine's throw and tagged the Osoeze runner.

"Out!" yelled the referee. "That's three out!"

Fillingham whooped from behind her. "We did it," he said as he came parallel to her. The two officers jogged off the field.

Back on the bench, the officers were thumped on the back and their hands pumped as the Dingbats celebrated the three outs.

"You guys are ringers," Ron said.

Christine and Fillingham pulled off their jerseys then put on their uniform jackets, despite entreaties to stay and bat. The players had arrived on the ferry during the inning and the game could proceed.

"We have to go," Christine said. "Our break is over."

Fillingham addressed the Osoezes before they headed onto the field. "Did anyone notice any garden equipment around?"

Gary Owen stood in a gray jersey. "What do you mean?"

"Property is missing from the Parks and Recreation sheds. And we're finding it all over the Island. Anyone see anything unusual today? People placing equipment in weird places?"

Owen shrugged. The Osoezes and Dingbat players shook their heads.

As the officers walked away, rolling their bikes, Christine said, "Maybe it was only on Algonquin Island." They passed the big willow tree at the southern end of the field, the one kids liked to climb. A wheelbarrow was wedged in the fork of two boughs.

Chapter 11

"Here it is," Christine said to Fillingham, who was following her on his bike.

The officers were on day shift, a quick change from afternoons. This always made Christine sleepy. She had gotten home last night at midnight after gathering the stolen gardening equipment from around the Island. And then she was up at five thirty to catch the 6:00 a.m. streetcar to the ferry docks.

They dismounted and leaned their bikes against the newly constructed fence around the Martins' yard. The white boards were over six feet tall, higher than any neighbor's fence. Most houses on the Island were not enclosed. On Ward's Island, the front yards were often too small to need the barrier. The Martins must have erected it this past week. It made their house look barricaded, like a prison.

Christine knocked on the gate. After listening for a few seconds, the officers unlatched the door and entered.

Christine scanned the yard. Judith Purnell had done a decent job filling in the holes with earth and raking the pockmarked gardens. The place no longer looked like a tornado had ravaged the place. It looked barren, but it was clean and swept.

"Did you see it before?" Christine asked Fillingham.

Her partner nodded.

They walked up to the porch. The two black urns on either side of the porch stairs had been replanted with begonias, but no other plants were visible.

The front door was closed. Islanders usually left their screen doors open to get a cross-breeze through the house. And kids were always running back and forth from home to camp, the beaches and the lagoons.

Christine knocked, hoping Mr. Martin was home. She had called the Parks and Recreation office this morning, but he hadn't been in his office.

The door opened six inches. A slice of Mrs. Martin's face appeared.

"Mrs. Martin," Christine began, "it's PW Lane and PC Fillingham. We were wondering if your husband was home?"

"He's not." She started to close the door.

"Can we speak with you for one moment?" Christine asked.

"What about?"

"Our investigation into your missing plants," Christine said.

Mrs. Martin tilted her head questioningly. She was wearing a tailored dress in peach and matching lipstick. "You found the culprit?"

"Not quite," said Christine.

Mrs. Martin rolled her eyes heavenward but opened the door wide. They followed her into the house. With one hand, she gestured to the living room on her left. Cream furniture sat on a blue and cream Persian rug. A white bookshelf rested against one wall. One corner was occupied by a squat television, the largest Christine had seen. The air smelled of paint. It was quite elegant—a living room from a well-off family in the suburbs. Ward's Island houses were usually full of second-hand furniture or furnishings handed down through the generations.

Several cardboard boxes were piled high in the corner. Three picture frames leaned against the wall under the side window.

"Have a seat," Mrs. Martin, indicating the couch. "We're not quite moved in yet."

"When do you expect Mr. Martin back?" Fillingham asked.

Mrs. Martin sat in a high-back blue tapestry chair across from them. "I believe Doug said Thursday, but he wasn't sure how many meetings he was booked for in Detroit."

"Is he there on business?" Fillingham asked.

"Why?" Mrs. Martin said, leaning back.

"Curious," he said, giving Mrs. Martin a wide smile. For once, his charm didn't seem to be working.

She harrumphed, then said, "He's meeting with the municipal government in Detroit and their harbor committee. Detroit recently revamped their downtown shoreline. Douglas is co-chair of the Toronto Waterfront Improvement Committee. He's reporting back to the commissioner and the mayor when he returns."

Christine said, "We were going to ask Mr. Martin about a break-in at the Hanlan's Point facility. We've found gardening tools and equipment scattered around the Island. Did he mention this theft to you?"

"No," Mrs. Martin said coolly.

"Mother!" a child's voice said.

The officers turned. A girl stood at the opening to the living room. She looked to be about ten or eleven, the same age as Christine's brother, Wayne. She was lean like her mother in her eyelet cotton dress but had the glossy black hair of her father.

"I'm busy," Mrs. Martin said. "Go play outside."

"By myself?"

"Where's your brother?"

The girl shrugged. "Upstairs playing with his cars."

Mrs. Martin waved a hand. "See if someone wants to go to the beach."

The girl frowned, her eyebrows puckered together. "No one will go with me. I don't have friends here."

Mrs. Martin said, "We just moved in, Matilda. It takes time."

"In Supervision," Matilda said, "no one would be my partner."

Mrs. Martin tilted her head. "That was one day. You need to try again."

The girl frowned. "They don't like me. They don't like our family. I don't know why we ever moved here." She turned and stomped up the stairs.

Mrs. Martin turned back to the officers, her expression neutral, as if the conversation with her daughter had never happened. "Did you find the culprits who vandalized the yard?"

Christine felt a seed of pity for Mrs. Martin. It must be hard to move to a place where your family wasn't welcome. And your children became the casualties of the conflict.

"We've looked around the Island to see if the plants were dumped by the marinas, meadows or tall grass areas," Fillingham responded. "We checked the beaches. Nothing found so far. The garbage collectors have found nothing in the bins either."

Christine wondered if Mrs. Martin's plants, the hydrangeas, roses and irises, were replanted in local gardens, as Mrs. Polotov had intimated.

"We are looking for connections," Fillingham said. "The garden vandalism and the shed break-in could be targeted acts against Parks and Recreation or your husband."

"Really!" Mrs. Martin said sarcastically. "I'm so glad our taxpayers' money is going to such crack investigators."

Fillingham and Christine met glances.

"Mrs. Martin," Fillingham continued, "if you think these acts have been intentional, who do you think are the perpetrators?"

Mrs. Martin pressed one hand to the collar of her neck, touching her opal necklace. "As you heard from Matilda, the Islanders dislike us. They are jealous of my husband's political position and refuse any change. They are squatters who have been allowed to stay on the Island unchecked. They are feral and tribal, and the Island would do well to get rid of them." Her right hand swatted the air.

The officers were speechless for five seconds.

"Do you have evidence against a specific person?" he asked.

Mrs. Martin's head tilted. "For which transgression? The garden? The break-in? Or for the pile of rotting fish left on my front porch?"

"When did that happen?" Christine asked, pulling her memo book out of her purse.

"Does it matter?" Mrs. Martin asked.

"Yes. I'll write an incident report," Christine said.

"You haven't figured out the first crime," the older woman said.

Christine waited, pen poised above her memo pad.

Wearily, Mrs. Martin described the pile of decaying fish she had discovered Friday morning when she had gone out on the porch. She had skidded on the slime, almost falling into the rancid mess. Her husband had to get a bucket and spade and make several runs to the lake to dump the smelly contents.

After Mrs. Martin's recount, Fillingham stood up. "Please let your husband know we will follow up on the break-in with the shed when he returns."

Mrs. Martin leaned back in her chair. "Come back when you have an arrest. You can see yourselves out."

Chapter 12

"She's a charmer," Fillingham remarked as they retrieved their bikes leaning against the Martins' fence.

"Like the husband," Christine replied.

"A match made in heaven."

"Why do you think Douglas Martin hasn't reported the break-and-enter?"

"Embarrassed?" he suggested. "Makes him look a fool. He can't even keep his equipment together."

She felt something swipe against her nylon legs. "Lifeguard!"

The dog wagged her tail, its rear moving back and forth with excitement. After Mrs. Martin, it was refreshing to have someone eager to see her.

Fillingham smiled. "Hey girl, where have you been?" He squatted and got a lick across the nose.

After patting the dog's long fur, the officers mounted their bikes, the dog trotting behind them.

As they rode parallel, he said, "Let's split up. You head to Ward's, question a few residents. I'll go to Hanlan's Point to check with Mallory. See if anything from the sheds is missing."

Christine nodded, trying to hide her disappointment. This morning had felt like their past camaraderie.

After Fillingham left, Christine pedaled over to a large maple tree and dismounted. Leaning down to pat the dog's head, she said,

"Want to go to the beach?" The dog bounded in front of Christine as she walked to the lake.

Christine headed to the firmer sand by the water. She didn't want to roll her ankle, especially since her sprain had healed. Families relaxed under sun umbrellas and the lake wind gently ruffling the fabric edges. People lay on towels, reading books, arms up to shade their eyes from the sun. A couple was playing cards. Teens at the far end were playing volleyball. She smiled. She'd talk to her mom tonight about their schedules and find a time in August when the family could ferry over for a day by the water.

Christine didn't see any local families on the beach. She wanted to ask residents about the garden vandalism, equipment theft and rotten fish. Likely, she'd get the same head shakes as she did at the baseball game, but it was her job to ask.

Halfway down the beach, she heard her name. Karl waved at her from the end of the beach by the rock pile. Phil, his coworker from the fisheries management project, was sitting in a beached rowboat beside him.

Great, she thought as she obediently headed in their direction. Time to relive her humiliation. The mutt bounded beside her. Christine smiled, her mood cheering. If she hadn't nearly drowned, she might not have met Lifeguard.

Christine made her way over in the sand and managed a cheery "Hello." Karl wore a tie-dye shirt with faded shorts and flip-flops. Phil was more conservatively attired in a white t-shirt, navy shorts and baseball cap.

"Returning to the scene of the crime," Phil said. He sounded grumpy rather than jocular.

Christine frowned. Up close, he looked ten years older than Karl, his lips thinner, shadows under his eyes.

Karl said, "You're hilarious, Phil." He turned to Christine. "I've been trying to get a hold of you. I dropped by the station, but you weren't around."

"I heard," she said.

"Got yourself a police dog?" Karl pointed to Lifeguard, who was splashing in the water after a ball someone had thrown.

She smiled. "Informally. The official uniform comes in next week."

Karl took a step forward, suddenly serious. "I wanted to thank you for jumping in to rescue me."

Phil removed equipment from the rowboat, placing the carriers on the sand. He grabbed two carriers and headed toward the trail to the Eastern Gap.

"He's way too intense," Karl said as he watched his coworker.

"Well, I won't water rescue him, then," she said.

Karl laughed. "Good call."

She said quickly, "You don't have to thank me. First, it's my job. Second, it ended in a farce."

He waved away her explanation. "It was very heroic. You risked your life to help me."

"Fine," she said. "You're welcome."

"How's your ankle?"

"Back to normal. The occasional twinge." Lifeguard trotted over, the fur on her legs and stomach wet.

"I should go," Christine said. "I have to patrol the residential area."

"Wait," Karl said, hand out in front of him. "I was wondering if you were around the Gala Day weekend?"

"I'm working. It's a busy time." Christine was scheduled to work all three days of the weekend and would bank overtime pay for the holiday Monday. And, she reminded herself, she had signed up for paid duty at the Adoption Barbeque, as Hawk had requested.

"The corn roast is on the Monday night." His face looked more bronzed than before, his cobalt blue eyes contrasting his auburn lashes. "I thought we could go together."

"I work until three that day," she said.

There was a piercing whistle. Phil stood in the grass by the sand's edge, one carrier on the ground, waving for Karl to follow.

Karl said, "The guy has three jobs, so he's always in a hurry to get to his next gig." He paused. "Back to the corn roast. If you're done in the afternoon, that gives us lots of time. We can swim, have a bite to eat and head to the fire for the corn roast at seven." He tilted his head, "Sound good?"

"Will you be wearing clothes?" When she first met Karl last year, he and his buddies were tanning nude on the roof of their houses.

"Only if you want me to."

She laughed. "I want you to."

"Okay. Great. Meet you at the beach at say, four o'clock?"

When she remained silent, he said, "What is it?"

"I'm a police officer. I can't be around anything illegal." She wasn't sure if Karl smoked pot, but she had certainly smelled it when called to his house last year.

"It's illegal to roast your corn with the husk off," Karl said, his tone serious, "so if you stick to the rules, so will I."

"I'm serious."

"No problem. Message received. I clean up good."

She thought he looked appealing now with his tanned skin and wavy hair, exuding health and smelling like the sun. "Okay."

Christine made her way back to her bike, Lifeguard trotting beside her. She told the dog, "Someone else likes my company."

Chapter 13

"Heading out?" Christine asked Wayne.

Wayne stood by the apartment door, a black-and-white sports bag slung over his shoulder with two baseball bats sticking out. A seam on the bag had come unstitched and patches of the black coloring had peeled. Wayne's birthday was in September. If she tucked away money from her extra shifts, she could buy him a new sports bag, one designed to accommodate bats.

"Yup," he said with a perfunctory smile. He was wearing an old pair of baseball pants and a blue jersey. Gosh, he seemed taller, like he had grown two inches over the summer.

"Which diamond are you at?" she asked, leaning against the hall wall.

He shrugged. "Not sure."

"Sorauren Park or the school?"

"Those are for babies."

She laughed. "My apologies, Hank Aaron. I forgot you needed extra yardage for your home runs."

He opened the door and headed out.

Christine ran down the hallway and stuck her hand out to prevent the door from closing. "Wayne! Where you headed?"

"I don't know."

She followed him out. "Wayne!"

Her brother paused on the stairwell, bag over his shoulder, glaring at her, wavy brown hair flopping over one eye. His stance reminded her of James Dean.

"You're not my mom," he said.

She felt a frisson of anger. She'd been like a mom to her siblings since they were born, taking care of them when Phyllis headed out to the track or passed out drunk with Eddie, their stepfather. Eddie had taken off six years ago, thank goodness.

"You're right," Christine said. "I'm not your mom."

Something in her tone made him pause.

She continued. "I am the one paying for your academy baseball training. But you're right. I should let Mom take care of that."

"Christie Pits," he mumbled, then ran down the stairs.

Back in the kitchen, Christine chastised herself. She didn't have to be so heavy-handed with her brother. Her job made her overly cautious.

She heard the bang of a drawer closing. Her mother was up. Phyllis had worked the afternoon shift yesterday and got home at midnight. She tried to sleep in if she could. After grabbing the kettle, Christine filled it with water for tea.

Wayne and Phyllis were similar. Both ran hot and cold. Excited and grumpy. Sometimes Phyllis let Wayne and Donna stay up late, even on a school night, and other times she ordered them to bed by eight with a scowl.

As Christine poured the boiling water into a teapot, she thought about her three days off before the hectic August long weekend. Today, she would make a nice dinner for her family and catch up on the laundry. Donna was in her room, reading, since she wasn't enrolled in camp this week. Opening the fridge, Christine checked for butter. *Yes.* She and Donna could bake this afternoon if the apartment wasn't too hot. Use the stovetop to make crispy rice squares.

"Tea's ready," Christine said as her mom entered the kitchen in her cotton bathrobe, brown-gray hair tousled from the sleep, eyes squeezed against the light.

Christine handed her mom a cup of tea with added milk and sugar and the two sat at the table. "Busy shift yesterday?"

Phyllis worked in a civilian department of the police force, typing the hand-written incident reports submitted by patrol officers. After six years in Records, she was not only a fast typist, but she was also adept at deciphering illegible scrawl.

Mondays in the summer could be as busy as Saturdays. Families crowded beaches. Yorkville and downtown Toronto were filled with young people at music venues, cafes and taverns.

Phyllis sipped her tea. "Yonge Street was hopping. Three loitering charges, a break-and-enter and a mugging. Just from the Strip."

"The Strip" was the name for a section of Yonge Street, a road that started at Lake Ontario and continued north to cottage country. It bisected the middle of downtown Toronto and was filled with record stores, vintage shops, restaurants, head shops, massage parlors and theaters. Grit and culture, side by side.

"Do you want toast and jam?" Christine asked.

Phyllis shook her head.

Her mother didn't eat enough. No wonder she was thin, her elbows pointy, her body swallowed up by the robe.

Phyllis patted her robe pockets, looking for her cigarettes. She must have left them in the living room. Christine was trying to get her mother to smoke outside when her siblings were around. She had heard that smoking wasn't good for you.

"Wayne's gone out to Christie Pits," Christine said. "He'll be gone until dinner. Donna's in her room, reading to her stuffed animals."

Phyllis pointed to the *News and Views* Toronto Police Association magazine on the kitchen table. "They've posted the Commendation Ceremony date in there. August 14th."

Christine frowned. "Did the announcement list the attendees?"

Phyllis tilted her head. "I'm sure he'll be there. You saved his daughter from the fire."

Christine took a sip of tea to calm herself. The Commendation Ceremony was to acknowledge the police officers involved in Project Niagara, the Yorkville undercover operation. Christine, Fillingham and Christine's three friends, Sarah, Gail and Julie, were being given plaques of appreciation. The chief and would be present. And so would Deputy Chief John Darlow, Christine's father.

No one knew the deputy was her father. Christine had found out herself a month ago. Phyllis had a relationship with John Darlow twenty-five years ago when he was engaged to a Forest Hill socialite. He got married and had a daughter. Christine did not see or hear from him for twenty-four years, although Darlow said he had kept tabs on her, sent money to Phyllis and paid for Phyllis's rehab. Now he wanted a relationship with Christine, albeit a secret one.

Christine wasn't having any of it. John Darlow hadn't been part of her life. She and Phyllis were raising Donna and Wayne. They didn't need Darlow. Just because had Christine rescued Darlow's daughter during Project Niagara, it didn't mean she wanted anything to do with his family. Darlow wanted his bastard to be kept a secret but to talk to her when he saw fit. She wasn't a marionette eager to dance to his tune.

"Could you accept the plaque for me?" Christine asked. "Say I had to work."

"No," Phyllis said. "You're expected to come in person. You. Geoffrey. Your friends. It would look strange if you didn't show up. The newspapers will be there. It will be good for your career." She paused. "I know it's awkward..."

Christine stared at her mother, but Phyllis sputtered to a halt. For all Christine's life, Phyllis had asserted that Christine's father had been a pilot killed in the war. Only when Kelly Darlow informed Christine about the truth did Phyllis admit her lie.

The telephone rang. Christine rose to get it, glad of the interruption.

"Julie," Christine said, "I was thinking about you guys." After a pause, she said, "Perfect timing for me. I have three days off. Yes, tomorrow for lunch would be perfect." She looked over at her mom to see if that worked with their schedule.

Phyllis nodded.

"That's great," Christine confirmed. "The Fearsome Four together again!"

Chapter 14

"This is fancy," Christine said as she sat down beside Gail at the cafe table, a vase of red carnations decorating the linen tablecloth.

Julie sat opposite them in a paisley summer dress, a white headband binding her blonde bob. "Nothing's too good for the ladies who serve Toronto!"

Christine wore a peasant skirt and loose white blouse, the best she could find. Beside her, Gail sported her usual attire of shirt and pants. The only time she wore a skirt was when she was in uniform.

"Sarah coming?" Christine asked, pointing to the empty seat across from her.

Julie nodded, then motioned for the waiter to bring the coffee carafe for Christine. "Ken is dropping her off. She said she might be a few minutes late."

Christine smiled before looking at the proffered menu. She hadn't seen her friends for a couple of weeks. During Operation Niagara, she had seen them daily. She missed that, especially since Fillingham was still miffed with her.

Sarah arrived, all freckles and smiles, her curly brown hair reaching her shoulders. She sat beside Julie and gave her friend's shoulders a squeeze. Leaning, she touched Christine's hand, then Gail's. "So nice to see you all. It's been so long since the Fearsome Four got together. What's new?"

Gail shrugged. "Summer in Toronto: giving directions to tourists; handing out parking tickets, attending fender-benders and dodging cars."

Julie said, "Gail, you caught that purse snatcher last week." The three friends worked at the Women's Bureau.

"I didn't know that," Sarah said. "Were you working for Morality?"

Gail shook her head. "I was ticketing on Queen Street, and this guy runs toward me holding a lady's purse. So I stuck out my foot. Guy hit the pavement like a sack of potatoes."

Christine laughed. "That'll do it." She paused. "Any progress with Petra's application?"

Gail's roommate and partner had been a doctor in Russia and had applied to practice in Canada. It was a tedious, drawn-out process.

Gail said, "Nah. Frustrating, but it is what it is." She addressed Julie. "How was the date with, what's his name, Frank?"

Julie said, "George, actually." She shrugged. "It was all right. We went to a swanky nightclub on College Street. The singer was talented. George was dull."

"Before I went on vacation, you were seeing that opera singer. What was his name...Carlos?" Sarah said.

Julie said, "Carmello. Yes, he was swoony, but he's moved on."

"Meaning?" Gail asked.

"His opera company travels throughout Europe and North America. He was here for a week."

"You're tearing through Toronto's bachelors quickly," Sarah said.

Julie said lightly, "I don't want anything long-term. Just looking for fun."

Julie had dated Fillingham for over a year, and he had broken up with her during the undercover operation.

"Leave a few men for Christine," Sarah said.

"Right," Julie said, looking at Christine. "You need all the help you can get."

Christine frowned at the dig. Julie sometimes made Christine feel like a dowdy matron.

"I have a date," she countered.

"Ooooh," said Sarah and Julie.

Julie said, "Who is it? Not the guy with the feathers?"

Christine froze. Was Julie referring to Hawk Johnson? Julie had seen him last summer when Christine and Julie worked the Mariposa Festival on Toronto Island. Hawk had greeted Christine after the dancing competition, resplendent in headdress, feathers and beads. Had Julie sensed a relationship between Hawk and Christine, even before they became secret lovers?

Hawk. She felt a familiar stab. They were never meant to be. But they were friends. Which was why she was attending the Adoption Barbeque this Saturday to look for Layla.

Christine said, "His name is Karl. He's working for a fisheries project on the Island."

Julie placed her chin on her hand. "Karl. Sounds Swedish. Or Danish. What does he look like?"

"Well, he's got long auburn hair. And a red beard."

"A hippie," Julie said dismissively.

"He's smart," Christine said defensively. "He's working on his PhD."

Sarah said, "That sounds challenging."

"That sounds boring," Julie said.

"Don't be like that," Gail chided Julie. "Everybody's looking for something different. We don't have to be like you."

Julie pressed a hand to her chest. "There's no one like me."

"Point made," Gail said. She turned to Christine. "You and Fillingham make up?"

Christine looked at her coffee cup. "No. He's asked to work with other partners."

Sarah said, "He broke up your partnership?"

Christine nodded. "Starting next month, he'll be randomly assigned to staff. We'll be on the same shift sometimes, but not regularly."

Julie sighed. "When I was his girlfriend, I never liked how chummy the two of you were. But you're meant to work together. Like Frick and Frack. The Odd Couple—"

"Can we talk about something else?" Christine asked.

The server came for their order, and the four women quickly perused the menu. When Julie said the brunch was on her, since she had her parents' credit card, Christine ordered waffles and fruit.

Christine said, "Sarah, you had a nice vacation?"

Sarah smiled. "Yes, it was wonderful. Ken's parents were up at the cottage for the weekend, but we had the rest of the week to ourselves to swim and barbeque and relax."

"Sounds great." Christine wondered if she'd ever have the money to go on vacation. Book a cottage or hotel somewhere. But not until she repaid Fillingham the money he had loaned her. Christine's mother had gone to a loan shark to pay her gambling debts. Fillingham had paid Phyllis's high-interest loan. Since then, Christine gave him money biweekly toward the repayment of the loan.

"You look healthy," said Julie to Sarah. "The tan suits you."

Sarah beamed. "I have news."

"Sergeant Anvil has the hots for you?" Gail said.

Sarah laughed. "Sergeant Anvil has the hots for every policewoman." She paused. "I'm pregnant."

The three women sat back in their chairs, surprised.

"That's wonderful, right?" Christine said, looking around the table. They all knew that pregnant policewomen had to resign from the force.

Sarah grasped Christine's hand from across from her. "Yes. Yes, it is!"

"What did Sergeant Carroll say?" Gail said.

Sarah shook her head. "It's early in my pregnancy. I haven't said anything yet at work." She smiled. "I had to tell you guys. I was going to explode."

"What does Ken think?" Gail asked.

Ken was a police officer out of the Etobicoke division.

"He's over the moon." Her smile faltered for a moment. "The only cloud is that I'll have to quit. And I won't see you guys as much."

Gail said, "That is such an unfair regulation." She lifted a hand in the air. "Does Ken have to quit because he's going to be a father?"

Sarah said, "They worry about pregnant women being hurt on the job."

Gail waved her comment away. "Put her on administrative duty. They do that all the time for injured policemen."

Christine asked, "Would you want to work after the baby?"

Sarah placed her head on her chin, considering. "Not right away. But I love my job. And my mom would help. I'd like to come back."

Gail said, "We should do something. Start a petition. Talk to our union representatives. This is unfair."

Christine said, "They changed the regulation forcing policewomen to quit after marrying a policeman. They could change this."

"I'll start a petition at the Women's Bureau," Julie said.

Christine said, "I could call Sam Malone." He was the head of the police union.

"I have a friend at the newspaper," Gail said. "She has a column in the women's section of the *Telegram*. I'll see if she can write about it."

Sarah blinked away tears. "You guys are the best." She raised her fist in the air. "Let's change the policy. When you guys have babies, you can go back to work too!"

The three women shook their heads. No one was having babies soon, except for Sarah.

Gail said, "You're our only chance for motherhood, Sarah."

Sarah said, "That settles it, then." She gestured with both hands. "All three of you will be godparents."

Chapter 15

"There'll be hot dogs and hamburgers and soda. Help yourself." The social worker gestured to the three barbeques lined up beside ten picnic tables covered in red plaid plastic tablecloths. "Oh, I see another family." She waved at a trio heading toward them, two adults and a toddler.

Christine walked around the perimeter of the party, greeting guests and introducing herself to the organizational staff. It was the annual Adoption Barbeque, sponsored by a local bank and newspaper; the location was a rectangular grassy section of High Park. As Christine wandered, she met the journalist who wrote the adoption column, social workers from the various adoption agencies, bank staff and families.

Hawk had spoken bitterly about the newspaper adoption column, noting than many children were Indigenous, taken from their families like Remi and Layla. He said white people were always trying to cure them of being Native, like they did in residential schools.

Christine didn't know what to think. As she leaned to throw a ball to a toddler, she thought that many of the children looked excited to be at the barbeque.

"Getting hungry, Officer?" a man said as he turned on a barbeque.

"Absolutely," Christine said. "There's a hamburger with my name on it!"

One child had leg braces, and another was tiny for his age. Looking around, she could see that several children had medical needs. There was something heartening about families stepping forward to provide support for these children.

Christine shook her head. She wasn't here to judge the adoption process. Her job was to locate Layla, Remi's daughter and Hawk's stepdaughter, and report back. And that was it. Her involvement would be finished.

As families joined, trickling in from the street and the parking lot up the road, the picnic area got more crowded. A group of fathers headed down the road and returned with more picnic tables. They placed additional seating by the playground that featured a slide, swing set and monkey bars.

The crowd had swelled to over a hundred. Christine kept her eye on the sidewalk, ensuring that park goers didn't crash the private event, enticed by the smell of cooking meat. High Park was busy on a Saturday with hikers, walkers, swimmers and tennis players. There was also a small zoo up the road that families were welcome to see after the barbeque. Christine had been there several times with her siblings.

A clown made animal balloons by one of the picnic tables, a group of excited children circling him. Farther down, a bank employee filled balloons imprinted with the bank logo with air from a tank. Children screeched as they hit balloons to each other, trying to keep them from striking the ground.

A few fathers set up a makeshift goalie net and were kicking a soccer ball around with a band of children. A trio of girls by the playground were holding bubble wands to the wind, the smaller children chasing the soapy bubbles and clapping them between their palms.

By noon, it was getting louder, with two hundred people in attendance. Food was served on paper plates, and families sat at the picnic tables or on blankets to eat burgers, hot dogs, coleslaw and potato chips, washed down with pop. With more people sitting, Christine had a better chance of surveying the children. There were more girls than boys, dressed in cotton dresses and mary jane shoes, sporting hair that had been plaited or pulled back into hairbands or ponytails. Boys wore cotton or dress pants and long-sleeved shirts as if ready for a church service.

Christine ate her hamburger standing up, surveying the crowd, careful not to drip ketchup onto her uniform. She wiped grease off her fingers and walked by the picnic tables, scanning for a girl with dark hair. Hawk was right. Quite a few adoptees were Native.

Some children had finished their lunch and were back on the playground or the field, kicking balls or playing tag. There! Christine spotted a dark-haired girl in a floral dress at a picnic table by the playground. Her hair was pulled into an intricate bun on her head. Two other girls sat at the table, backs to the girl as they watched the antics of the other children, smiles on their faces.

Slowly making her way to the girl, Christine stopped on the way to hit a balloon and pick up a toddler who had fallen.

Ten feet away, Christine scrutinized the girl. It was Layla; she was sure of it. The same heart-shaped face. Dark hair. About eight years old. She looked well cared for. As Christine moved to the side of Layla, she spotted white frilly socks and mary jane shoes. Her dress had layered sleeves and three rows of ruffles on the skirt.

The two girls who had been sitting at Layla's table ran over to the swings.

Christine sat down across from Layla. "Is it okay if I take a break here?" she asked.

Layla stared at her with intent brown eyes and then gave a slight nod of assent. Her glance moved past Christine and alit on one of the picnic tables where four adults were talking. One pair must be her adoptive parents.

"I'm Policewoman Lane," Christine said. "You're Layla, right?"

The girl's eyes flared wide, jaw dropping. After a few seconds, she said in a low, astonished voice, "How do you know my name?"

Shoot. Christine gestured to the table where Layla's adoptive parents sat. "People were chatting about their children. I thought I heard your name."

"I'm not allowed to say that name ever again," Layla whispered. "It's my old name."

"I'm sorry," Christine said, shocked that the adoptive parents had changed the girl's name. "What's your new name?

"Margaret," the girl said. "Margaret Campbell."

Christine said, "Hello, Margaret Campbell. How are you liking the picnic?"

Layla stared at Christine. Her hair was shiny, but there were hollows under her eyes, as if she didn't sleep well. And she exuded not misery, but a blankness.

Christine schooled herself to keep the conversation short. She had gotten what she came for. Layla was here at the picnic, which meant she had been adopted in Toronto or the vicinity. Christine now knew the surname of the parents. That was enough. Her mission was complete. She should get up and continue patrolling.

Moving so that she blocked Layla's sightline to her adoptive parents, Christine said, "I'm a friend of Hawk's."

Layla's eyes widened, tears filling them. Her chest heaved visibly.

What had Christine done? She was interfering. Making a mess of things. But Layla had looked so desolate. She needed to know that she was loved. That people were thinking about her.

"Where is he?" Her voice was an anguished whisper.

"With your mom," Christine said.

"He's...he's dead?" Layla asked, mouth pulled in a horrified twist.

"No," Christine said quickly. "No. He spends time with your mom in Whitefish."

"My mom?"

"Yes, Hawk comes back to the reservation when he's not working in Toronto."

"My mom?" The girl's hands shook.

"Layla. Margaret," Christine began. "I'm sorry if I upset you."

"My mom's not dead?" Layla's voice was barely above a whisper.

"Dead?" Christine responded. "No, of course not."

The girl shuddered, her shoulders turning in. She turned away from Christine, bent over, and threw up.

Christine ran over to the girl, who vomited once more on the grass. Christine rubbed her back. Scanning behind her, she saw a man and woman stand up from a picnic table and hurry over.

"What happened?" the woman said, her tone horrified. She was tall and lean, hair in a bun like Layla's, wearing a skirt and blazer. The man stood ten feet behind her as if he didn't want to get any nearer.

Christine smiled. "Probably ate too many hotdogs."

"Margaret," the woman said, approaching the girl, "I told you to have one hot dog. One. And to eat it slowly." She turned to Christine. "She eats too much. And too fast. Like an animal. She has no manners from where she came from."

Christine watched as Layla sat back up, silently taking the tissue offered by the woman to wipe her mouth.

"It's the heat," Christine said. "I see it all the time at Centreville. It doesn't agree with children's stomachs."

"Well, she's ruined the day for the rest of us," the woman said. She looked over her shoulder. "Howard, get the car, please. We're leaving. I need to say goodbye to Mrs. Fitzwilliam."

Christine said, "I'll walk Margaret to the sidewalk and wait there for the car." The parking lot was a three-minute walk up the road.

With a withering look at Layla, Mrs. Campbell left.

Layla stood up, eyes on the ground, and followed Christine across the grass to the sidewalk.

They waited by the side of the road. After a few minutes, a car honked as it approached.

Layla said quickly, "They told me my mom died in the accident. That's why I was being adopted."

Christine closed her eyes for a second. Hawk had been right.

As the car slowed to a stop, Christine hurriedly pulled a necklace from underneath her work blouse. Hawk had given her the medicine bag last year containing a shell, button and pinches of sweetgrass, sand and tobacco. It was to keep her safe on the job and help her act with integrity and bravery.

"This is from Hawk," Christine said. "It will protect you."

Layla snatched it and quickly looped it over her head, hiding it under her dress. Mrs. Campbell approached. Silently, the two got into the car and it sped away.

Two hours later, Christine called Hawk from a payphone at the Centre Island ferry dock.

"It's Christine," she said. She had wanted to call him as soon as possible. To be finished with it.

"I know who you are," he said, his tone warm. She remembered that timbre. It was how he spoke to her when they were in bed together.

Snap out of it. "I saw her. Layla. She was at the picnic."

There was a long pause. She could hear him swallow. "How…how is she?"

Christine reminded herself that Hawk and Remi hadn't seen Layla for months. For them, she may have disappeared forever.

"She looks cared for. Wearing a nice dress. She…" Christine didn't know how to say this.

"What's wrong?"

"She looked empty. Like she didn't care about anything anymore." She could hear a quick intake of breath.

"I got her name," Christine continued. "They changed it. She's Margaret now. Margaret Campbell. That should help find her, right? The dad's name is Howard Campbell."

"That will help."

"From what I could tell, the families were from Toronto, or a nearby town like Milton, Burlington, Oshawa. The child and family services agencies were from Toronto, Peel and Durham. I don't know where the Campbells live."

He exhaled. "That helps too."

The ferry gate clanged open, and passengers surged onto the boat. "I have to go to work," she said.

"Christine. I cannot thank you enough. Remi cannot thank you enough."

"You asked for my help, and I gave it. I did it for you. Now I'm done."

"Thank you."

"One thing I should tell you. Layla was told her mother had died in the accident. And that's why she was adopted. I told her the truth. She was very upset."

There was silence for several seconds. In an angry but controlled voice he said, "They do that sometimes. Tell them the parents are dead. Or that they didn't want them anymore. They lie so the child doesn't fight. Doesn't run away."

The ferry's horn blasted its final boarding signal, and Christine ended the call. It felt like she was saying goodbye to Hawk forever.

Chapter 16

Christine enjoyed working Gala Day weekend. Sure, there were swarms of people, but most were current and past Island residents, and it was one large, joyous reunion. Christine knew most of the locals by sight, if not by name. There was a warmth to the gathering as old friends greeted each other and people danced, ate and talked. There were musicians and performers on stilts and a bonfire. The proceeds of the raffles, bake sales and games paid for Supervision, the Ward's Island summer camp.

Gala Day patrol was preferable to policing the Caribana Festival taking place concurrently on Centre Island. Christine had done a shift once for Caribana and swore never to do it again. Gala Day dealt with hundreds of people; Caribana attracted thousands. The Caribana costumes were fabulous as was the food, but the ferry system couldn't handle the droves of visitors. By the late afternoon, there were hundreds waiting for the ferry back to the mainland. For some, it was a three-hour wait, even with private taxis picking up passengers. The lack of transit was hectic and frustrating for party-goers and police. When a ferry did dock, the police stood as a human barricade around the ferry docks to stop people from trampling each other to get on the boat.

Now that it was Gala Day Monday, Christine and Fillingham were on day shift, with Nelson scheduled to start at noon.

"A bake sale! And a party and games?" Nelson said when she arrived at the station. "When can we go?"

"I'll finish this lost wallet report," Christine said from her perch at an office desk. "Then we'll head over to Ward's. Most events start after one."

"I'm starving," Nelson said, clutching her flat stomach.

"You should eat more," Fillingham said. He walked over to the counter. "You're so slender."

Nelson walked across the waiting room and leaned her elbows on the counter. "I eat like a horse." She showed them her bicep in the narrow sleeve of her uniform. "I'm strong as an ox, too. If you need anything lifted or moved, I'm your girl."

Fillingham chortled. "I'll let you know when we rearrange the station furniture."

Nelson smacked the counter. "What can I do now?"

Christine stood up from the desk and placed the incident report in an envelope for the courier. "Can you get our bikes out from the garage and water the front bed flowers?"

Nelson disappeared out the front door.

"She's got a strong work ethic," Fillingham said.

"On one hand, she's a dynamo, and on the other hand, she is so innocent," Christine said.

"I admire her energy," he said.

"There are worse combinations." Christine thought of Morano and the other woman-hating officers she had met during her career.

"Bring your pocket change," Fillingham said as he walked into the waiting room.

Christine's hope flared. Last year, they had competed against each other in the Gala Day games: the dart throw, bottle toss and fishing pool. Were they back to normal?

Fillingham continued, "I promised Cadet Nelson a game or two."

Christine sighed and followed him out the front door. This weekend was her last partnered schedule with Fillingham. After today, he would be randomly assigned to officers. Since returning to Island patrol three weeks ago, she hadn't been able to dent his armor. Were they even friends?

The three officers biked eastward toward Ward's Island, Nelson chatting the whole time. Christine was glad to have her on shift. She was a buffer between Christine and Fillingham, allowing the trio to function.

Fillingham gestured to a hand-painted sign on the grass to their right. It read: *Is the water safe?*

Nelson asked, "What does that mean?"

Christine said, "It's about the duck deaths. You heard the community at the TIRA meeting. People are concerned about water quality and its impact on wildlife."

Nelson asked, "Is the water at the police station okay? I'm used to well water."

Fillingham said, "Tap water is treated at the filtration plant on the Island. It's fine."

The three rode side by side until a pedestrian came along, and they slid into a line behind each other.

"Another sign." Christine pointed to a white cardboard square attached to a flat piece of wood: *Save the animals. Save the Island.*

Nelson asked, "Who's writing the signs?"

Christine said, "Could be the advocacy groups we saw at the meeting. Operation Pollution. Or Greenpeace. Friends of Toronto Wildlife."

They passed another sign about water safety. Fillingham said, "Could be Islanders. They're worried about water quality."

Christine shook her head. "If the ducks had died from toxins in the water, wouldn't other organisms such as fish be affected?"

Fillingham said, "Unless they're the canary in a coal mine, warning of increased toxicity."

As Christine rounded a bend, she could hear the jubilant twang of a fiddle. Last year, Gala Day showcased local musicians, ranging from big band musicians with brass instruments to fiddlers and folk singers. One teenager sang an opera aria. They had ongoing performances all day long.

And there would be items for sale by Island artists: knitted blankets, macramé plant holders, textile art, jewelry, pottery and hand-dyed silk scarves.

The ferry docks and field came into view. They passed a few more signs. One said: *Is this grass safe to sit on?*

There was the thwack of a ball. Christine spied tennis players competing in a doubles game behind the community center. From beside the tennis court came the clunk of lawn bowls colliding.

The field used for the Monday night baseball league was populated with tables of food in one corner—the bake sale. The rest of the green contained a variety of children and adult games, from ring toss to casino games to a water dunk tank.

A small stage at the north end featured two fiddlers, the sound that she had heard earlier. Fifty spectators stood or sat on the blankets and mats in front, cheering the duo. The fiddlers were battling each other, each musician taking turns playing.

"Lucky draw here! Get your tickets for the lucky draw!" a man barked.

The officers dismounted and placed their bikes against the far wall of the community center. Bikes leaned against the fence surrounding the tennis court and lined the pathway south to the lake.

"Nelson," Fillingham said, "let's try the ring toss."

With a whoop of agreement, Nelson followed Fillingham out onto the field.

"See you later," Christine said. She took a deep breath in and out. She didn't need Fillingham or Nelson to enjoy herself. Gala Day weekend was built-in fun.

Heading into the heat of the community center where tickets were being sold, Christine introduced herself to the event organizers, letting them know that three officers would patrol the field. Despite her protests, she was given a handful of free tickets.

Tickets in hand, Christine chatted with the women supervising the food tables, asking for suggestions. She ended up with a chicken salad sandwich and a butterscotch square. Her mom sometimes made the brown sugary treat. Plate of food in hand, Christine scanned for a place to sit. Benches and chairs were in use. She might have to sit on the grass, which was fine, except for the risk of grass stains on her skirt.

By the baseball diamond, Christine spotted a stretch of empty bench. Beelining for the seat, she passed the baby pool filled with plastic fish and a magnetic fishing rod, the toilet paper toss and a track for tricycle riding.

A family sat at one end of the long bench created for baseball teams. As Christine neared, she recognized Mrs. Martin. She was smoking a cigarette while her two children sat several feet away from her, munching popcorn.

Christine was too close to turn around and find a different seat. It would be obvious she was avoiding the superintendent's wife.

"Mrs. Martin," Christine said as she sat at the far end of the bench. "I'm looking for a place to eat my lunch. The place is crowded."

Mrs. Martin watched her sit down. After another puff and exhale of her cigarette, she said, "No one will sit by us, so take all the space you want." She was wearing a mint-green dress with a shallow string of pearls and low-heeled pumps. She looked ready for high tea.

Christine didn't know what to say to that. Locals disliked Douglas Martin because he supported the plan to evict them from their houses. Did Mrs. Martin expect any other response from residents? It seemed unwise for the Martins to live on the Island, even if it was protocol. It was a source of conflict.

After swallowing a bite of her sandwich, Christine asked, "Is your husband here, Mrs. Martin?" She scanned the area. That would be bad. The superintendent's presence would surely lead to an argument, if not fisticuffs.

Mrs. Martin shook her head. "He's with the mayor at the Caribana festivities."

Christine turned back to Mrs. Martin, relieved. "I patrolled the carnival last year. Busy, but fun."

"Yes, it was my preference to go with him." The superintendent's wife looked at her children. "But Matilda and Reginald insisted." She waved the smoke of her cigarette away. "The camp children had been talking about Gala Day all week. "

Either Mrs. Martin was devoted to her children, out of touch or didn't care what the Islanders thought of her. All three, Christine hazarded.

"Have you tried the desserts?" Christine asked the children. She held up her butterscotch square. "Two tickets."

Matilda shook her head. "Mother said we could have ice cream later. If we behaved."

The siblings looked well behaved to Christine, silently eating their popcorn as they watched children whooping and running around the field.

"Hello, Mrs. Martin," a male voice said. Christine turned. Fillingham.

"Where's Cadet Nelson?" Christine asked.

He gestured behind him. "She wanted to join a country dance called the Madison. I have no idea what she was talking about, so I let her go."

Over the megaphone, a man's voice announced that the three-legged race for females would begin in fifteen minutes, followed by the males. Participants should meet at the starting line by the community center.

"Mother," Matilda said excitedly, "be my partner for the race. All the camp kids are doing it."

"Go with your brother."

"I can't," Matilda said. "It's girls only and boys only races." She pouted. "Please, Mother."

"Look at me, Matilda." Mrs. Martin's voice was stern. "I am not dressed for a race." She took a puff of her cigarette. "It's not dignified for a woman of my position."

Christine met Fillingham's glance. What position? The most hated woman on the Island?

Matilda's face fell, brown eyes blinking tears.

"I'll do it," Fillingham said.

"What?" Mrs. Martin regarded him with suspicion.

"I'll race with your son." He addressed the boy. "What's your name?"

"Reginald!" The boy stood up, spilling his popcorn.

"And PW Lane will pair up with Matilda."

Matilda's eyes widened, mouth hanging open. She stood up and said, "Let's practice!" She ran toward the community center. After ten feet, she turned, waving to Christine to follow her.

Christine looked over at Fillingham. "I'm not a fast runner."

"You'll be paying for ice cream then. Best finisher wins. The loser pays for two scoops. Medals are awarded to the top five finishers."

Before Christine could protest further, Mrs. Martin said, "That's very nice of you." She looked away, then back at the officers. "Thank you."

Fillingham's smile widened, and he tipped his hat. A feeling of warmth spread through Christine. It was like old times—her partner conniving her into an activity, hooking her in by making it a competition. Maybe things would be okay after all.

Chapter 17

Matilda held out the potato sack. Christine placed a leg inside the burlap and bunched the material in her fist to hold the sack. Matilda followed suit. Their first attempt at walking in the sack was disastrous—they fell to the ground in a heap after three steps. They were out of rhythm—Christine's stride was so much longer than the girl's.

"Let's tie our legs together," Matilda said. She grabbed a handkerchief from her mother and tied her left leg to Christine's right. After a few tries, they were able to walk together, counting out each step: 1-2-3-4, over and over.

"We need to take bigger steps," Matilda said.

"Why?" Christine asked.

"To win." The girl hooked her left arm through Christine's right arm. "Hold my arm," she commanded. "Jump me forward with each step so I keep up with your step. Like leapfrogging."

They practiced for a minute, tumbling a few times, but they got the hang of it. Mind you, Christine's wool skirt now had grass stains and her nylons had a run.

The announcer's voice sounded, calling the female three-legged racers to meet at the community center.

The grass had been painted with a yellow starting line. Racers were to run the width of the field to the white finish line. As the pairs lined up for the three-legged race, Matilda smiled excitedly at Christine.

Christine said, "I don't care if we win. Let's have fun. If we fall, just get up. We'll get ice cream either way."

Matilda nodded.

The girl reminded Christine of her sister Donna, who was so enthusiastic about her passions: dinosaurs, animals and volcanoes. Matilda was a kid in a difficult situation. And every kid deserved fun.

The starter pistol blasted, and the racers moved ahead, some tumbling immediately.

Christine called out, "One, leap! Two, leap!" as she grabbed Matilda's arm to launch her ahead. They were doing well until the middle of the field, when Matilda stumbled in a divot and the two tumbled to their knees.

"Get up! Get up! Get up!" Matilda yelled.

Christine restarted her count. "Look ahead," she advised. "We're almost there!"

They frog-leaped through the last quarter of the race, pairs laughing, falling and screaming around them.

"One, leap! Two, leap!" Christine and Matilda chanted together.

They passed the finish line. A volunteer said, "Fourth!" and handed each of them a green ribbon.

Christine staggered to a halt, then leaned over to catch her breath, the burlap bag falling to the ground.

Matilda untied the kerchief binding their legs together, then squeezed Christine in a hug. "We were fourth! Fourth!"

Matilda took off to show her mom the ribbon, while Christine returned the potato sack to the organizers for the next race. The three-legged race for males was announced. Matilda ran to the starting line to give her brother the kerchief in case they wanted to tie their legs together too.

Christine excused herself to get a drink of water. A table in the food section had free glass bottles filled with water, with a caveat to return the empty bottle before you left the festival. As Christine waited in line for a bottle, someone behind her said, "That woman stole my house."

Christine turned. The woman looked familiar: mid-thirties, light brown hair tied behind with a hair clip. Then she remembered. Carol Merriweather, the previous owner of the Martins' house.

"I'm sorry," Christine said. "What did you say?"

The woman gestured to the race finish line. "The Martins. I saw you with the family. They're thieves and liars. When our lease was up, they said we had to leave, that the house would be demolished like the other Lakeshore houses. So we left, and the Martins moved in!

"This is my husband, Albert," Mrs. Merriweather said, pointing to the tall, lean man with wispy brown hair behind her. "We're trying to find a house on Ward's or Algonquin. Right now, we're living with my daughter in Leslieville."

Christine nodded at this barrage of information, and then her turn was next. She gratefully received a water bottle and stepped off to the side to take two large gulps. She wiped her forehead with her hand, hot from the race.

The Merriweathers received their water bottles and walked back to Christine. "A word of advice," Mrs. Merriweather said. "Stay away from that family. The Martins are going to hell in a handbasket." Her tea-brown eyes bored into Christine's.

The Merriweathers moved on. Christine stationed herself at the finish line to watch her partner and Reginald race. After the bang of the starting pistol, pairs tumbled and rolled in the burlap sacks, screams and shouts and howls of laughter as they traversed the grass.

Fillingham and the boy raced across the field, their pace frenetic, Reginald's face tense with effort. The boy's steps were so fast, Fillingham couldn't keep up and they tumbled to the ground. After two more falls, Fillingham grabbed Reginald, placed him on his shoulders and they ran the rest of the race with Reginald waving the potato sack in the air like a flag.

The pair crossed the finish line third, with a few good-natured protests about the pair's unconventional method. Fillingham bent over and the boy jumped from his shoulders. They were handed bronze medals.

"He shouldn't be allowed a medal," a teenage boy said as he stepped out of his potato sack.

Fillingham frowned.

The boy with floppy hair addressed the crowd. "He's a Martin. They want to take our homes. Kick us off the Island. Make money by building new houses right where our houses are now. He doesn't deserve a medal. He should be tarred and feathered." A smatter of applause from the onlookers.

Reginald's face had gone white.

Fillingham put up a hand. "He's just a boy. He has nothing to do with Island politics."

The teen approached Reginald. "Hand it over. It doesn't belong to you. Nothing on the Island belongs to you."

Reginald clutched the medal to his chest.

"That's enough from—" Fillingham began.

Matilda marched over to her brother, her dark hair bouncing. She grabbed the medal from his clenched fist. "We don't need your dumb medals or ribbons." She flung the medal to the ground, then threw her green ribbon on top of it. "And this is how I feel about your stupid bloody Island." She stomped on the awards, the heel of her mary jane shoe grinding them into the grass.

Chapter 18

"Did you see me? Did you see me dance?" Nelson asked after she ran over to Christine and Fillingham.

Christine shook her head.

"We were doing the Madison," Nelson explained. "Forty of us. It was so much fun." She clapped her hands together. "This Gala Day festival is the bomb." Her hands lowered. "What's wrong? Why so glum?"

Christine met Fillingham's glance. Neither one of them wanted to recount the debacle at the end of the three-legged race.

Fillingham said, "All good here." He glanced at his watch. "Two thirty. We need to head back for shift change."

"I'm working until eight," Nelson reminded them. "I can stay here."

"Are we permitted to leave a cadet on patrol unsupervised?" Christine asked Fillingham. They had left Nelson at the station on her own for half an hour, but patrolling was different.

Fillingham said, "The next shift will be here at three. They could drive directly from the Centre Island ferry dock to the festival."

"It doesn't make sense for me to return to the station, then come all the way back with the next shift," Nelson protested. "That leaves the festival unsupervised."

"True," Christine said. She didn't foresee issues on Gala Day, but with the underlying tensions, one never knew.

Nelson clapped in excitement. "It's settled." She looked around. "I'm hankering for ice cream."

Christine shook her head. "You can have your break later. If you're the only one here, you need to be constantly monitoring the crowd, checking that people are getting along, that there hasn't been an injury or a child lost. Ensure that the field is not overcrowded, including the ferry docks. Be visible and check in with the organizers so they know you're here. Take my radio." Christine unbuckled the belt that held her miter and handed it to Nelson.

Nelson buckled the belt around her slender waist. She stood up tall. "Now I'm a real officer."

"Remember to act like one," Christine cautioned.

Nelson stood at attention and saluted them.

Fillingham and Christine grabbed their bikes and pedaled back to the station.

The phone rang as they stepped into the station office. "I'll get it," Fillingham said.

Another officer, recruited from 52 Division for the busy long weekend, sat in the kitchen with a cup of coffee. He raised his mug to them in greeting.

"It's for you," Fillingham said, holding the black receiver toward Christine.

Christine frowned. No one called her here. It could be her policewomen friends, but Fillingham knew them and would have chatted.

"PW Lane," she said as Fillingham went into the kitchen.

"Karl Olsen. Toronto Fisheries Management Project."

She smiled at his fake-serious tone. "Mr. Olsen, how can I help you? Are you drowning?"

"No, no," he said. "I barely survived my last water rescue. But thank you for your offer of help."

"I'm here to serve," she replied. Thank goodness she could laugh at herself, although the memory still stung with embarrassment.

"I wanted to see who could eat the most roasted corn after a vicious game of Frisbee, but I've run into a problem."

Christine felt a stab of disappointment. She wasn't deeply interested in Karl. He was knowledgeable about the natural world, which was interesting. And had an easy-going manner. But he wasn't really her type. It was just nice to have someone interested in her. And now he was canceling their date. She had brought a change of clothes and makeup bag to the station. "That's okay. It's been a long day—"

"Wait! Whoa! We're still meeting. I'm a little delayed. My coworker Phil hasn't shown up for work for the last five days. I'm collecting water samples on my own. I have two stops at Hanlan's Point, and then I'm ready to Gala Day with you."

"Okay," she said, relieved. "When should we meet?"

"Let's say five o'clock. In front of the Ward's Island community center."

"See you then."

After hanging up, she headed into the kitchen.

The officer from 52 Division got up, stretched and told them he'd head out to the patrol car. Fillingham said he'd be there in a minute.

"Who was that?" Fillingham asked Christine, gesturing to the office phone.

Christine shrugged. "A friend." Her partner had made it clear he didn't want to associate with her. She did not feel inclined to gush details of her life.

"Heading back to the Gala Day events?" Fillingham asked.

She frowned. He must have been eavesdropping, although it was hard not to in the open room. "Yes. Why?"

He shrugged. "You can keep an eye on Cadet Nelson."

Christine said, "I'll try, but I'm off the clock. And other officers will be there."

"Be careful," he said.

"Of what?"

The doorbell tinkled, and Judith Purnell walked in with her cleaning equipment.

Fillingham greeted her, then headed out the door.

"Hi, Judith," Christine said. "Working a holiday Monday?"

She shrugged. "It's just another Monday to me."

"I thought you might be at the Gala Day celebrations."

The housekeeper placed her bucket on the floor. "Not much fun when you're a pariah."

The conversation was eerily similar to the one Christine had that afternoon with Mrs. Martin.

Christine said, "People must understand your situation, Judith. The economics." Having enough food to feed her family had been a worry for Christine most of her life.

Judith sprayed the rag with furniture polish. "My kids are there. The oldest one is big enough to help with the younger ones."

"Are the Islanders so black-and-white in their thinking?" Christine asked.

Judith paused, rag in hand. "They call me Judas now, not Judith. You're either with them or against them. It's that simple."

Chapter 19

"Are you two on a date?" Cadet Nelson asked, staring at Christine and Karl.

Christine ignored the recruit's comment. She and Karl had finally met up at Ward's Island. Christine had changed into a pair of navy capris with a short-sleeved cotton blouse tied at the front. Karl sported a graphic shirt with patterned orange and yellow circles and khaki shorts.

Christine said, "Did you check in with Sergeant Bard and PC Morano?"

"Yes, yes, yes." She addressed Karl. "What are you going to do?"

Christine shook her head to indicate that Karl did not have to answer.

"First," he said, slipping off his backpack and pulling out a Frisbee, "to the beach!"

With a wave to Nelson, the pair headed toward Ward's Island Beach. Christine and Karl threw the Frisbee, the sand softening their dives. One of Karl's roommates called them over to join his beach volleyball team. Christine wasn't an experienced player, but when they put her beside the net, she was tall enough to tip the ball over.

After several games of volleyball, they went in search of drinks.

Christine said, "Let's get lemonade." Kids from Supervision camp were selling glasses by the beach entrance.

"Do you want a beer or a mixed drink? We can buy them at the community center," he said.

"I'm not a big drinker," Christine said, "but you go ahead."

They sat at a picnic table, Christine with her lemonade and Karl with a beer. They had bought hot dogs too since their beach exercise had made them hungry. Christine noticed another flag in the grass beside them: *Is your drinking water safe?*

Christine said, "It's frustrating that we haven't received the cause of death for the ducks yet. It makes the hysteria continue."

Karl nodded. "I've been working on this fisheries project since May. The water quality in the lagoons, Inner Harbor and Lake Ontario hasn't changed over the summer. Lake Ontario isn't the cleanest lake in the world, but the ducks didn't die of sudden water contamination. It must be disease or something they ate."

"Whatever it is, it's making the Islanders edgy. It's an environmental problem, someone harming wildlife or an agitator trying to portray the Island as toxic."

"How'd you end up on the Island?" he asked. Before she could answer, he said, "Actually, how did you end up as a police officer?"

"My mom had gotten a job in the civilian Records Department of the force. After I graduated from high school, I joined too. It was shift work, which is hard because I have younger step-siblings, but we've managed. While I was in Records, the force got funding to hire more policewomen. I applied because the pay was better."

"No grand ideas to save the world?" he teased. He took a bite of hot dog.

"You saw how great I was at saving you," Christine said. "But," her expression got serious, "I think it's important to serve the community."

"You like being a police officer?"

She nodded. "I do. It's challenging, especially the changing shifts and the difficult situations, but it's rewarding: finding a lost child, arresting a purse snatcher, returning a lost wallet. And I love Island patrol. After being away from it for a couple of months, I appreciate it more. The natural beauty. The sound of water. And the residents are so interesting: creative, eccentric, but always helpful in a pinch."

"How about your colleagues?" He had finished one hot dog and was starting the second.

"I'm friends with a group of policewomen. I've known them since police college."

"And the guys?" he asked, wiping ketchup off his mouth with a serviette.

"Most are fine. Some have problems working with women."

"I wish I worked with a woman. She'd be more reliable."

"Did you hear from Phil?" she asked. Karl's coworker had seemed so serious about his fisheries management job. It seemed strange that he hadn't shown up for work.

Karl shook his head. "I've called him twice. So did my boss. I'm not sure what the issue is. I mean, he's humorless, but he works hard. He's got a wife and two kids to support. The guy has three jobs and he's writing his PhD thesis. When he's finished his shift on the Island, he drives an airport limousine. And he works for a scientist in a research lab."

She drained her glass of lemonade. "You're doing your PhD as well?"

He nodded. "I've completed the course work a while ago. I have to finish writing my thesis paper. My father thinks I've been taking my sweet time. That's one reason I got the fisheries job. To get him off my back."

"They must be proud of your academic accomplishments," she said. Christine hadn't made it past high school. She hadn't even thought about doing postsecondary. Where would she get the tuition?

He swiveled his hand. "Yes and no. My mom was a high school science teacher before she met my dad, so she's great. My dad, not so much. He's a business guy, self-made. Education is not as important to him. He's not as interested in the natural world. He wants to know when he can stop paying my tuition and when I'll start my career."

"My mom doesn't like me working as a policewoman," Christine offered. "She thinks it is dangerous. She'd much rather have me back in Records filing incident reports."

"What about your dad?"

Christine's hand scrunched the serviette in her palm. "I don't have a dad." When she didn't elaborate, Karl asked if she wanted to head over to the beach to see the bonfire.

It was twilight, the sun low on the horizon, the light soft. The games and activities had been packed up and cleared off the field, leaving food vendors and a trio of musicians setting up on the stage. Clusters of people stood around the stage and community center, chatting, children running back and forth between the adults.

Christine and Karl followed the line of people making their way to Ward's Island Beach. As she walked on the sand, shoes in hand, she admired the enormous fire in the middle of the beach. People stood or sat around the flames, chatting and drinking. Christine could smell weed but purposely did not look for the perpetrator. Twenty feet away, a smaller fire burned under a rectangular grill that was covered with corn husks, their threads burning into curls, the cook rotating the cobs with long metal prongs.

Karl pulled a small towel from his backpack and placed it on the sand. They sat down on it with their corncobs smeared with butter and spices. Christine licked the butter off her lips. It had a smoky

Cajun flavor. After finishing a second cob, they angled their blanket so they could watch the fire and look out over Lake Ontario.

"Look who it is!" Christine said.

Lifeguard came sniffing around, looking for errant corn kernels on the towel. After nuzzling Karl's beard, the dog settled beside Christine, curled up in a circle, her back pressed against Christine's leg.

Eventually, Christine checked her watch. It was after ten o'clock. She'd have to get up soon and head home.

After shaking sand off their clothes, they crossed the beach and walked down Withrow Avenue toward the dock. Lifeguard wandered off, probably in search of food or treats. Music blared out of the open doors of the community center. In the lamplight, couples slow-danced in front of the building. Others talked in small groups, the red ember of cigarettes like glowing eyes in the dark.

As they passed in front, Karl asked, "Do you want to dance?"

Christine scanned the couples moving rhythmically to the ballad being strummed inside.

Wait. Who was that in uniform?

Cadet Nelson was dancing with PC Morano, her head on his shoulder, his arms curled around her back. *Morano.* Her least favorite officer. He was bigoted. Mean. And didn't think females should be officers.

And he was married.

"Hey, Cadet Nelson," Christine exclaimed. A few couples looked over.

Nelson's head jerked up.

"I thought your shift ended at eight."

Morano and Nelson jumped apart.

"PC Morano," Christine greeted.

He regarded Christine with a flat brown stare.

Christine said, "I'm heading back to the mainland. Want to join me on the ferry, Nelson?"

Before the cadet could respond, Morano said, "I'll walk her back."

"I know the last hour of shift gets busy, PC Morano," Christine said. "You wouldn't want to be late coming home to Mrs. Morano."

"Don't tell me what to do, PW," Morano said.

Nelson twitched, looking from one to another. "It's okay, PW Lane. I...I...can get the ferry on my own."

"Are you sure?" Christine asked.

"I'm okay," Nelson replied.

Christine paused, waiting for her to change her mind. With a shake of her head, she rejoined Karl and hastened toward the ferry.

"What was that about?" he asked.

"A snake with a mouse," she said. Aside from kidnapping Nelson, Christine didn't have a choice other than to leave the two together. Tomorrow, she'd talk to Nelson again and be explicit about her own experiences with Morano.

As they waited for Christine's ferry on a bench by the dock, Karl reached for her hand. "I had fun today."

She let her hand stay loose in his. "Me too." The Frisbee-tossing, volleyball game and corn roast were fun.

"You don't have to take the ferry home," he said. "You could come to my place."

She looked at him. He was fit, attractive and smart. Easy to talk to, to be with. She wondered if his beard tickled. She didn't love him and probably never would. But wasn't that the point? Wasn't that why she was relaxed around him? Nothing was at stake.

Slowly, she shook her head. "I work the morning shift. Perhaps another time."

He smiled. "I'll put you in my calendar."

She smiled back.

"How about coming to a barbeque with me next weekend?" he asked.

Fillingham had tossed her aside as a partner. Hawk was married, with his own family problems. It was time to move on. "Sure," she said, squeezing his hand, then standing up as the ferry approached.

On board, she waved at Karl standing on the dock, then headed to the second floor to watch the city lights loom brighter and brighter.

Chapter 20

"Late night?" Fillingham said. He was leaning against the patrol car in his raincoat, a plastic protector over his police hat. He must have seen her yawn as she exited the ferry with a straggle of people heading to Centreville. The day was stormy, which meant few families or tourists would venture to the Island.

"Not really," she demurred. She would not discuss her date with Karl.

Christine jerked as something wet rubbed her leg. It was the dog.

"Hey, Lifeguard," Fillingham said. "Did you follow me from the station? You're all wet."

Christine regarded the dog with her cream, white and brown hair pressed flat against her body. She looked so small without the silky fur fluffed around her.

"Does she recognize the patrol car?" she asked.

He squatted down to rub the dog's ears. "How are you doing, Lifeguard? Are you a smart dog? Did you follow us?"

The driver's door opened, and Sergeant Bard got out.

Christine stood at attention. "Sir."

"PW Lane," he said amiably, "you have an admirer."

"Did we find the owner, sir?"

Bard shook his head. "Don't know if we will. There's been so much coming and going of residents, tourists and sailors over the summer. One of them must have left her behind. We'll have to call the humane society to pick her up and take her to the shelter." He tilted his head toward the ferry. "I'm getting out of this drizzle. PC Fillingham, give report."

Christine frowned. Lifeguard didn't need to go to a shelter. They were taking care of her. She was an Island dog.

Fillingham straightened and pulled his memo book from his raincoat pocket. His shift was ending and hers was beginning.

She took her memo book out too. They could be two strangers or two work colleagues who rarely saw each other.

"Yes," she said, businesslike.

"Fitzgerald called in sick," he said.

She nodded. She hadn't seen another officer disembark from the ferry. "Who's coming?"

He shook his head. "No one. Everyone's tapped out after staffing for Caribana and Gala Day. There's no one left at 52 Division to fill in. Cadet Nelson started at noon, so she's at the station. Not sure if that's a help or hindrance."

She gave a small smile. At least Nelson would make the day interesting. Rainy days were quiet. And it would give Christine an opportunity to lecture the young woman about Morano.

"And," he continued, "two geese were found dead."

"Oh, no," she said, "where?"

"Near Trout Pond."

"By the water filtration plant," Christine said. "Do you think that's a coincidence?"

"Not sure. Sarge and I cordoned off the area. Both were ganders. I'm not sure if that's significant. We looked for suspicious food and signs of predator or human interference, but we didn't find anything noteworthy."

"Any other wildlife found dead?" she asked.

He shook his head. "Just the geese. Parks and Recreation came by and roped off the area. There are healthy females on nests nearby. Sarge says Wildlife Conservation was called in. He contacted the inspector from 52 Division, too."

"When did this happen?"

"The call came in at noon. Right now, they have a Parks and Rec employee guarding the site. If journalists get wind of this, you might find a horde coming over. You may have to guard the area, ensure no one crosses the tape. The ganders have been taken for examination. We searched the area for toxins, garbage or rancid food. Nothing notable." He flipped his notebook closed.

"Wait until the ecological groups hear about this," she said. "The whole Island will have signage."

The dog shivered against her leg.

"Hey, Lifeguard," Fillingham said. "Let's get you a blanket." He went to the back of the patrol car and pulled out a blanket.

She picked up the dog and placed her into the blanketed arms of Fillingham. As she tucked the cover around the dog, Lifeguard licked her nose. Smiling, she looked up into Fillingham's blue eyes.

"Christine," he began, his expression serious. "I want to talk to you—" The ferry horn blasted, drowning out his words, the last warning for people to embark. He looked at the boat. "Shoot. I gotta go."

She took the dog and watched Fillingham walk onto the ferry ramp. He disappeared into the main deck cabin without turning around.

Chapter 21

The woman stood on the pathway, waving her hands over her head as the rain misted.

Nelson?

Christine pressed on the gas pedal until she reached the cadet. Braking, she hopped out of the car, engine running, the dog following behind, barking.

"Nelson? What is it? Are you okay?" They shouldn't have left her at the station. She wasn't experienced enough to be on her own, even for a short while.

Nelson grabbed Christine's rain jacket by the sleeve. The cadet's wool uniform was sodden. Water dripped from the brim of her hat.

"We got a call to the station!" Nelson said.

"Okay. Is it an emergency?"

Nelson leaned forward. "There's a fight."

"An assault? Where? What's the address?"

Nelson fumbled in her uniform pocket and examined an ink-stained note. "Fifteen Second Street."

"Who is the complainant?"

Nelson's brown eyes widened. "I...I don't know."

"You don't know who called?"

"I forgot to ask. I was so excited. I had to find you."

"Hop in," Christine said. "Second Street is on Ward's Island. Lifeguard, in the back."

Christine dropped by the station to pick up her radio and grabbed a tea towel for Nelson to dry off. Lifeguard followed them back to the car. Christine was afraid she'd run the dog over, so she let her in the back seat.

As they headed toward Ward's Island, Christine said, "Tell me what the caller said, word for word."

Nelson nodded. She had taken her hat off, and her hair lay in wet auburn strands as she dried the ends with a tea towel. She looked fourteen.

Nelson said, "He said, 'Is this the Toronto Island police station?'"

"After that," Christine said.

"He said that a neighbor was being aggressive. That several people tried to calm her. That her place was a disgrace. And so was the woman."

"What was the assault? By the woman? On the woman?"

"I don't know," Nelson said, biting her lower lip.

"Next time, ask the name of the caller or the complainant. Ask if they know the name of the aggressive neighbor."

"This is so exciting," Nelson said.

"With domestic and neighbor calls, emotions run high. The first thing I do is separate the combatants, whether they are spouses, roommates or neighbors. Got that?"

Nelson nodded. Freckles were stark on her pale face.

Christine looked over at her. "You need to be careful. Domestics can be dangerous. Sometimes a knife is pulled. Or a police officer gets punched or hurt in the melee. You must have your wits about you. Most of the time, no one wants to press charges. Sometimes it's unclear who started an assault. Both may have taken part in the physical altercation. In this situation, our job is to mediate, to lower the emotions and set a plan of action for the next twenty-four hours where the two people can stay out of each other's way. One of them could visit a friend or relative."

As Christine turned onto Second Street, she recognized the house from patrolling Ward's Island. The front yard was cluttered with wood, bins, boxes, tubs and lumpy piles covered in tarp. The roof had gaps of missing shingles, and the yellow paint on the sideboards was peeling. Mrs. Polotov had told her an older lady lived there, a Mrs. Buckley. A hoarder. Christine had never seen her. Occasionally, Mrs. Polotov coaxed her older neighbor out of her home for a cup of tea and butter tart.

This must be Mrs. Buckley. A stooped, gray-haired woman in a man's yellow mackinaw over a house dress stood in front of her lawn, arms up protectively as if to ward off intrusion.

Christine recognized the man in the navy rain jacket opposite the old woman. Gary Owen, TIRA president. He held a pink notice in his hand.

He turned to the police officers. "Thank goodness. Authority." He waved the pink paper. "I'm trying to help Mrs. Buckley. Metro Council posted this notice of by-law infraction on her door due to the state of her front lawn. I am offering to help her clear it up."

"I don't need your help," Mrs. Buckley said in a quavering voice.

Owen sighed. "Mrs. Buckley. The place is a mess. And a fire hazard. And has been for years. Your rain barrow leaks and floods your neighbor's garden. You have rats and who knows what else living in the rotting wood. It's too much for one person to clear. Your neighbors are happy to help."

A woman with long black braids exited the house across the street. It was Rachel Conroy, the city counselor who had co-chaired the TIRA meeting with Owen. "I can help, Mrs. Buckley. Inside or outside the house. That way you can avoid a fine."

Owen turned to Conroy. "Let's focus on the outside. Island homes need to look cared for. Metro Council is happy to have an excuse to evict us." He turned to Mrs. Buckley. "You want to stay in your home, right, Mrs. Buckley?"

"Of course," she said, brown eyes glaring at him.

Owen's arms opened wide. "We're trying to help you do that. We don't want your place condemned."

"My house is fine," the older woman said, but her tone was unsure.

"Hi, Mrs. Buckley," Christine said, standing in front of her. "I'm Policewoman Christine Lane. I'm here to assist. Other people are too. I'm strong. I could help move things."

"Nobody touches anything!" Her voice was querulous, her hands clamped into fists. "It's my property. My things. They're not for sale."

"Nobody's buying this mess," Owen said.

Lifeguard came over to the group, tail wagging. Christine bent to give her a scratch behind her ears. "Do you like dogs, Mrs. Buckley?" she asked. "This is Lifeguard. We found her wandering the Island. Do you want to pet her? She's friendly."

"I used to have a dog," Mrs. Buckley said.

"Can Lifeguard sit with you on your porch while I chat with your neighbors? We won't touch anything until we get your permission."

Mrs. Buckley stood for a minute, glaring, but then said, "Okay."

Christine turned. "Cadet Nelson, can you help Mrs. Buckley to the porch out of the rain? Lifeguard wants attention."

Mrs. Buckley let Nelson lead her by the elbow to the solitary chair on a front porch that was piled floor-to-ceiling with boxes.

Christine turned to Owen. "Did you call in the complaint, Mr. Owen?"

He shook his head. "Someone must have heard us talking."

Conroy said, "You were arguing. Your voices were very loud. She's an old lady, Gary."

Owen turned to her. "The state of her house, and all our houses, influences our application to stay on the Island. They've accused us for years of having derelict housing. Metro Council wants to frame it as a health hazard. It's one more reason to evict us. We can't give Metro any ammunition. Our community must look tended and kempt."

"What's happening with Edith?"

Christine turned. It was Mrs. Polotov. She was wearing a lavender floral poncho, hood up against the misty rain.

Owen showed her the notice.

"She's refusing to clean up her property?" Mrs. Polotov asked.

Owen nodded. "Yes. Her mess impacts all of us. Remember when the mayor and Metro Council toured here last spring, pointing out homes in need of repair?"

Mrs. Polotov said, "I've known Edith for a long time. Although she's a bit set in her ways, she will listen to reason. She knows she can't manage anymore. Since Bill died, she's been overwhelmed."

Own heaved a sigh. "That may be the case, but it doesn't change the city infraction notice. Or that her yard has to be cleared."

"Let me talk to her," Mrs. Polotov said, "see if I can get her to agree to a tidy-up."

Christine said, "In my experience with people who hoard, it's difficult for them to see their belongings taken away, even if it's old magazines and rubbish. It has meaning for them or is tied to a memory. Or it's something they want to get to someday. If you can get Mrs. Buckley to leave for a day or two while people clear, it's easier for everyone."

"Smart idea, PW Lane," Mrs. Polotov said, patting Christine on the forearm before heading over to the front porch.

Conroy said, "If Mrs. Buckley left for a day, I could round up a team of volunteers. We'd get a dumpster and a fire permit to burn the rotting wood. If vermin are an issue, we have an exterminator on the Island."

Christine nodded. "I also think that Mrs. Buckley needs help to cope."

Conroy said, "There's a social worker on Algonquin. Vanessa Torrins. She'll have a list of resources and services for seniors. I'll ask if she can drop by."

Christine walked up to the porch, where Mrs. Buckley sat with Lifeguard on her lap.

"Making friends, Lifeguard?" Christine said.

"She really likes Mrs. Buckley," Nelson said, smiling. The cadet was leaning against a column of cardboard boxes, since there was only room on the porch for Mrs. Buckley's chair.

"I know exactly where she likes to be scratched," Mrs. Buckley said, head bent over the dog. "I grew up with dogs."

"I can see that," Christine said. She squatted in front of the seated woman. "Mrs. Buckley, people want to help you so you won't get in trouble or have to pay fines. So your house won't get condemned."

"I don't like people touching my stuff," Mrs. Buckley mumbled into the dog's neck.

"Understandable. Mrs. Polotov is going to talk to you about a day when you can take a break and your neighbors will tidy your yard. And then you can stay in your home. Does that work?"

Mrs. Buckley reluctantly nodded.

Christine continued, "Cadet Nelson and I are going to leave." She straightened. "But I need a favor from you first."

Arms slack around the dog, Mrs. Buckley looked suspicious again. "What?"

"I can see you are best friends with Lifeguard. And he will insist on another visit. Can I drop by the next time we're on patrol for a pat from you?"

Mrs. Buckley gave a weak smile. "Okay. I might have a treat for her in the kitchen."

"Then we're definitely coming back," Christine said.

Chapter 22

The rain had slowed by the time Christine and Nelson left Mrs. Buckley. They drove to Hanlan's Point to check the cordoned area where the ganders were found. The taped-off square near the filtration plant was deserted except for the Parks and Recreation staff standing morosely under an umbrella. They drove to the station to grab an old raincoat for Nelson before heading to patrol the amusement park. It would be a quick walk around the grounds and then dinner break.

The rain had slowed to a mist as the two officers walked around Centreville. It was still relatively warm, so Christine wasn't cold, just damp. It was eerie observing the rides at a standstill, the Ferris wheel seats rocking in the wind. A ghost amusement park. A few customers were shrieking on the Scrambler ride, and the Antique Cars were in motion. Parents held umbrellas over picnic baskets or huddled with their children under the canopied edges of the buildings out of the rain.

Lifeguard followed the two officers, darting away to follow a smell and then returning to trot by them again. Nelson caught the dog licking a foil hamburger wrapper and pulled it out of her mouth.

"I don't know much about dogs," Christine said to Nelson. "Do you think she's hungry?"

Nelson tossed the foil into the garbage. "Dogs are always hungry. It's hard to tell if Lifeguard is fed regularly. Her ribs aren't sticking out. She looks small, but that's her breed."

They paused to let the train go by that ran through Centreville. It was full, which was not surprising, since its overhead canopy protected riders from the rain.

Christine's stomach grumbled. "Did you bring dinner?" she asked the cadet. It was five thirty. Christine's supper was in the police station fridge: a sandwich, banana and cut carrots.

"I have pot roast!" Nelson exclaimed.

"Wow!"

"My landlady sometime makes me a meal, especially if I'm on shift. I'm staying at a ladies' boarding house."

"Is that part of your rent?"

They walked toward Far Enough Farm. "Not really," Nelson said. "She's supposed to provide breakfast. That's it. She's a little grumpy, but I'm friendly. And she feels sorry for me. A farm girl in the big, bad city." Her eyes rolled.

"Imagine that," Christine said, trying not to laugh. "Let's show our faces in the office, see if there's anything that needs our attention."

They meandered past the empty Swan and Boat Rides and then headed toward the office inside the main building.

"Where's the dog?" Nelson asked.

Christine looked around. "She wandered off."

"Is she the station dog?" Nelson asked.

Christine shook her head. "We're hoping someone comes looking for her. We've posted notices and called animal services to see if someone reported a lost dog, but no response."

"Why can't we keep her, then? The fire stations have dogs."

"I don't think Sergeant Bard would allow it." Perhaps Fillingham could convince Bard that Lifeguard could be the Centre Island police station mascot. Guard the premises. Get petted by tourists. Be part of a public relations strategy to show the human side of policing. She had a feeling that Fillingham didn't want Lifeguard off the Island any more than she did.

The dog wasn't around when they exited the amusement park office and headed back to the patrol car. Nelson whistled loudly through her two fingers. After a minute of waiting, the officers returned to the station without the dog.

No one had called the station, or Dispatch would have notified Christine. The news of the dead geese hadn't been made public yet. Thank goodness. Christine was on her own after eight o'clock when Nelson left, and she hadn't relished dealing with the media on her own. Her evening would be quiet, and she was thankful.

Nelson sat at the station's kitchen table with her plate filled with reheated pot roast, potatoes and turnip. Christine tried to ignore the delicious smell of gravy as she bit into her bologna sandwich. She couldn't remember the last time she or her mom had cooked a roast. It was too expensive. Perhaps they could buy a cheaper cut, shoulder roast, and use the bone for soup.

Christine smiled as the cadet dug into her meal. She was telling the truth when she said she could eat like a horse. Nelson was a fun partner on patrol. She was sensible and practical in ways Christine could relate to. And she was glaringly gullible.

"Can I give you advice?" Christine said.

Nelson swallowed a bite of potatoes, nodding rapidly. "Of course. You're my mentor. That's your job."

Christine laughed. "A different type of advice. I'm no expert on men, but I know one thing. You need to stay far away from PC Morano."

Nelson frowned. "He's my mentor too. I learned how to complete incident reports, check the security on houses, move tourists along toward the ferries."

"He's a wolf in sheep's clothing."

"He's been really nice to me."

"With a wife."

"I know," Nelson said, blinking rapidly.

Was she going to cry?

"He...he thinks I'm pretty," Nelson said.

"You *are* pretty. You don't need him to confirm it."

"I'm not." She shook her head vigorously. "I'm the carrot-head. The ginger. Pippi Longstocking."

"Morano is a married man who wants something from you. And when he gets it, he won't be your friend any longer."

Nelson said, "It's harmless fun."

"He's not harmless."

Nelson sat there, staring wide-eyed at Christine. After a few seconds, she said, "Did you hear that?"

Christine wondered if the cadet was trying to change the subject. Then she heard it too. She put her sandwich down. "It's the door. Probably Lifeguard scratching to get in."

Christine opened the door wide. Lifeguard lay on the ground, tongue out, a pile of pink vomit beside her.

"Lifeguard! What's wrong?" Christine bent, placing her hand on the furry back. The dog tried to get up but staggered and fell back on her stomach.

"Nelson!" Christine yelled.

Christine heard the quick patter of feet. Nelson was beside her. "Lifeguard's sick," Christine said. "She can't stand up."

Nelson squatted beside the dog. "Lifeguard, buddy. What's going on?" The dog looked at Nelson, her brown eyes glassy, her breathing slow and laborious. "She's not herself. She's so lethargic."

"Nelson," Christine said, "put Lifeguard in the car. We'll take her to Dr. Hapler. He has an office on the Island. I'll find his number and tell him we're heading over."

Two minutes later, they were driving to the vet's, the dog on Nelson's lap in the back seat.

"Do you think she ate something bad? That's why she threw up?" Christine asked.

"I don't see any cuts, and she's not acting like a bone is broken," Nelson said. "She could have hit her head. Fallen off something. That makes you sick." She paused. "Dogs get into everything: rat poisoning, ant traps, laundry detergent."

"The last time I saw her was the Swan Ride," Christine said, "where they found the dead ducks."

Chapter 23

It was getting dark, the hazy twilight softening the bright crimson of roses to burgundy and the Kelly-green leaves to olive. The rain had stopped, and a weak band of sunlight filtered through the damp tree leaves. The two women rolled down the patrol car windows to get fresh air as they headed back to the station from the vet's house.

Christine and Nelson had left Lifeguard in the care of Rob Hapler, who was hydrating the dog with an intravenous line. If the dog's situation worsened, the vet would send her to an emergency clinic on the mainland.

"The vomit was strange," Nelson said from the passenger seat. The cadet had cleaned up the dog's mess but had the presence of mind to keep a sample to show the vet.

"Do you mean the color?" Christine asked.

"Yes. Pink. Strange, unless the dog ate beets."

"Or candy floss," Christine hazarded. "There's a lot of that in Centreville. Would bubble gum look pink?"

"I don't know. The texture wasn't like bubble gum."

"Was it blood?" Christine asked. Poor Lifeguard, her insides torn up.

Nelson shook her head as they drove slowly along the lagoon. "I don't think so. The texture was spongy, like bread or pizza."

"A pink donut? Would that make her woozy?"

Nelson shook her head. "I hope no one left out radiator or windshield wiper fluid. They do that to kill raccoons or rats."

Concern gripped Christine's stomach.

Nelson gave a little smile. "The good news is that Lifeguard vomited. That means she got rid of some of whatever was making her sick."

"Is it a coincidence we last saw her at the Swan Ride where the ducks were found?" Christine had to get this idea out of her head.

Nelson shook her head. "I don't know."

Christine braked. "Let's check Centreville before it gets too dark." She would have a tough time sitting at the station anyway. She was jittery with worry for Lifeguard.

They left the patrol car by the amusement park entrance and retraced their walking route from earlier that day. Crowds were sparse due to the damp weather. And by eight in the evening, most young families had headed back to the mainland.

"Let's check in with the office," Christine said, "see if anything weird was found after we left."

The manager had gone home for the day, but the office staff said they had no reports of animals being sick or substances found.

At Far Enough Farm, they found an employee forking hay into the horse's enclosure. According to him, the farm was running normally. No complaints. No sick animals.

"You wouldn't leave antifreeze or cleaner around, would you?" Christine asked.

The man made a face. "No! We have chickens, peacocks and other animals roaming the farm. We'd never leave that out."

"Can you show me where you keep your chemicals?" Christine asked.

"Did more ducks die?" he asked.

Christine shook her head, although she thought of the dead ganders by Trout Pond. "No."

The man in coveralls unlocked a shed with wooden shelves full of engine oils and bottles of flea and tick lotion. He gestured inside. "We don't have antifreeze. Most are products for animal care and for equipment maintenance."

"Thanks for your time," Christine said.

As they walked around Centreville, Nelson said, "They had steering fluid for the tractor. It's pink." She shrugged. "A lot of chemicals on a farm are poisonous to animals and humans if ingested."

Christine sighed as she and Nelson walked past the goats. Nelson made clucking noises and a goat ambled over.

"We're not supposed to touch them," Christine said.

"We had goats. They liked to be scratched right here." Nelson leaned over the wooden railings and gave the goat a scratch around the back of the horn. It stood stock-still.

"See?" Nelson said, turning to Christine. "Heaven."

"We have about half an hour until it's too dark to search," Christine said. "Let's check around the waterways, ponds and lagoons for any sign of a pink substance Lifeguard might have gotten into." After a pause, she added, "She may have eaten pink cotton candy and something else toxic, so the pink color might be misleading. Let's look for anything suspicious, regardless of color."

They paused at the farm's exit.

Christine said, "I'll head right and check the water rides. You go left around the lagoon by the Carousel restaurant. Yell if you see anything interesting." Nelson didn't have a radio. "Otherwise, we'll meet at the patrol car in thirty minutes."

It wasn't quite dark enough to use her flashlight, but the beam was helpful when examining the shadowy places under rocks and docks by the water rides. An employee was gathering the empty swan boats into a ring to lock them up for the night. He hadn't seen food or liquid around the ride. Or any wildlife that seemed sick.

Christine walked along the lagoon near the entrance. Lots of geese poo, she observed as she placed her foot carefully on the grass. The rickety wooden dock bisected the ribbon of water. It was slightly angled and hadn't been used in a long time. A gull currently stood on it, fluffing up its feathers.

Christine ventured to the water's edge and hesitantly placed her foot on the wood. The dock jostled with her weight, and she yelped. She didn't want to fall into this weedy pond, getting her uniform soaked for the second time this month. Directing her flashlight beam along the dock, she searched for a telltale pink stain. The wood was a dark, mossy brown, wet from the day's rain. Should she risk walking to the other side of the pond?

"PW Lane!" shrieked a voice far down the lagoon.

Christine started, almost losing her balance on the dock. It was Nelson.

"I'm coming!" Christine roared.

She turned and leaped off the dock onto the bank. "Where are you?" She ran back to the farm and turned right on the path where she and Nelson had parted.

"Here! Over here!"

Christine ran along the lagoon, trying to locate Nelson amongst the tall pine trees. It had gotten darker. She couldn't see anyone. "Where are you? I'm halfway down the path to the restaurant."

"Here! Here!" Nelson yelled.

Christine followed the cadet's voice to a dense grove of trees, branches scraping her uniform, breathing in the smell of pine.

"I'm under the spruce tree," Nelson said.

"Which one is that?"

"You don't know your trees?" Nelson's voice was incredulous.

Christine aimed her flashlight at the tree trunks around her. She spotted nyloned legs and the soles of a pair of feet. "I see you."

Nelson was lying flat on her stomach underneath the lowest boughs of the tree.

"Here," Nelson said, "shine your light where I'm pointing."

Christine lay down beside Nelson on the damp grass, pine needles sticking to her uniform. Her light beam illuminated a pile of soggy pink bread on a tinfoil plate.

"This must be it," Nelson said excitedly.

"It was placed here," Christine said. "The poisoning was intentional."

Chapter 24

"You've been to the Royal Canadian Yacht Club before?" Karl asked Christine as they sat in the canopied cockpit of the *Kwasind*, the Canadian flag flapping loudly from the stern.

He looked handsome with his auburn hair tied back, his beard trimmed close to his face, eyes cobalt-blue under blonde eyebrows. He was wearing khaki pants, white loafers and a long-sleeved cream silk shirt. It was the first time Christine had seen him in clothes that weren't faded or rumpled. She hadn't known Karl was a yacht club member. He didn't act or dress like he came from money. She was having difficulty reconciling Island Karl with Yacht Club Karl.

"A couple of times," she answered, her brown hair whipping across her neck in the wind. "I was interviewing people in the line of duty. I've never come as a guest."

A red hairband tied her hair back to show ears adorned with pearls, loans from Julie. Christine's white linen dress, borrowed from Sarah, was picked to match the red and white theme of the yacht club's Canada Cup party.

Christine sat on the bench seat of the boat with her legs crossed tightly. The dress rose a bit too high up her thighs, especially when she sat, since Sarah was shorter than Christine. Christine's one inch, bone-colored mules made her a smidgeon taller than Karl when they stood side by side.

When Karl had asked Christine out after the corn roast, she thought they would go to a café or music club. Karl's choice of the RCYC had surprised her. The club had a boat in the Canada Cup sailing race, a competition between American and Canadian yacht clubs. The RCYC was hosting a party to cheer on their racer, *Mirage*.

As the watercraft chugged across the Inner Harbor, Karl said, "There's been a lot of chatter in the news about the Island."

"I know," she responded. Information about the dead ganders by Trout Pond and the pink substance found in Centreville had splashed headlines across the Toronto newspapers. Media had gotten wind of the possible toxin when people saw police photographers and the Identification unit hustle over to Centreville. Television, print and radio journalists swarmed the Island, dropping by the police station in search of more information. Thank goodness Christine didn't have to speak to anyone. Sergeant Bard directed the officers to say that the incidents were under investigation. The ganders were being examined by a vet and the substance found in Centreville was at a lab for evaluation.

And thank goodness, Lifeguard had recovered. Christine had picked her up the next day at the vet's. Lifeguard's tail was wagging so hard, it was making a thwacking sound on the wooden floor. She whimpered as if she hadn't seen Christine in a month. And other than the advice to keep the dog's diet bland for a day or two, Lifeguard would be back to normal.

Karl said, "I knew the water was clean. That it hadn't poisoned the ducks. This makes more sense. That someone left tainted food around, which the ducks found."

"How does that make more sense?"

"I don't mean the rationale or motive, but it's more logical that the ducks ate or were fed toxins than the conclusion that Lake Ontario water is poisonous or that pesticide run-off is the culprit."

Christine hooked her borrowed white leather purse over the shoulder. It was small, able to hold a comb, lipstick, powder and a small wallet. "So the chemicals used on Island grass and gardens have no negative impact on water quality?"

He tilted his head back and forth. "Yes and no. It didn't cause the ducks to die, but that doesn't mean that lawn care products have no effect on marine life and aquatic plants. There's not enough analysis done on Toronto Island's natural environment to answer that question. Studies show that strong chemicals like agricultural pesticides affect the water table and water quality. That much we know."

The boat's drone lowered as it approached the lagoon leading into the yacht club.

"Should I be worried about swimming on Island beaches?" she asked.

Karl shook his head. "Island beaches are safe. The issue for swimmers is sewage runoff after a rainfall. This happens to the western beaches and Woodbine Beach, not the Island. As for Toronto's drinking water, the treatment plants filter bacteria and contaminants."

Christine smiled. "I feel better after talking to you."

He bowed. "Karl Water Quality Olsen, at your service." The boat slowed as it prepared to dock. "And I feel better knowing that if I ever get robbed, lose a wallet or have a killer after me, I can count on you."

Christine stood up to disembark. "I'm not sure about that. I almost arrested you the first time we met. And the second time, I almost drowned you."

He smiled. "Third time's the charm."

The Canada Cup celebration was an elaborate event sprawled around the green lawns of the yacht club and inside the grand clubhouse. Outside, children splashed in the swimming pool and teens served on volleyball courts. Several staff were leading children in an on-land sailing lesson. There was face-painting and flag-making and a craft table where people could build replicas of the *Mirage*. One area had a life-size chessboard with pieces as tall as the children.

The clubhouse and lawns were festooned with Canadian flags and pennants. Red and white ribbons decorated the two-story veranda of the clubhouse in scalloped lines, accented by pots of red and white flowers. The RCYC blue-and-white flag flapped from the flagpole.

Karl and Christine wandered around with glasses of white wine offered by wait staff circulating amongst guests. Christine was awed by the ambiance: the beautiful view of the Inner Harbor, the jazz music being played by a quartet by the front staircase, the groups of well-dressed men in summer suits and women in dresses and floppy hats. It was like a movie scene.

Inside the clubhouse, Karl and Christine headed to the rooms dedicated to the Canada Cup race. Tanned men with dress shirts rolled up to their elbows listened intently to CB reports from sailing members who were following the competitors in motorized boats. In another room, maps and navigation equipment were laid out on tables, with markers for the two boats, plotting their latitude and longitude.

"It's intense," she said as they wandered through the bar to the back patio and sitting area. The north side of the club looked out onto the Inner Harbor, revealing a panoramic view of the cityscape with white-capped waves in between.

Karl directed them to a table. "I'm hungry. Do you want to eat?"

Christine nodded, and they sat down.

A waiter refreshed their wine glasses. Christine asked for water as well. Two glasses of alcohol would be enough for her.

"There's a special dinner menu today," he said. "Lobster sandwiches. Is that okay? It's simple fare, since they are feeding a large number."

"Sure," she said. She felt embarrassed to tell him she'd never had lobster. And that it didn't seem casual to her. She had tasted the chef's food at RCYC before; it was delicious.

"Dear, this is where you are." An older woman with deep auburn hair in a coiffed bun came over, placing a hand on Karl's shoulder. She was tanned, her jade dress making her eyes look emerald green.

Karl looked up and smiled. "Mom." He motioned across the table. "This is Christine."

"Welcome, Christine," Mrs. Olsen said, leaning over to take Christine's hand. She gestured to the backyard, where throngs of people were playing croquet, standing in conversational circles, drinking or sitting by the fire pit. "It's quite an event today."

"It certainly is," Christine said. "I hear the *Mirage* is doing well."

"Yes. She won the first race, so fingers crossed for the second." She turned to her son. "Do you two want to join your father and I later for drinks?"

He smiled, shaking his head.

She tilted her head. "It's just a drink, Karl."

"You know what'll happen," he said.

"You don't always argue."

"Don't we?" He paused. "Why don't you join us for coffee and dessert later, Mom?"

Mrs. Olsen said, "I think we're supposed to sing the anthem, recite our allegiance to RCYC and then cut the Canada Cup cake. Assuming we win the second race today, of course." After a pause, she asked, "How's work?"

"You read the news, Mom. Water quality is on everyone's lips."

She smiled. "That makes you a superstar, dear."

He laughed at that. "Yes. I'm the rock star of water quality and fisheries management. I'll put that on my business card. Impress even Dad."

"Your father will be impressed when you finish your thesis," she remarked.

The smile left his face. "Can we table the lecture for another time?"

"Of course. I'll leave you two to your meal." She looked at Christine. "Nice meeting you, Christine. Enjoy your day." She headed inside.

Christine took a sip of her wine. "She's very gracious."

"Yeah, minus the nagging. She's the one who got me interested in science."

"You said your father was in business?"

He nodded. "Yup. Dad never turns it off. Always working on a deal. Money is the mecca."

The waiter came back with their food: a lobster sandwich nestled between a mixed green salad and an artful array of fruit, cheese, meats and dates. The pair was silent as they ate their meal.

"That is delicious," Christine said, taking her last bite of lobster roll.

"Do you want any more to drink?"

She shook her head. "I'm on days tomorrow, so up at five. Any more alcohol and I'll be foggy all day."

"Ready to wander around?"

"Sure."

They headed outside to the south lawn. They made several fabric flags that Karl wrapped around her headband. He stuck two flags like chopsticks through his ponytail.

"We look very patriotic," she said.

Karl convinced her to try lawn bowling. After a few ends, where her bowl either crashed angrily into the other bowls or passed wide of the mark, they moved on.

"Didn't expect to see you here, Lane."

Christine turned. It was Fillingham. He was wearing a navy suit jacket, white dress shirt and white linen pants with loafers, every inch the sailing elite. He held a full glass of whisky.

Christine smiled perfunctorily. She had been hoping to avoid him, knowing that he spent a great deal of time at the club. "It's an exciting event to attend." She gestured beside her. "You remember Karl."

Fillingham took a drink from his glass. "The guy who almost drowned you."

She frowned. "He cut the wire from my ankle to save me."

"I thought you said hippies weren't your thing," Fillingham commented. He took a large gulp of whisky, half emptying the glass. "Or were you lying about that as well?"

After a pause, Karl said, "What's your problem?"

"No problem." Fillingham emptied his glass and handed it to a waiter walking by. Turning back to them, he said, "Got any weed on you, Karl?"

Karl crossed his arms. "You selling or buying?"

"That's enough," Christine said, shaking her head. Fillingham's eyes were shiny, cheeks flushed. This wasn't his first tumbler of whisky.

Karl said, "Yeah, move along."

Fillingham snorted a laugh. "Move along?" He pressed his hand to his chest. "I'm part of the Canada Cup support team. My family has been club members for a hundred years. What back door did you enter?"

Before Karl could retort, Christine held out a hand to Fillingham. "I don't know what you're doing," she said softly, "but please stop."

"Just looking out for you, partner." He smiled widely.

"Ex," she said. "Ex-partner."

Fillingham said, "Maybe I should give Karl a heads-up." He gestured to Christine. "Serious money problems," he said in a loud whisper. "Friend to friend, I'd hide the silverware."

"We're not friends," Karl said.

"You're being a jerk," Christine said. She could feel the tears prick her eyelids.

"Making conversation."

Christine stood in front of Fillingham, four inches taller than him in her heels, hands clenched. "Then stop. Stop talking to me. Stop being my partner. Stop being my friend. We're done."

Fillingham's mouth pinched tightly. "You two deserve each other."

"Yes," Karl said. "We do."

Chapter 25

"PW Lane!"

Christine braked her bicycle and looked over her shoulder. Mrs. Polotov waved at her from her front lawn, a carrot bunch clutched in one hand.

Christine smiled and pedaled back. The Islander sometimes gave her fresh vegetables from her garden. This summer, Christine had returned home with leeks, red peppers and potatoes.

Placing the carrots in her bike basket, Christine said, "I'll ask my mom to make carrot cake and bring you back a slice," she said. "She's a better baker than me."

"Have time for tea?" Mrs. Polotov said.

"That would be great," Christine said. She could use a burst of caffeine. Last night she had gone to bed late after her date with Karl and had been bleary-eyed as she patrolled the Ward's Island streets. She wheeled her bike to the backyard. Sitting down at the patio table, she angled her chair to be under the shade of the overhead umbrella.

Christine stood up when her friend came out the back door.

"Take this, love," Mrs. Polotov said, handing Christine a tray. "I'll pop inside for the rest."

Christine placed the tray holding the tea set on the patio table.

"You spoil me," Christine remarked as her friend returned with a plate of butter tarts, lemon squares and walnut fudge brownies.

The older woman shrugged and sat down, tucking her long floral skirt underneath her. "Who else to I have to dote on?"

"You feed the entire neighborhood." When Hawk Johnson was Mrs. Polotov's neighbor last year, she kept him in constant supply of zucchini loaf.

Hawk. She didn't want to think about him. Had he found Layla? Was his family reunited? Christine had read nothing in the newspaper about a child abduction. She shook her head to clear her thoughts.

"Anything wrong, dear?" the Islander asked as she poured them tea.

"No," Christine didn't want to involve Mrs. Polotov in Hawk's situation, even though they were friends. "Trying to clear the cobwebs."

"Did the Canada Cup event go late?"

Christine sat back in her chair. "How did you know I attended?"

Mrs. Polotov smiled. "A few Ward's Island residents are yacht club members. Someone mentioned they saw you there." Her eyes widened as she looked at Christine.

Christine put two teaspoons of sugar in her milky tea. "Say whatever it is you want to say."

Mrs. Polotov chuckled. "They mentioned you had an escort."

"He's a PhD student working on the Island for the summer."

"Karl or Sandro?"

"Do you know everybody?"

"Not quite everybody, dear. But a few people."

"Karl. His family are club members, so he thought it would be fun."

"And was it?"

Christine nodded. "It was. I've been there before, with Fillingham. It's lovely. The clubhouse is a grand building with a wraparound patio and so many rooms inside. The backyard has a spectacular view of the harbor. You've seen it, right?"

The older woman nodded. "Yes, dear. But it's been a while." She placed a lemon tart on her plate. "How is young Fillingham? I'll save dessert for him."

Christine tried to keep her face neutral. "I don't know. We're not on the same shift any more. Or at least not very often." Thank goodness for that. After his remarks last night, she'd be happy never to work with him again. The sooner he made it onto the Harbor Police force, the better.

A bark made the two women turn.

"Lifeguard!" Christine exclaimed. The dog bounded in, as exuberant as ever.

The dog ran over to sniff Mrs. Polotov's hand.

"You look as right as rain," the older woman said to the dog, giving her a pat on the head. "Ready for a treat?"

Lifeguard barked as Mrs. Polotov stood up.

When her friend returned with crumbled bits of bacon, Christine said, "No wonder Lifeguard found me. Or should I say you. She knows a soft touch when she sees one."

"The pot calling the kettle black." Mrs. Polotov got the dog to sit and then give her a paw. "It's amazing she recovered. Was it really poison she ingested?"

Christine said, "I'm guessing. We're waiting on lab analysis."

"And the ducks? Was it the same poison source that killed them?"

Christine shrugged. "I'm guessing that they're linked. But we're awaiting those reports as well."

"Is someone targeting wildlife? Or pets? Or any animal?"

Christine shook her head. "I'm not sure." The papers had been full of conjecture. Members of Operation Pollution had picketed the Parks and Recreation facility on Hanlan's Point, concerned about the dead ganders found nearby. Local birding associations had been demanding that the government classify the Island as a bird sanctuary in need of protection.

Christine looked at her watch. "Thanks so much for the tea and treats. I should get going. I'm on shift with Pilkington, and he'll kill me if I leave him alone with Cadet Nelson. She's too much energy for him." She retrieved her bike.

Mrs. Polotov came out with a small cardboard box. "A few tarts for Fillingham."

Christine placed the box in her bike basket beside the carrots. "I'll leave them in the fridge and put a note on them."

"Have you two made up?" Mrs. Polotov asked.

"No." Her tone was definite. "And we won't."

The Islander regarded Christine silently.

"It's hard for me to accept too," Christine protested, although Mrs. Polotov had said nothing. "I'm sad we're not friends any more. He was a great partner. And my friend. You know how much he helped my family. I won't forget that. But things change. Things end. It's what we both want."

"If you say so," Mrs. Polotov said.

Chapter 26

"How did Annie Oakley get invited?" Julie asked Christine as they stood in front of Edith Buckley's front yard, cluttered with towering boxes, wood piles, broken furniture and tarp-covered mounds. Julie's gaze was on Nelson, who was attired in denim coveralls and a hair kerchief.

Last week, Mrs. Polotov had called the station to see if Christine would help clear the Buckleys' place, and Cadet Nelson had volunteered as well. Christine was able to corral Sarah and Julie for the morning with the promise the friends could head to an Island beach for the afternoon.

Six other residents gathered around the front yard with the policewomen.

"Welcome, everyone," said Gary Owen. "It's going to be a busy day. A busy two days. Mrs. Buckley left this morning. Mrs. Polotov's sister Audrey was kind enough to host her for two days at her house on the mainland." He looked at the house, the patchy roof and the cluttered front lawn. "We have our work cut out for us.

"Our goal is to clear the outside premises," Owen continued. "The Parks and Recreation commissioner and his cronies from Metro Council lead spontaneous walks around our community—trespassing through our yards. If properties look destitute or in disrepair, they record them. Unkempt houses are fodder for their campaign to evict us and pave the way for a shiny new development that will make them money and gild their reputations. We cannot give Metro Council any leverage."

"Gary, dear," Mrs. Polotov said, from beside him, "it's important to clear the inside of the house, too. Vivian, our social worker, paid Edith a visit. She said the inside is a health hazard. No room to cook. Limited space to sit or stand. Barely a path to the washroom. It's a miracle she hasn't fallen."

Owen waved away Mrs. Poltov's concern. "If we don't clean up the outside, there won't be any inside. For any of us."

"Gary," Mrs. Polotov remonstrated, "I'm counting ten people here now at nine o'clock in the morning and a second shift to come later. And tomorrow the same. Surely, that's enough people to address interior and exterior clutter. This gathering is to help Mrs. Buckley."

"Fine," Owen conceded. "I'll get the men to help with the front yard. It's got the heaviest items. I'm hoping Far Enough Farm will lend us a tractor for a couple of hours so we can dump garbage into the two bins we rented. Wood debris can go in a separate pile to be burned. I got a fire permit for today and tomorrow. The wagon here is for donations."

Second Street was too narrow for the ten-foot bins that had been placed at the southern end of the street near the beach.

"Ladies," Mrs. Polotov said, addressing the policewomen, "let's head to the back. Edith had a garden at one time. Let's see what we can salvage. We'll need bags for the garbage. We'll pile the twigs and branches together to be burned. Larger garbage, like broken chairs, can be brought to the front for the tractor to carry to the bins."

Sarah, Christine, Julie and Nelson followed the short, round form of Mrs. Polotov to the backyard. Sarah paused by the side door that was blocked with weeds and debris. The concrete step in front of the door had crumbled into large chunks of stone.

Sarah said, "It's a fire hazard to have the door blocked. I'll start here." She grabbed several bags and an empty box.

"Nothing too heavy," Christine warned. "Limit yourself to weed-pulling and tidying. Call me for any lifting."

Sarah touched Christine's sleeve. "Look at you, being a concerned godmother already."

Mrs. Polotov assigned the women jobs. Despite being the kindest person Christine knew, the Islander certainly was a no-nonsense manager. Christine was asked to haul the heaviest and largest items away so they could see what was underneath.

"I'll help," Nelson said as Christine held one end of a moss-covered couch.

"Should I call one of the men?" Mrs. Polotov asked.

"I'm strong!" Nelson protested.

"Like an ox," Nelson and Christine chorused as they lifted the couch.

The backyard crew carried the larger items: broken kitchen chairs, a loveseat, a bed frame and a rusted patio table to the front. They uncovered many sodden cardboard boxes spilling out their contents, as well as wooden crates and open piles of debris. Mrs. Polotov hazarded that the backyard took the overflow from the house.

They worked diligently on the box contents, piling items into three piles: donation, garbage or fire. Mrs. Polotov cleared the corner of the yard that used to be a garden.

A thundering rumble got louder. Nelson stood, her overalls soiled at the knees from kneeling in the dirt. "That's the tractor! I drove one on the farm!" She ran to the front.

"She's very enthusiastic," Julie said as she squatted by a box of old kitchen dishes.

Christine chuckled. "A bit overpowering, but her energy is conta-gious. More fun to be around than some Island policemen." Christine was thinking of Morano and Pilkington. And, of course, Fillingham. "She says what's on her mind. Sometimes a police officer needs tact."

Julie carefully plucked out shards of broken crockery and placed them in a cardboard box for the garbage. "Nelson thought I was a beauty pageant star. Nothing wrong with her observations." Squatting in her black chinos and polka dot shirt, hair in a black bandana, mascaraed eyes, Julie looked fashionable, albeit grimy.

"You *are* a beauty pageant star, Julie," Christine said as she placed a pile of old magazines on the fire pile.

"That's high praise from you," Julie sniffed.

"And somewhere in that platinum beauty, deep, deep down, is a heart of gold," Christine amended.

"Not that deep," Julie said. "I'm here today, aren't I? I have better things to do. Men to meet. Boys to charm."

Christine grabbed a bag of garbage and headed to the front. She picked another bag from Sarah and deposited both on the large mound of garbage piled on the road. Craning her neck, she spotted the tractor at the end of the road. Nelson sat in the bucket chair, expertly switching gears and levers as she dumped a couch into a large metal bin.

Mrs. Polotov walked up to Christine. "That girl is surprising."

They both smiled.

"I'll go get the lemonade I made this morning," the older woman said. "I'll be right back."

"Need any help?"

Mrs. Polotov shook her head. "I'll attach the wagon to my bike."

As soon as she left, Julie yelled, "Break time!" She grabbed wooden crates and the three women sat down.

"While the cat's away..." Christine began.

"The mice will pause and dust themselves off," Julie said.

"Got the side doorway cleared, at least on the exterior," Sarah said. "I'll go inside and see if I can clear a path to the door and unlock it."

"Feeling okay?" Christine asked.

"I'm hot," Sarah replied, wiping her forehead with the back of her hand. She placed a hand on her belly over her cotton t-shirt. "Did you hear that the union is considering our petition?"

"Really?" Christine said. "That's great news."

Julie took a sip of lemonade. "We got over four hundred signatures on the petition."

"Wow," Christine said, "I didn't realize that so many other officers would support the policy."

Sarah waved away Christine's comment. "It's only half police officers. We opened the petition to others: women on city council, advocates, politicians. Doctors and community agencies. Gail ran with it."

"It's too bad Gail had to work today," Christine said.

"Is Geoffrey showing up?" Julie asked as she retrieved a compact mirror from her purse.

Christine's cheerful mood evaporated. "I have no idea what he's doing."

Sarah and Julie met glances. Julie opened the compact and dabbed her nose and forehead, then closed the compact with a snap.

"What?" Christine said. "We're not partnering anymore. We're not on shift together."

Sarah said, "Okay."

"It is okay," Christine said. Why was her tone so defensive? "It's better this way. Lately, he's been—"

"Mean," Julie answered. She removed her hair band, shook out her short blond bob and put her hairband back in.

"How did you know that?" Christine asked.

"He told me," Julie said.

"You talked to him?" Christine said.

"Yes, he came over yesterday for dinner."

"You're on speaking terms?" Christine asked.

"He still calls me every week, even though we broke up. I know we didn't end well. We both made mistakes. But we've calmed down now, apologized to each other. We've found a way to be friends."

Christine almost said, *Good for you.* So Fillingham was friendly and apologetic with his ex-girlfriend but had nothing but vitriol for her. She shook her head.

Julie faced her, brown eyes wide. "He feels bad about the way he's treated you."

"He should," Christine said.

Sarah turned to her, her curly hair askew. "He knows he messed up, Christine."

"How do you know that?"

"I dropped by Julie's for dessert," Sarah said, "when Geoffrey was there."

Christine said, "Are you ganging up on me? Is that why you came today—to talk about Fillingham?"

Sarah and Julie were silent.

Oh, for goodness' sake. Christine said, "He's crossed a line. We can't go back."

A loud male voice called, "You don't belong here!"

A woman's voice yelled back, words indistinguishable.

Christine ran to the front yard.

Gary Owen and the Merriweathers stood on the road facing Judith Purnell and Mrs. Polotov on her three-wheeled bicycle with attached wagon.

Judith said, "I have the right to be here." She pointed at the house. "I've known Edith all my life. I want to help. I clean houses for a living."

Owen said, "We don't need help from a Judas like you, licking the superintendent's shoes. Taking his money."

Judith pressed her lips closed, furious.

Mrs. Merriweather said, "Judith, that man stole our house. I can't believe you agreed to work for him."

Mrs. Polotov said, "Judith has a right to choose her jobs. To feed her children. We don't have to agree with her choice to accept her help here today."

Owen crossed his arms. "I don't want help from traitors."

"Good thing Edith isn't as picky." Mrs. Polotov dismounted. "Carol, can you distribute the lemonade? Judith, I could use your help in the kitchen." Mrs. Polotov grabbed Judith by the elbow and headed toward the front porch.

Julie came up beside Christine, hooking her arm around Christine's. "There's a Jack and Jill baby shower for Sarah planned on the 31st," she whispered. "It's a surprise. Book the day off, fellow godmother."

Turning Christine around, the two women returned to the backyard with a purloined jug of lemonade. "One more hour," Julie proclaimed, "and we're heading for the beach!"

Chapter 27

"Mrs. Martin!" Christine greeted the woman.

The superintendent's wife stood in the station waiting room, a large wicker basket over her arm, wearing a cream dress. Her daughter followed her in, also in a cream summer dress, a miniature version of her parent.

"Ew!" said Cadet Nelson from behind the counter. "What's that smell?"

Without speaking, Mrs. Martin heaved the basket contents onto the counter. Dark green seaweed slid from the basket onto the counter.

Nelson covered her nose with one hand.

"Dumped on my front porch this morning," Mrs. Martin said.

"Dumped?" Christine echoed.

"Yes. My husband said about a hundred pounds of seaweed. He had to get Mallory to fork it into a wheelbarrow and throw it into the lake." Her mouth was a flat line.

"Somebody did this on purpose?" Nelson said.

Mrs. Martin's eyebrows rose as if the answer were obvious. She retrieved a piece of paper from her handbag. "My husband wants to file an official complaint about ongoing acts of harassment. The details are here. We'll need a copy of the police report. Please forward a copy to Metro Council as well."

It was interesting that the Martins were reporting the seaweed, given that Mr. Martin hadn't called in the gardening equipment theft. She guessed he had had enough.

Mrs. Martin's note was penned in elegant black script. Beside the date, July 17, was the statement that the front and backyard gardens had been removed. The next event occurred on July 26, when a pail of rotting fish was left on the front porch. On four separate dates, the Martins' milk bottles had gone missing after the milkman confirmed delivery.

Cadet Nelson retrieved an incident report form, the one meant for the public. Christine wrote Mrs. Martin's information on the triplicate carbon form.

Mrs. Martin waited for her copy of the completed form, arms crossed, refusing to take a seat in the waiting room, playing with her gold wedding rings.

"Mom," Matilda said, "I'm bored."

Mrs. Martin frowned. "You're bored because you refuse to go to camp."

"No one likes me there."

"You need to grow thicker skin, Matilda."

Matilda's face clouded.

"Your brother made friends at Supervision," Mrs. Martin said. "You need to try harder."

"Can't I go to camp at the sailing club?" Matilda asked.

"We're not RCYC members yet. Daddy has his application in, but we must wait."

Matilda sat on the bench, back to her mother.

Mrs. Martin turned to Christine. "Are we done here?"

"Almost," Christine said. "Confirm the information you gave me." She placed the form on the counter, away from the seaweed. "Then sign at the bottom." She handed Mrs. Martin a pen.

"What do we do with this?" Nelson asked, indicating with her chin the noxious-smelling mound of seaweed beside them.

"Keep it," Mrs. Martin said, smiling. "As evidence."

"We'll take it outside and dump it in the lagoon," Christine said.

Mrs. Martin folded the form into her purse.

"Mrs. Martin," Christine said, "I'll get a patrol car to drive by your house during each shift. Monitor for suspicious activity."

Mrs. Martin sniffed, then turned around, grabbing Matilda's hand. "Yes, I'm so glad local police are on the case. They've done a wonderful job so far."

"Head out," PC Morano told Christine. "Cadet Nelson and I can hold the fort."

The three officers stood in the office of the Island police station. Christine had been on day shift with Morano. Nelson had come on duty at noon.

Morano smiled at Christine, who stared back at him, unsmiling.

"It's okay," Nelson said. "We're fine. I'm fine," she amended.

"She's got me to take care of her," Morano added, putting one arm loosely on Nelson's shoulders.

"That's what I'm afraid of," Christine retorted, but she turned around and exited the office. She didn't have time to lecture Nelson again. She had to make the twelve thirty ferry back to the mainland.

In ninety minutes, Christine, Fillingham, Sarah, Gail and Julie would receive commendations for their undercover work in Yorkville in a ceremony at headquarters. The top brass and media would be in attendance.

As a team, the undercover officers had identified and captured the biker gang leader selling hard drugs into Yorkville. The untold story was that they also found a missing teen, Kelly Darlow, Deputy Darlow's daughter.

During Operation Niagara, Christine had been asked to search secretly for Kelly. Christine had found her. Kelly then revealed that Deputy Darlow was Christine's father and used Christine to blackmail him. The girl was a manipulative, self-centered addict.

Christine blew out a big breath as the ferry chugged across the Inner Harbor. She needed to get through the ceremony, take her plaque and beeline it out of there. Go out for a coffee later with her friends who knew about Darlow but were sworn to secrecy. Darlow wanted to keep his illegitimate daughter hidden, which was fine by Christine, since she wanted nothing to do with him.

The five officers sat in the front row of the main floor conference room at police headquarters. Fillingham sat at one end and Christine at the other. Fifty people were scattered around the eighty chairs, journalists and police staff mixed with civilians.

Julie leaned forward. "Christine, there's your mom."

Christine turned around. Her mom sat in the back row with her hair neatly pressed back in barrettes, Donna and Wayne beside her. All in their Sunday best. Wayne wore dress pants and a white shirt that was short at the wrists, and Donna sported a summer dress.

Christine said to Sarah beside her, "I'll be right back."

Christine greeted her family. Touching her mom's shoulder, she said, "Mom, you didn't have to come." Her mom was working afternoons, starting after the ceremony. Turning to her siblings, Christine said, "Anything to get a little air conditioning."

"That's right," Wayne said, although he looked in awe of the police paraphernalia in the room, ranging from portraits of past chiefs and photos of dramatic rescues to display cases of evidence collected at crime scenes.

Donna said, "Are you going up to the podium? Do you have to say a speech?"

Christine laughed. "Let's hope not. I'll accept my plaque, shake everyone's hands and be on my way." She addressed Wayne. "If you two are going home on your own, you need to be careful."

Wayne grimaced. "I know."

Christine headed back to her seat. Fillingham turned around to wave at Wayne. They had met before and were buddies.

After Christine sat back down, Sarah said, "Ken said he'd spring for dessert after. How about we line you up with a slice of pecan pie?"

Christine smiled. "You know me well." Any dessert made with brown sugar was a sure-fire way to her heart.

Christine hoped Fillingham wouldn't come to the café, but since he was chummy with her friends, she knew he would be asked.

Stop! Stop letting Fillingham affect your mood. She would have fun with her friends, with or without her ex-partner in attendance.

The audience hushed as Chief Benson and Deputy Chief Darlow walked up to the front of the room by the podium. Sergeant Buckman from Morality Squad joined the senior officers, standing a deferential distance away. Buckman had led Operation Niagara. Several cameras behind Christine clicked. Journalists pulled memo pads from their pockets, pens in hand.

Christine gazed at the tiled floor. She would not look at Deputy Darlow, *her father.*

The chief was introduced, and the burly man took the podium. Christine focused on him.

"Good afternoon," the chief said. "It is my great pleasure today to discuss the success of Operation Niagara."

The chief summarized the number of arrests, the quantity of drugs seized and the positive impact this would have on the community. Yorkville residents, visitors and tourists could feel safe in the neighborhood again.

Turning to Sergeant Buckman, the chief highlighted the dedication of the Morality Squad. He acknowledged the long hours worked by the undercover officers during Operation Niagara, a sting that had ended in the dramatic takedown of a biker gang and shutdown of their drug business.

After applause from the audience, the chief asked Sergeant Buckman to distribute the plaques, which recognized the officers' bravery and service. Fillingham went up first, shaking the hands of the three senior officers. The officers filed up, received the plaques and handshakes and sat back down. When it was Christine's turn, she smiled as she shook Buckman's hand and then the chief's, then averted her eyes as she took the deputy's outstretched hand.

"Can I see you after the ceremony for a moment, Officer?" Deputy Darlow said, holding her in the handshake.

She was about to refuse when she saw Chief Benson look over.

"Yes, sir," she managed, and then sat back down.

Chief Benson closed the commemoration. Christine said goodbye to her family, and the officers were asked to pose for photos. Christine stood away from Fillingham for each shot, even when the newspaper photographer got him to lie across the laps of the policewomen.

"Can we drop him when we're done?" asked Gail. The women pretended to tip him to the floor. Fillingham was able to roll off and land on his hands and feet, like a cat. The photographer clicked a picture of that as well.

As the group of friends gathered to leave, Christine said, "I'll meet you at the café in fifteen minutes."

"What's up?" Fillingham said. This was their first direct communication.

She averted her eyes from his searching blue stare. "I have something to take care of. I'll be there soon." She turned to Sarah. "Save me a seat."

As the group left, Christine caught the deputy's glance and trudged over.

"PW Lane," Deputy Darlow said, "if you could come to my office for a moment, please."

Silently, she followed him to the elevator and the sixth floor that hosted the chief's and deputy chiefs' offices.

As they passed his secretary's desk, Deputy Darlow said, "Hold all calls."

"Yes, sir," the woman said.

Christine followed Darlow into the large office that had light streaming through its west-facing windows. She stopped.

Kelly.

Christine turned to leave.

"Wait!" the deputy said. "She just wants to talk."

Christine paused.

"Please," the teenager said from the tan leather couch beside the large oak desk.

Reluctantly, Christine took a seat in a chair across from the couch, a coffee table between them holding tomes about the history of policing and city neighborhoods.

Darlow sat at his desk, leaving Christine and Kelly in the sitting area.

Kelly regarded Christine with a small smile.

She looked different. The Kelly that Christine knew in Yorkville had been a skinny teenager, unwashed hair in stringy strands down her back, dressed in baggy clothes, with acne and a missing tooth.

The teenager in front of her was dressed simply in cotton pants and a t-shirt, clean hair pulled back with a red hairband. She was still thin, but her acne had lessened, and her tooth had been fixed.

"Thanks for coming," Kelly said.

Like she had a choice.

"I'm in rehab," Kelly continued, clasping and unclasping her hands on her lap. "I'm trying to get better."

Christine felt a twinge of empathy. Her mom and her stepfather had been drinkers and gamblers. It was a hard thing to kick.

"That's good," she managed.

"I got special permission to come today," Kelly said, "so that I could watch the ceremony."

Christine hadn't seen her. She must have stood at the back. Christine looked over at the deputy behind his desk. How long did she have to stay?

Kelly held up a hand. "I won't keep you long. I wanted to thank you, in person, for what you did for me. For finding me. For saving me."

"I would have done it for anybody."

Kelly said, "I know I did things that put you in danger."

Christine frowned at the memory. Kelly had a biker kidnap Christine so they could blackmail John Darlow for Christine's safe return.

Kelly continued. "And that was wrong. I was an addict. Really messed up. I'd do anything to get drugs." She wiped her palms on her pants. "I'm still an addict, but I'm getting better. I'm eating better. Sleeping better. I see a psychiatrist. I know I need to make amends." Her brown eyes looked into Christine's, their almond shape similar to her own. "I'm sorry."

Christine nodded, then stood up.

"Wait," Kelly said, standing up too. "I know it's too soon, and you have no reason to trust me, but maybe we can see each other again." She gave a hopeful smile.

"I don't think so," Christine answered. She had enough challenges in her life with her mom and raising her stepsiblings. She had no intention of adding a secret stepsister to the mix alongside being the hidden, illegitimate daughter of the deputy.

She turned to the deputy. "I came here because I thought it was something to do with policing. Please do not mislead me again. Speak to me only about police duties."

And she walked out.

Chapter 28

Sarah waved Christine over to the rectangular table where she had saved her a seat. Sarah and Julie were sitting by the window. Gail, Fillingham and Ken sat across from them.

Christine slid in beside Sarah, greeting Ken across from her. Everyone had coffee in front of them. The waitress had noticed Christine's entrance and filled her empty cup.

Julie said, "We were telling the boys about Cadet Nelson on the tractor!"

Christine smiled. "At least we could put her skills to use on the Island."

Gail said, "You got to like a woman who handles machines."

Sarah said, "From a person who sailed a tanker."

Gail said, "I didn't sail one. I trained for it. I could if I needed to."

Sarah said, "Noted."

Fillingham looked over at Christine. "Nelson's quite gung-ho."

Christine averted her eyes but answered the question. "Too enthusiastic. I think she's going to get herself into trouble."

Sarah turned to Christine, "She's young...barely eighteen. What were we like at that age?"

Gail said, "None of us joined the police force that early. Ken, how old were you?"

Ken said, "Twenty-one."

Sarah said, "I was a social worker before joining, Julie did temp work. Gail was a navy officer, and Christine, you worked in Records. We have to give Olivia Nelson slack."

Christine wondered if she should mention her concern about Morano and Nelson but decided she'd keep quiet. Nothing had happened between them. It was just a niggling worry.

The group chatted and laughed for the next hour, reminiscing about Operation Niagara, the fund-raising wrestling match between Christine and Fillingham, the volatile scene at the bikers' den before it was set on fire. Christine didn't say too much; she still felt awkward with her partner there. Everyone else seemed on agreeable terms with him. Was she being oversensitive?

No, Christine thought, as she chewed a forkful of pecan pie. Fillingham had been a jerk since Yorkville. Look what he had said at the Canada Cup event. She was tired of people, Fillingham, Deputy Darlow and Kelly Darlow, thinking that an apology was sufficient reparation for terrible behavior. She didn't have to forgive anyone. After finishing her pie, she made an excuse to leave.

"See you at work," Fillingham said.

Christine let the door close behind her.

The next day, the door of the police station banged open, the bells above it clanging. An older man in a straw hat entered with two scowling young boys in tow. A woman in a blue sun hat followed the trio in.

The man pulled each boy by the elbow toward the counter where Christine stood. "Here's where you two hooligans belong. At a police station." The man wore a short-sleeved plaid shirt and khaki shorts. A pair of binoculars hung from a strap around his neck.

Christine said, "Hello. I'm PW Lane. Toronto Police. How can I help you?" She looked closer at the boys, who were trying to pull away from the disgruntled man. Both had straight brown hair and triangular faces. They must be brothers.

"These thieves tried to sell us goose eggs," the man said. The woman came up beside him, nodding vigorously. She was about fifty, with gray, blonde chin-length curls. Probably his wife.

Christine came out from behind the counter into the waiting area. "Let's sit down for a chat. Boys, you can sit beside me."

The man reluctantly let go of the boys, who scooted to Christine's other side. The two groups sat kitty corner to each other on the benches.

"We were out birding today," the man began, "looking for migrant bird nests in the shallows, when these boys offered us goose eggs for fifteen cents apiece."

The woman said, "We're Mr. and Mrs. Applegate." She pressed a freckled hand to her chest. "We are members of the Toronto Ornithological Club. My husband is the treasurer."

Mr. Applegate said, "As a club, we disagree vehemently with the selling of bird eggs in unlicensed settings. That is how species become extinct." He gestured toward the boys. "I want these boys arrested."

Christine turned to the boys. "I've seen you two around. Do you live on Algonquin Island?"

The older boy clutched the younger boy's hand, squeezing it hard. They looked at her with large brown eyes, mute.

Christine leaned back against the bench seat. "I can bring you to Algonquin, knock on anyone's door and they'll tell me exactly who you are. I might have to handcuff you."

The younger one let go of his brother's hand. "I'm Kevin."

The older one said quickly, "I'm Thomas. His brother. Thomas Ancaster."

She addressed Thomas. "Tell me what happened."

Thomas shrugged. "It's like they said. We tried to sell them eggs. To make money to buy comic books. We weren't hurting anyone." He glowered at the Applegates.

"Well, young man," Mrs. Applegate sputtered.

Christine interrupted. "Let them finish."

Thomas continued, "We sometimes take eggs from a bird's nest if no goose or gander is around. That's it. People buy from us to have fresh eggs for breakfast."

"What species do you take?" Mr. Applegate asked angrily. "Was it a yellow-tipped lark? An English grouse? Because there are very few of them left, I'll let you know."

Christine placed her palms together and pointed them at the siblings. "Boys, can you understand that removing eggs from birds' nests is not only illegal, but it can impact a bird population, especially for a species under threat?"

"It was geese," Thomas said. "Not the yellow whatever he said."

Christine stared hard at both boys. "Agreed?"

"Okay," said Kevin quickly.

Thomas said, "Okay."

"And if I ever hear that you are stealing eggs again," Christine said, "I will have your whole family come into the station to discuss the community service you will be assigned, which will undoubtedly include cleaning the toilets at Manitou Beach."

The boys looked horrified.

Christine turned to the Applegates. "I'll talk to their parents. Let them know what happened here today. I think the boys have learned their lesson. Thank you for bringing them in."

"You're not going to arrest them?" Mr. Applegate said.

"We don't arrest children under twelve," Christine said. "But we will tell their parents, which can have as much impact."

With a harrumph, the Applegates left.

Cadet Nelson appeared at the counter. She had been on lunch break in the kitchenette. "What's going on?"

"We're taking these boys back to Algonquin to have a chat with their parents about their egg-stealing tendencies."

"Can I drive?" Nelson asked.

Christine wondered if cadets were allowed to drive patrol cars. But surely, if Nelson could drive a combine and a tractor, a utility vehicle would be a piece of cake. "Sure."

The boys stood up to leave.

Nelson pointed to Thomas's back pocket. "They used a sling-shot."

Tucked in the back pocket of each boy's pants was a slingshot.

"They shoot the goose to get it off the nest," Nelson said. "My brothers did it all the time with the chickens when it was their turn to gather eggs."

Thomas flushed red while his younger brother's eyes widened.

"Sit back down," Christine said to the boys.

"Where do you get your eggs?" Christine asked.

Thomas's eyes shifted left and right. "Different places."

"How about Trout Pond?" Christine asked.

"Not really," Thomas said, his tone hesitant.

"They did it!" Nelson shrieked, arms gesturing to the children. "That's how the two ganders died. The boys hit them with rocks from their slingshots and grabbed the female's eggs."

Christine turned to the boys. Kevin's face scrunched up, then he burst into tears. "We didn't mean to kill them. We only wanted to scare them away."

"They started coming after us," Thomas said, "attacking us. It was self-defense."

Nelson turned to Christine. "The ganders weren't poisoned. We've found our culprits!"

Chapter 29

It was another beautiful July day, Christine thought as she exited the ferry with Nelson. The late afternoon sun warmed without scalding, the heat moderated by a southerly wind. It was so much cooler than her Parkdale apartment with its stale air and windowless bedroom. She wished she lived on the Island in the summer.

"What's this fluff?" Nelson commented, swatting at the white fibers floating around them.

"It's from the cottonwood tree," Christine remarked. "When there's a breeze, the seeds blow off the branches, and it makes the Island into a snow globe."

"It's soft," Nelson said, catching one in her hand.

"Islanders hate it," Christine said. "They clump together and become a fire hazard." Fire was a concern on the Island. She remembered seeing old photos of grand hotels and stadiums on Hanlan's Point that had burned to the ground.

As the women neared the patrol car, she heard Sergeant Bard tell Pilkington to head onto the ferry. He'd be along in a moment.

Christine and Nelson stopped in front of their commanding officer. Ferry passengers flowed around them in noisy groups on their way to the amusement park. Those with wicker baskets would head to the green lawns, barbeque pits and beaches.

"PW Lane. Cadet Nelson," Bard greeted them.

"How was day shift, sir?" Nelson asked.

Bard raised his bushy gray eyebrows. "If you'd give me a second to give report, Cadet, then you'd have your answer."

"Yes, sir. Of course, sir." Nelson's freckled face was grave, her brown eyes serious. She looked like a child practicing being an adult.

Christine scanned the crowd. "Sir, I don't see PC Ulster."

"He had an appointment," Bard answered. "He should be on the next ferry."

Christine stared at her sergeant. Ulster was a buddy of Bard's. They had started on the force around the same time. Christine found him affable, although not hardworking, and he was sometimes tardy for shift, which was unacceptable in policing. Your pay got docked. And everyone knew Ulster tippled from a mickey in his uniform jacket throughout the day. By the end of shift, he was mildly soused.

But Bard had a soft spot for Ulster.

Bard said, "The vet's report came in regarding the two geese found dead near Trout Pond," Bard said. "They were killed by—"

"External injuries!" Nelson shrieked, clapping her hands.

Christine had informed her sergeant about the brothers who sold eggs and shot at the ganders. The confession was forwarded to the vet.

Bard nodded. "The first gander had a head contusion, leading to death. The second one had a broken trachea. The vet didn't see the need to order extensive lab analysis or blood work. It's reasonable to conclude that the ganders were killed by the boys slingshooting rocks."

"Skillful work, Cadet Nelson," Christine said, "noticing the slingshots in the boys' pockets. Getting them to confess."

Bard smiled at Christine's praise, her ruse obvious, but he nodded in agreement. "The vet's report will be released tomorrow. Hopefully, this will reduce hysteria and get Operation Pollution and the birders off our backs."

Nelson said, "I don't think the Applegates will be happy to hear that the boys killed the ganders."

Christine asked, "Sir, did the toxicology report on the Centreville geese come in? It's taking such a long time."

He shook his head. "The stomach contents and bloodwork were sent to a provincial lab for analysis. They're always slow. Then we have the pink substance you two found in Centreville at the lab as well. There's been so much fuss about the ducks that they're double-checking to make sure the final report is accurate and impartial."

Christine sighed as she got into the passenger seat, allowing Cadet Nelson to drive them to the station. To be truthful, she wasn't impartial about the Islanders' situation, even though Bard had advised her to stay out of local politics. She had a soft spot for the residents of Ward's and Algonquin Island. Many families had lived on the Island for over fifty years. These weren't summer cottages. They were all-year homes for many people.

Residents watched out for each other, helped each other, like they did with Mrs. Buckley. They shared food and tools. They played sports and celebrated together. The communities were part of Toronto's history. Why evict them to create more parkland when there was ample parkland already? The green areas of the Island were never crowded. And if the goal were to build a new, modern community, why evict people who currently lived on the Island, who took care of it and had history here? It made little sense to Christine.

At the station, she slipped an envelope into Fillingham's secure locker—her biweekly repayment of the money she and her mom owed him. Whether she loved or hated the man, she still needed to repay him for the loan. She reviewed the log entries and made a few calls. As she hung up the phone, Nelson approached her desk and handed her a cup of tea.

"Thanks, Nelson."

"Can I talk to you for a minute?" Nelson said, looking serious.

"Sure."

Nelson brought a chair over and sat across from Christine, knees together, hands clasped tightly on her lap.

"Anything wrong?" Christine said.

"I...I want to talk to you about Gala Day."

A flashback to Nelson dancing in Morano's arms in front of the community center. Christine shouldn't have left her there.

"Did something happen?" Christine asked.

Nelson's face contorted. "Yes...no."

"Did Morano do something? Did he hurt you?"

She averted her eyes. "He tried to get fresh. I pushed him away, but he pushed back."

Christine waited. Morano should be reported. He was a bully and an abuser.

"Until I told him," Nelson explained. "Then he stopped."

"Told him what?" Christine asked.

Nelson's cheeks flushed red. "I...I..." She grabbed a pen from the nearby desk and fiddled with it, kneading it between her fingers.

"It's okay," Christine encouraged.

"I told him I was in love with someone," she said.

"That stopped him?"

She placed the pen back on the desk. "Not at first. Until I told him who it was."

"Who?"

"A woman," Nelson said. "I said I loved a woman. And that made him stop."

"Oh." Christine knew from the Women's Bureau that some women had relationships with other women. Look at Gail and Petra. "That's okay—"

"It's not true," Nelson interrupted. "I'm not in love with anybody. I don't love women."

"At least it made him stop. That's the important thing. And that he'll leave you alone."

"That's not the problem." Nelson looked beseechingly at the older officer.

"What's the problem?" Christine asked.

"When he asked me who the woman was, I panicked. So...so I told him it was you."

Christine's mouth hung open.

Nelson held her hands up. "You're the first name that popped into my head."

Christine rubbed her face with her hands. "What did he say to that?"

Nelson said, "He said it figured. No wonder she wouldn't leave us alone."

Christine closed her eyes. Her love life was a farce. Policewomen were stereotyped as either lesbians or promiscuous. Now the station officers would think she was both, since they had seen her with Karl.

Christine shook her head. Wait until her friends got wind of this. They'd crack a rib laughing. "That's okay."

Nelson said, "Really? 'Cause he might say something to you. Ask you about it."

Christine managed, "I always liked red hair."

The doorbell tinkled. The two women stood up to see who was in the waiting room.

Fillingham. In uniform.

Christine looked at him questioningly.

"Ulster's not coming in," Fillingham said. "I'm filling in." He didn't look happy about it. Neither was Christine.

He levered the counter open and headed to the kitchen. Nelson followed him in, offering him tea.

The phone rang. Christine got up to answer.

It was Sergeant Bard. "Do you know who called me at home right now?" he howled.

Christine held the receiver away from her ear. "No, sir."

"The chief of police."

Christine waited.

"Chief Benson received a call from Douglas Martin. The family received a death threat."

"Goodness," said Christine. She motioned the other two officers over and held the receiver for them to hear.

"The note said," Sergeant Bard paused, "*You're next.*"

"You're next," Christine repeated. "And they perceived that as a death threat?"

"Yes, PW Lane. They did." Bard's tone was sarcastic.

"Sergeant, there was no record of a call from the Martins to the Centre Island police station. We checked the logbook when we arrived."

"Mr. Martin made it clear to Chief Benson that Island police have been ineffective in solving and preventing incidents of harassment and persecution."

"We wrote an incident—" Christine started.

"And that this lack of progress," Bard continued, "has allowed further escalation by the perpetrators."

"That's not—" Christine tried.

"PW Lane, let me finish," Bard said. "Is Fillingham there yet?"

"Yes," Christine said. He stood beside her, but she didn't meet his glance.

"The two of you go to the Martins' and collect the note as evidence. Interview the family regarding who found the note, where and when. Follow protocol to the letter. Put the note in an evidence bag. Handle it with tweezers. Don't touch the note yourself. Note anything remarkable about where it was found, condition, dampness, time of day."

"Yes, sir," Christine said.

"And you'll be polite, both of you. You'll listen to their complaints about the police force, how they are going to sue us, lambaste us to the media, get you fired, and you'll nod in the right places. Inform them the note will go directly to the lab for analysis. And that a patrol car will drive by their house several times each shift as additional security."

Christine said, "I told Mrs. Martin last week that the police would check on their house each shift. I'm sure that's been happening."

"That didn't stop someone from dropping a death threat on their front porch." Bard paused. "Get on your way. They're expecting you. Leave Nelson at the station."

Nelson pulled away from the phone, her glance confused.

"Why, sir?" Christine asked.

"The Martins are fed up with the shenanigans on Toronto Island. And so is the chief. We need diplomacy and maturity. It's not a time for babysitting."

Bard ended the call and Christine looked over at Nelson.

"It's fine," Nelson said. "I'll bike over to Centreville. That's a fun patrol. You two head to the Martins'."

Fillingham said, "You'll have a much better time than we will."

Chapter 30

A white-faced Mrs. Martin led Christine and Fillingham into the living room. Mr. Martin sat in a high-back chair, smoking a cigarette. He wore a steel-gray suit, slightly wrinkled, and a black-and-gray tie loosened at the neck.

Mrs. Martin gestured to the couch and the officers sat down.

The note lay on the coffee table. It featured cut-out and glued letters, similar to the ones used in ransom notes.

YOURE NEXT

The capital letters were inked in black except for the first "E" and the "T," which were crimson. Newspapers did not use colored ink, which meant the red letters originated from another newsprint source such as a weekend magazine or weekly. Christine wondered why they hadn't included an apostrophe for the contraction. Perhaps they couldn't find one in a headline.

"There it is," Mr. Martin said, glancing at the note. "Take it."

"We'd like to ask a few questions," Fillingham said.

Mr. Martin gestured through his cigarette smoke to start. He was an imposing presence: dark hair lightly oiled with Brylcreem; piercing green eyes; jaw starting to jowl with an air of a man who made important decisions.

Christine took out her memo pad and pen, her signal for Fillingham to start the interview. Fillingham could talk to Martin man to man.

A knock rattled the front screen door.

"Who the hell is that?" Mr. Martin said.

Mrs. Martin looked at her watch, a slim gold band on her wrist. "It must be the housekeeper. I forgot."

"Tell her we're busy."

The officers waited as Mrs. Martin got up and answered the door. After an exchange, Judith walked in with Mrs. Martin. Judith scanned the people in the living room, expression guarded.

Mrs. Martin said, "Judith is booked for this time to clean. She can't come later."

"Can't you see we're busy?" Mr. Martin said. "You'll have to wait until tomorrow."

Judith frowned. "I'm booked tomorrow. You'll have to pay for today. I reserved this time for you."

Mr. Martin leaned back in his chair. "I'm not bloody paying for a job that's not done."

Judith said in a conciliatory tone, "I can't get a client for this time slot on short notice. So I lose the money."

"I'm not sure why you're being difficult. What did you say your name was?" Mr. Martin asked.

"It's Judith. Judith Purnell."

"If it's so damn difficult to clean my house," Mr. Martin said, "then we'll find another cleaner. Good day."

Judith paled, eyes wide with alarm.

Mrs. Martin said, "Douglas, she has a point—"

"Out," Mr. Martin said, pointing to the door as if Judith were a dog.

Judith stared at Mr. Martin, her brown eyes hard, then turned and walked out.

Mrs. Martin slowly sat down. The officers looked at the note on the coffee table between them.

Fillingham said, "Mr. and Mrs. Martin, tell me what you know about this note."

Mr. Martin jerked a hand to Mrs. Martin.

Her hands were clasped in the navy skirt of her lap. "I noticed the note at two o'clock this afternoon. It was on a front porch step."

"When's the last time you or a family member were on the porch?" Fillingham asked.

"I've been alone in the house since nine o'clock," Mrs. Martin said. "Douglas was in the city for meetings and the kids were in Supervision camp."

Mrs. Martin must have figured out how to get Matilda to camp, Christine thought.

"I had lunch on the front porch at noon," Mrs. Martin continued, "as well as a coffee. I sat there until approximately twelve thirty."

"You didn't notice a note?" Fillingham said.

Mrs. Martin shook her head. "There was no note on the steps. I wandered around the yard with my coffee. I would have stepped on it if it were there."

Christine said, "So the note was placed on the steps between 12:30 and 2:00 p.m.?" She scribbled down this information.

Mrs. Martin said, "That's my assumption."

Fillingham said, "Did you hear any noises during that interval?"

Mrs. Martin shook her head. "I cleaned the kitchen. Washed dishes. Marinated chicken for dinner. I hand-washed two blouses and hung them in the backyard. I went for a short walk."

"Where?" Fillingham asked.

"Does it matter?"

Fillingham waited.

Mrs. Martin continued, "I went to see how Matilda and Reginald were doing in camp."

"How are they doing?" Christine asked.

Mr. Martin leaned forward. "What does that have to do with the note? We're wasting time here."

"Continue, please," Fillingham said.

"I went to the field and came right back," Mrs. Martin said. "The campers had already gone to the beach for the afternoon."

"What time did you return to the house?" Fillingham asked.

"One thirty," she said. "I came in the back door. I had a glass of iced tea in the kitchen, then watered the backyard grass. I came out the front door to water the potted flowers and found the note."

"Satisfied?" Mr. Martin growled.

"Did you touch the note?" Fillingham asked.

"Yes. I picked it up."

"Then what did you do?" Fillingham asked.

"I brought it inside. I was quite upset, as you can imagine. I called Douglas right away. I had him pulled from his meeting with the commissioner. And he called Chief Benson." She reached for her cigarettes on the side table, glancing at her husband, who nodded.

Did she need her husband's permission to smoke?

"What did you notice about the note, Mrs. Martin?" Christine asked.

Mrs. Martin frowned. "What did I notice? I noticed that someone was threatening our family."

Fillingham said, "A threat to do what, Mrs. Martin?"

"For God's sake, man," Mr. Martin said, gesturing with both hands. "Are you daft? It's a threat to harm. Ducks were poisoned. Dead fish dumped in our front yard. Our plants and mail and milk have been stolen. It's an escalating strategy to intimidate us into leaving. To protest Metro Council's progressive plans for the waterfront, including the revitalization of Toronto Island."

Fillingham did not cringe at Mr. Martin's tone. Turning to Mrs. Martin, he asked, "How do you interpret the note?"

"It's a threat. To me. To my husband. To my children. I wish we never moved here."

Mr. Martin bellowed, "That's what they want! To pressure us to leave! To instill fear so that the city gives up on our plans." He shook his head. "They're not getting the better of the Martins. Or Parks and Recreation. Or Metro Council." His pointer finger rose in the air. "We will never bow to these primitive scare tactics. This persecution makes me more determined to remove this renegade group from the Island so we can welcome a more progressive urban community."

Mrs. Martin looked away from her husband at the framed lake scene hung over the small fireplace. It must be their Muskoka cottage. She must be wishing she were there. A second painting hung beside Mr. Martin's leather chair: a formal painted portraiture of the Martin family, the parents standing behind their children, hands on their offspring's shoulders.

Christine felt a frisson of pity for Mrs. Martin. She had no friends on the Island. She was home alone or in the company of her unhappy children. Clearly, she followed her husband's wishes. And clearly, she was afraid for her family's safety.

Someone had once threatened Christine's family, and she remembered the overwhelming fear and anger choking her, making it hard to think.

Christine leaned closer to the letter to examine it. The uneven edges of the letters showed they had been cut with scissors. The black letters could have originated from newsprint or magazine print. Even a book. The background looked like white typewriter paper.

"Does the lettering look familiar to you?" Christine asked.

Mr. Martin said, "What do you mean?"

"Have you seen this typography before? In a magazine you've read. Or a newspaper, journal, poster, pamphlet?"

Mr. Martin frowned. "What does that have to do with anything? Are you intimating that the criminal used paper from our house?"

Mrs. Martin took a drag on her cigarette. "She's checking if we wrote the note ourselves."

"That's not what I—" Christine began.

Mr. Martin stood up. "Get out! You are not only the most useless officers I've met, but the most insulting."

"I'm checking—" Christine said.

"Don't come back," Mr. Martin roared. "I need real investigators, ones recommended by the chief. Not you two insolent buffoons."

Fillingham stood up. "Okay. We're leaving. I need to secure the note as evidence."

"Don't mess that up," Mr. Martin said.

Fillingham pulled a manila paper bag out of his jacket pocket alongside a set of tweezers. Shaking the bag open, he then picked up the note with the tweezers and inserted it into the bag.

"The courier will pick it up from the station tomorrow morning," Christine said.

"It better," Mr. Martin said.

The officers let themselves out.

Fillingham handed the evidence bag to Christine and the duo got into the patrol car.

"That went well," he said.

"I'm sorry if I messed it up. I was just asking—"

Fillingham said, "A logical question. I don't recognize the font from the note. I can't tell if it's from a particular newspaper, the *Telegram, Star* or *National Post*, but it may be. Or perhaps *Maclean's* or *Saturday Magazine*. You were checking if the typesetting was familiar to the Martins. This would be a clue."

Christine's shoulders relaxed in relief as they slowly drove onto Cibola Avenue.

"We should get the note back to the station and lock it up," she said, waving the envelope.

"I have a better plan," he said.

If they were on friendlier terms, she would joke that she'd heard that line before. For now, she said, "What?"

"Let's pick up Nelson from Centreville. Goodness knows what mischief she's got into. She's probably on the Log Flume ride. We'll grab dinner while we're there and have a sit-down together. We need to figure this out." He pointed at the evidence bag.

"Do we need to keep the note with us?" she asked.

"For now. It will be couriered to Identification tomorrow for fingerprints."

Christine wasn't sure what Fillingham was up to, but it felt comforting to be chatting like this. They used to sit across from each other in the police station kitchen, sipping coffee and bantering ideas about suspects, alibis and investigative strategies.

They turned back toward Ward's Island.

"Where are we going?" she asked.

"You'll see."

He parked in front of the covered ferry waiting area and motioned for her to get out of the car.

"What are we doing?"

"We're looking for newspapers and magazines discarded by people before they get onto the ferry. We should grab them now before the garbage gets collected."

"I see one," she said. It was tucked under the shelter's bench.

"Bring it with you. Look around the entire dock while I check the garbage cans."

Christine found two more newspapers, a *Globe and Mail* and a *Telegram,* as well as a *Chatelaine* woman's magazine. And several copies of the *Ward's Island Weekly*. She didn't stray far from the vehicle. She didn't want the evidence bag out of her sight.

Fillingham returned with an armful of papers. "Got mustard on my jacket."

"Wouldn't it be great to find a magazine with cut-out letters?" she said.

He placed his haul into the back of the patrol car with Christine's collection of print. "Unlikely. Even if we don't find the original newspaper or magazine, if we can find the same typesetting, then we know the perpetrator is local."

"Not really. A tourist or a mainlander could have brought a paper over," she said. "How many garbage cans are on the Island?"

"Let's focus on Ward's Island first. There's one by the washroom. And the beach."

"And the field," she added.

"You take the women's washroom," he said. "I'll take the men's. They're gloves in the back we can use, not only to keep ourselves clean, but also in case we find the original."

"Elbow-deep in garbage," she said as she got into the patrol car.

"Like old times," he said.

Chapter 31

"What are we doing?" Nelson asked, wiping ketchup from her mouth. The three officers sat around a picnic table, eating French fries. At the far end of the table sat the manila evidence bag. Parked beside the group was the patrol car with its back hatch open, a mound of papers in its maw.

"Are we finished eating?" Fillingham asked from across the two women.

"I'm still hungry," Nelson said.

"You had an ice cream cone before the fries," Christine observed.

Nelson shrugged. "It's okay. We can start."

While Nelson collected the empty food containers and balled serviettes, Fillingham grabbed an armful of newspapers and magazines from the back of the car and dumped them on one end of the picnic table. He placed another garbage bag full of paper beside them.

Sliding along the bench, Fillingham grabbed the envelope and retrieved the note with tweezers. He placed the note on the evidence bag. They leaned in to study the words on the paper.

"The letters are relatively large," Christine said. "It's from a caption, headline or ad."

Fillingham nodded. "I read the *Globe and Mail*. The font doesn't look familiar to me."

Christine said, "The black letters look like they originate from the same source. The typography seems similar. A serif font."

Nelson placed her chin on her hand. "Why no apostrophe? Can't the writer spell?"

Christine said, "Is the writer less educated?"

Fillingham shook his head. "I don't know if it's a grammar error. They're cutting out letters for a threat. Are they really going to spend the time trying to find a large apostrophe? Is that their concern?"

"Nelson," Christine asked, "how large is each letter?"

Nelson peered at the note. "Three quarters of an inch."

Christine said, "Let's keep that measurement in the forefront as we look."

"If anyone one sees a page with letters cut out, yell, 'Hallelujah,'" said Fillingham.

"Record the name and date of the paper, book or magazine you examined that is not a match in your memo book," Christine said, "so we can exclude publications."

Five minutes later, Christine wrote *Chatelaine, July 1969* in her memo book and let the magazine drop to the ground. The pages were shinier than the letters on the note. She felt something brush her calf and jerked her leg away. Looking under the table, she spotted Lifeguard. "She's found a French fry."

Fillingham called the dog over for a pat. "You have a nose for policing."

"If only she could sniff out the note writer," Christine said.

Lifeguard got strokes from the three officers and then settled on the bag of papers beside them.

Christine asked. "Should we move her?"

Nelson laughed. "That's her bed. She won't pee on it. And the papers are inside the garbage bag. It's fine."

After an hour, their eyes were bleary. They paused, taking sips of the pop they had bought with their fries.

Christine shook her head. "A paper expert at Identification would know this immediately, but the letters are not newsprint. It's from thicker material."

"A brochure?" Fillingham asked.

Christine nodded. "Or a poster or book."

Nelson said, "There's a notice board by the Ward's Island ferry stapled with flyers, ads and notices."

"And by the school," Christine continued, "the washrooms and the Algonquin Bridge."

Fillingham said, "If they took a poster for the letters, the original will not be there."

"There could be similar flyers," Christine said. "Or more than one."

Fillingham stretched his arms over his head. "Let's round up a list of suspects."

"Okay," Nelson said, smiling.

"We have obvious local suspects," he said. "The Ward's Island and Algonquin Island communities. But that's three hundred adults. That's a lengthy list. So let's narrow it to people like the TIRA executive."

"Gary Owen's a hothead," Christine said. "Rachel Conway seems more reasonable."

"The Merriweathers," Christine added. She remembered the angry way they had spoken to Judith Purnell, how heartbroken they were to be evicted and replaced by the Martins.

Fillingham said, "Martin threatened to cut electricity to ten families on Ward's Island who were complaining about his residency in the Merriweather house. Who were they again? The Munros,

Hamiltons, Owens, Conways and the Stines. We should find the names of the other families."

Christine said, "The bird watcher groups can be fervent." She thought of the Applegates. "They think that Parks and Recreation are destroying the natural bird habitat with their chemical use."

"Mark Fraser from Operation Pollution," Nelson exclaimed, looking happy to suggest a suspect.

Fillingham said, "We should consider other ecological groups as well. They can use unorthodox strategies."

Christine said, "The residential community on the Island has held animosity for the superintendent and commissioner of Parks and Recreation for over ten years, since they started razing Island houses. And we haven't touched on the locals who were forced to leave, like the Merriweathers. They must hold a grudge."

Fillingham pressed his hands together. "There's a lineup to get at Douglas Martin. We saw that today with Judith Purnell. She wanted to strangle him with her bare hands. He wins no popularity contest. And he's vulnerable because he is the only one of the Waterfront Improvement Committee who lives on the island, a wolf among the sheep. Now the sheep are plotting the wolf's demise."

"Are we being presumptive?" Christine said. "He could be having an affair, and the threat is from a disgruntled lover."

Fillingham shrugged. "A possibility, but unlikely. It's life or death for Islanders. Many of them have stayed so long, they have passed the date to receive compensation for their homes. They have nowhere to move to on the mainland and no money to buy a replacement house. Leaving the Island not only means giving up a cherished home, but economic hardship as well."

Nelson said, "Did Douglas Martin write the note?

Christine and Fillingham looked at her.

Nelson continued, "It makes people sympathetic. The family is being persecuted. It makes Islanders seem threatening and violent. "

"The thought crossed our minds," Christine said. "Mrs. Martin seemed truly afraid. I don't think she's in the mix of suspects. She would leave the Island in a second if her husband let her."

Fillingham looked around. "It's getting dark. Let's head back to the station. Whatever print we don't get to, I'll bag and place in the station's garage. We can continue picking through the papers tomorrow."

"How about the notice boards?" Christine asked.

"It will have to be tomorrow," he answered. "We'll come in early. Before our afternoon shift. All of us are working, right?"

"Ulster is scheduled," Christine said.

Fillingham waved that away. "He's on a bender. He won't be in all week. I've picked up his shifts."

"When we get back to the station, I'll type up our notes so we can chart the journals, newspapers and brochures we've already reviewed. Nelson?"

Nelson perked up at her name.

"How are your sketching skills?" Christine asked. They didn't have a mimeograph at the station.

Nelson's eyes were wide. "Fair. I did art in grade school, ma'am, but that's about it."

Christine said, "Tonight is the last time we have access to the original note. Nelson, can you draw it to scale so that we have our own copy to refer to?"

Nelson clapped her hands. "We're going to find this person. The three of us. Like the Mod Squad."

"Or the Three Stooges," Fillingham said as they headed to the patrol car.

Chapter 32

Sergeant Bard stood in front of the vehicle, back straight. He looked ready to salute. Christine looked at Fillingham and Nelson as they walked toward the police car from the ferry, ready for their next shift. What was going on?

When the officers neared the patrol car, Bard said, "Did you see him?"

"Who?" Christine asked. "Identification? Are they coming to retrieve the papers we collected?" She had called her sergeant at the station that morning to notify him of the newsprint collection in the station garage.

"No," Bard said brusquely. "Deputy Darlow."

Christine's horrified eyes met Fillingham's glance.

"Why is the deputy here?" Fillingham asked.

Nelson's eyes were wide. "I've never met a senior officer. Do I salute?"

"You curtsy," Fillingham said.

Christine shook her head at Nelson. "Don't listen to him. Salute if it's formal. Say 'sir' if he addresses you. Otherwise, be quiet."

"Yes, ma'am," Nelson said.

"As I told you yesterday," Bard said, "the chief is concerned about the politics and incidents on the Island, including the threatening note to the Martins. Officers canvassed the neighbors this morning, but no leads. I'm staying on shift to drive Deputy Chief Darlow to the Martins' so he can confirm the force's commitment to finding the culprit."

"Or culprits," Fillingham revised.

"Your bikes are in the back," Bard said as he walked closer to the ferry. "I could only fit two. One of you will have to walk back to the station."

Fillingham retrieved the two bikes and handed them to the women. "I'll jog. You two bike."

Bard walked quickly forward. "Deputy Darlow. Sir, this way." He gestured to the patrol car.

The three officers stood off to the side as the deputy followed the sergeant to the car, nodding at the officers, eyes on Christine.

The two senior officers drove away.

"What was that about?" Nelson asked Christine.

"What do you mean?" Christine asked.

"He was giving you the eye." She looked from Fillingham to Christine. "The evil eye."

Fillingham pressed his lips together.

Christine said, "I've met Deputy Darlow before. He doesn't always approve of me."

"But didn't you get an award?" Nelson asked.

"Yes, we did," Fillingham interjected.

Christine changed topics. "Let's check the posters, flyers and ads on the bulletin boards. There's one by the ferry passenger shelter. Another by the Centreville entrance."

Nelson said, "The copy of the note is at the station."

Christine said, "We'll do it by memory. Grab any poster or announcement that has the same letter size and material."

Fillingham said, "Let's take a cursory look at the boards here and then head to the station to pick up our radios. We should be available in case Sergeant Bard or the deputy request us."

Christine rolled her eyes at this but conceded. They split up to look at the respective bulletin boards and agreed to meet back at the station in thirty minutes. Brochures, pamphlets, posters, flyers, letters, magazines, newsletters, newspapers, journals, business cards and books littered the police station's kitchen table, surrounding the officers in a mound of paper. They had hauled the bag of paper from the garage and collected a pile from the announcement boards.

Sergeant Bard had come by the station an hour into the shift to pick up Fillingham, who would drive the two senior officers to the ferry docks and return with the patrol car to the station. Christine was glad that she was not asked to drive Deputy Darlow to the docks.

After, the three had patrolled on bikes, passing by the Martins' place and returning to the station to eat. Now that it was after dinner, they were digging through their collected material. Most of the posters had very large lettering and were discarded.

Christine pointed to a pile of shredded paper. "I got excited when I saw the cut paper, but from the gobs of glue, Supervision camp was making papier mâché puppets."

"We'll be able to do that by the end," he said as he lifted a brochure, examined it and then tossed it to the floor. He rustled around in his uniform pocket. "Anyone want a Rolo?" He proffered the chocolate to Nelson sitting beside him at the table.

"No thanks," Christine said.

Nelson asked Christine, "Are you allergic?"

Christine said tersely, "No."

Fillingham put the chocolate back in his pocket. "It's her favorite. She doesn't want to accept it from me."

Nelson said, "Why not? You're best friends."

Christine and Fillingham met glances and looked away.

Nelson licked the lingering chocolate from her lips. "You've had a fight or something, right?" Her arms widened to gesture to them.

Sitting in the middle of Christine and Fillingham, she looked like a referee. "But I can tell that you're best mates. Like my dog Ralph and my cat Coco. Sometimes they ignore each other, sometimes Coco spits at Ralph, but one doesn't go anywhere without the other. And they protect each other when they're outside so they don't get eaten by wolves or coyotes."

"Am I Ralph or Coco?" Fillingham asked Nelson. "I have a slight preference for Ralph."

The phone rang. With relief, Christine got up to answer. After she introduced herself, a man's voice said. "They've broken in."

"Broken in where, sir?" she asked. "Who is this?"

"I was closing for the night, locking the equipment in the garage, and I saw the cupboards. They were hanging open. Empty."

"Sir, what garage? Who is this?" Christine asked again.

"Ollie Mallory. Toronto Parks and Recreation."

"Mr. Mallory. I remember you. You were retrieving equipment on the Algonquin bridge. It's PW Lane."

"The tall one?"

"Yes," Christine said. Everyone identified her by her height. "Can you repeat what you said? Is there something missing from your facility?"

"When they took the rakes and wheelbarrow, it was from the carport—an open building. And we found the equipment around the Island. This time they raided the garage, where the tractors, cars and dump trucks are parked."

"Are any of the vehicles missing?"

"No. But one wall has cupboards filled with fertilizers, lawn sprays and machine oil. They cleared out every bottle, can and jar."

"Any of the products toxic?"

"I don't know. But if they dumped this stuff into the lagoon, it would kill more than a few ducks." He coughed.

"Stay where you are," she said. "We'll be there in ten minutes."

Chapter 33

After Mallory's call, the three officers drove to the Parks and Recreation facility at Hanlan's Point, passing hordes of tired visitors wending their way to the Centre Island ferry after a day of swimming, picnicking and amusement ride fun.

"What do you think the thief is going to do with the garage chemicals?" Christine asked from the passenger seat.

"You got me," Fillingham said.

Nelson was in the back seat. "How about if they want attention?"

Christine turned to look at Nelson. "How so?"

Nelson leaned forward, elbows on her lap. "It's like the threatening note to the Martins. Do we think someone is really going to kill them?"

Fillingham put in, "So, the purpose of the note is to evoke sympathy for the Martins and antipathy for the Islanders?"

"Maybe," Nelson said.

"In that case, the Martins and their allies, which would be Metro Council and the commissioner of Parks and Recreation, would be the note writers," Christine said. "Isn't that a stretch?" She shook her head. "Back to the chemicals. Someone stole them because they think Parks and Recreation poisoned the ducks or is allowing toxins into the water. So they stole their chemicals. If that is one theory, who are the suspects, Nelson?"

Nelson pondered. "Residents, because they live here. And those groups interested in the environment and wildlife: the birders, the anti-pollution groups, the animal activists."

"Or," Fillingham posited, finger in the air as he drove slowly on the Island of the Americas, "Theory Number Two. Someone wants to make the Island seem toxic. Make people afraid to live here. And having dangerous chemicals at large will do the trick."

Christine sighed. "Again, that makes the government, including Parks and Recreation, suspect."

Nelson said, "The person who wrote the note isn't necessarily the person who stole the chemicals."

"Or the person who harmed the Centerville ducks," Christine added, "if that was intentional."

"Three separate unrelated incidents?" Fillingham queried.

"It's possible. Probable," Christine amended.

"*Quomodo hoc erit finis*?" he said as he drove into the driveway of the Parks and Recreation facility.

"What does that mean?" Nelson asked.

"How will this end?" he replied.

"Mr. Mallory." Christine greeted the Parks and Recreation worker as the three officers got out of the car.

"Is the gate to the facilities always open?" Fillingham asked Mallory, looking back at the open double gate the patrol car had driven through.

Mallory stood in the driveway, faded overalls stained with paint, sporting a baseball cap sweat-stained around the edges. He had gray-and-white stubble, as if he hadn't shaved in three days. He looked pale for a man who spent so much time outdoors. Could be the shock of the theft. Christine wondered if he would get in trouble with Superintendent Martin for the break-in.

"It's not always locked," Mallory answered. "Vehicles are in and out all day long. We lock up at night at the end of the last shift. Nine o'clock in the summer."

Turning around, Mallory headed up the roadway of flattened grass and gravel. He had a strange gait, leaning slightly to the left as he walked. Christine tried to guess his age. Fifty? Sixty?

Boxy buildings stood on either side of the driveway, ranging in size from a shed to a large garage.

Mallory gestured to the open, oversized door of the garage, and the four stepped inside. The air smelled like manure, wood chips, engine oil and chemicals. Inside were parked lawn mowers, golf carts, pick-up trucks, a van and dump truck.

Immediately, Christine noticed the yawning cabinet doors on the right wall. As she approached, she saw that every shelf was empty.

"Wow," Fillingham commented, coming alongside. "That's quite a few items. What exactly did they take?"

Mallory walked over to the cabinets and read the labels out loud. "Insecticide, fertilizer, bone meal, sulfur, ant traps, weed killer, moss cleaner, fungicide, toilet cleaner, disinfectant, bleach, ammonia, lye, hand soap, grout cleaner, baking soda, vinegar, steering fluid, engine oil, antifreeze, windshield wiper fluid." He coughed, bracing himself with one arm on a worktable.

"Are you okay?" Christine asked.

He waved her off, pulling a handkerchief from his pocket.

"Shall we go outside for fresh air?" she asked.

He shook his head. "I'm used to the smell."

Fillingham gestured to the empty cupboards. "What happened tonight?"

Pulling out a stool from underneath the worktable, Mallory sat down. "I was watering plants on Centre Island. Staff had gone by then. We have staggered shifts that end at three and at six. Tonight,

Ron and I were the only workers on until closing at nine. Ron pinched his hand in the van door. It bled a lot, so he took the ferry home early to deal with it. I drove back to the yard with the water truck just before nine. I parked it in the garage and saw the empty shelves." He paused. "Then I called police."

"What's your explanation?" Christine asked.

He shook his head. "I have no idea what's going on here."

"Is someone trying to paint Parks and Recreation in a poor light?" she asked.

Mallory wiped his forehead with the edge of his handkerchief. "Because we have poor security? I hope not. I hope they don't pin this on me."

"Not on you," Fillingham said. "On Parks and Recreation. Show that you don't store chemicals responsibly."

"Make people afraid that stolen toxins will be dumped into the water or poison wildlife," Christine added.

Fillingham said, "So people are afraid to live here. Or visit here."

Mallory shook his head as if he were trying to shake off their assertions. "I don't know what you're talking about. Somebody broke into the garage. What about the buffoons who stole the gardening equipment and hung it around the Island? Have you found those guys? Wouldn't they be suspects?"

Christine flushed. "Superintendent Martin chose not to file a police report on that break-in, since all items were found."

"Found by me," Mallory said grumpily.

Fillingham asked, "Who have you notified of the theft?"

Mallory said, "I called Superintendent Martin. He wasn't home. I talked to the commissioner. He said to call the police. And not to talk to anyone else about the break-in."

"Sage advice," Fillingham said.

"Can you compile a list of the stolen items," Christine asked, "including the quantity of bottles and volumes? I know it won't be exact, but Poison Control and Toronto Water will want numbers."

Fillingham said, "I'll have a look around with Mr. Mallory, check that nothing else was stolen. PW Lane, Cadet Nelson, can you head back to the station and call Sergeant Bard?"

"Does this look bad on us?" Christine asked as she walked out of the garage with Nelson and Fillingham.

Fillingham shrugged. "We haven't solved the duck deaths, the threatening note or the harassment of the Martins. We don't come off smelling like roses."

"Kind of like manure," Nelson concluded.

Chapter 34

"What was that?" Christine asked Nelson as they drove back to the station.

"What?" Nelson said, turning to her.

"I saw something run across the grass toward the lagoon." Christine peered out the driver's window into the murky darkness.

"An animal?" Nelson asked.

"Bigger. A person."

"You told me the last ferry leaves at eleven. People are still here," Nelson said.

"It's ten o'clock at night and pitch-black away from the pathway lights. Centreville is closed. No one is swimming or picnicking." Christine swerved the car onto the grass and parked the car.

"Do you think someone needs our help?" Nelson asked. "Or is up to mischief?"

"I'm not sure." Christine opened her door. "Let's walk to the lagoon edge. You check right toward the police station. I'll head left. Yell if you find anything. Here, take my flashlight."

Christine left the car headlights on and jogged toward the lagoon in its yellow beam.

There! A person, lying flat on the ground, arms hanging over the lagoon. Were they putting something in the water?

"Stop! Toronto Police!" Christine yelled. She approached the figure thirty feet away. "Nelson, over here!"

As Christine neared, she could see the outline of a man's body illuminated by the light from Centreville on the other side of the lagoon. The man had his arms out of the water now, bent against his side.

"Stay where you are," Christine said. She approached cautiously. "Toronto Police," she repeated. She could hear running steps behind her and see the bounce of Nelson's flashlight along the ground.

"Fisheries Management," the man's voice said.

Nelson stopped beside Christine, breath labored, aiming the flashlight at the man.

"Stand up, hands in the air," Christine directed.

The man slowly obeyed. He was wiry, wearing a t-shirt, wrinkled shorts and sandals, hair cut short to the scalp. The beam hit his face, and he turned from its glare. "It's me. Phil Merton. From the Fisheries Management Project. I work with Karl, remember?"

Christine relaxed for a second. "What were you doing, Phil?" She took the flashlight from Nelson and checked the lagoon where Phil had been lying down.

"Retrieving equipment," he said.

"Why are you removing it in the dark?" She knew from Karl that the last collection was at five o'clock.

Phil shrugged. "They're mine."

She handed the flashlight back to the cadet. "Can you check in the lagoon? Look for the water-sampling frame. Or anything else."

Nelson took off her jacket and rolled up her blouse sleeves. Lying on her stomach, she immersed her right arm in the water. "I feel a metal cage." With a grunt, she pulled it up. "And a bottle."

"Anything else down there?" Christine asked.

Nelson shook her head.

"Pull the equipment out," Christine directed. "I want to have a look." She turned to Phil. "Why are you doing this late at night?"

When Phil did not answer, she said to Nelson, "Put the equipment in the patrol car."

Phil raised a hand. "No!" He paused, then at a lower volume, he said, "No. I'll tell you. It's because, it's because, I don't work for the project anymore."

"You were fired?" Christine asked. She remembered he had missed quite a few days of work.

He shook his head. "No. No, I quit. But I left some equipment here. My collection bottles, sample vials and carrier. I wanted them back, that's all."

"Why didn't you retrieve them during regular hours? If they're your equipment, there shouldn't be an issue."

Phil sighed. "Because the manager wasn't happy with me. I hadn't been to work in a while. For a week. Then I quit. And the project is supposed to be finished by the end of August. I left them short-staffed. They're miffed."

I'd say so, Christine thought. She remembered Karl running around on Gala Day, working two people's jobs. "We'll hold on to your equipment until we've contacted your boss at Fisheries Management.

Phil shook his head, incredulous.

Nelson stood by Christine, the light illuminating the three of them.

There was something weird going on here. She could sense it. Could Phil be putting something toxic in the water? But what was his motivation? "Why did you quit?" Christine asked.

"Why is that your business?" he said, chin jutting out.

"Karl said you were an industrious employee. Knowledgeable. Diligent. Aren't you working three jobs to pay the bills? You're married, right, with a wife and kids?"

He remained silent.

"Why quit a full-time job when you need the money?" she asked.

"I can get another one."

"Why did you leave this one?"

He looked at Christine, his brown gaze flat. "I don't like the Island. Or the people. They're always in each other's business."

Chapter 35

Two days later, Christine was placing a radio on her belt when the station phone rang.

"I got it," Fillingham said.

Christine tilted her head for Nelson to follow her out on patrol.

"Mrs. Martin!" Fillingham said loudly. He held one hand out for the female officers to wait. His eyebrows raised. "They're there now?" He listened for a moment. "What do you mean around your house?"

Mrs. Martin must have delivered a caustic comment, because he grimaced. After a pause, he said, "Yes, ma'am, we'll send someone over." After another pause, he said, "What's that? Bring evidence bags?" There was a loud click.

He hung up, sighing loudly.

"Trouble?" Christine asked.

"It's," he checked his watch, "eight fifteen in the morning, and protesters are surrounding the Martin house."

"Are they on the Martins' property?" Christine asked.

"I'm not sure." He opened a drawer and pulled out evidence bags of varied sizes and three pairs of tweezers. "She said to bring evidence bags, whatever that means."

Nelson said, "Is there another note?"

"I hope not," Christine said. As she left the station, she said, "I'll tell Dispatch we're responding to a call at the Martins'."

Nelson said, "Am I coming with you?"

Fillingham nodded. "We need officers to talk to the Martins and deal with the crowd."

The trio headed to the garage to retrieve their bikes, which were stacked against the wall.

"Nelson," Fillingham said as he rolled the white bike toward the cadet. "Lane," he said, as he moved her bike off his. Something fell to the ground.

"Is this yours?" he asked, holding up a necklace.

It was Christine's leather medicine bag, given to her by Hawk. The one she had given to Layla for protection.

Christine blinked at it several times, her mind churning. *Hawk has Layla. They took her. She's back home.*

"Is it?" Fillingham repeated impatiently, shaking the bag in his hand.

She grabbed it, quickly putting it around her neck under her blouse.

As the three exited the garage, Fillingham said, "You seeing him again?"

Christine glanced over at Nelson, who was watching them, wide-eyed.

"Do you want to ride ahead, Cadet?" Christine suggested. "We'll catch up. Cut through by the Shaw House. It's faster."

"Yes, ma'am," Nelson said and hopped on her bike.

Christine waited until Nelson was thirty feet up the path. Turning to Fillingham, she said, "My life is none of your business." She mounted her bike and followed Nelson.

Fillingham glided beside her. "Let sleeping dogs lie."

Christine's brakes squealed. "Stop. I don't want your advice. About Hawk. Karl. My family. My job. You don't have the right to do that. We are not friends anymore."

"I'm just saying—"
"I don't care what you say," she cut in, pedaling again.
"I still care," he said.
"Too little, too late."

Chapter 36

Christine's knuckles gripped the handlebars of her bike. She made herself breathe slowly in and out as she pedaled. She was too emotional. The necklace had thrown her. At first, she had felt a stab of fear. What if her superiors found out she was involved with Layla? Then, exhilaration. Had Hawk really done it? Contacted Layla? Got her back?

And then there was Fillingham. She was going to kill her partner—her ex-partner. Acting as if he had a right to comment on her choices. She was having none of it.

Fillingham's tires whirred behind her. He was smart enough not to glide up beside her. But where was Nelson? Christine pressed hard on the pedals, accelerating. The cadet shouldn't be alone with the Martins. They would eat her for breakfast.

Pushing faster, Christine shook the cottonwood fluff off her face.

There she was. Christine spotted her straight back as she pedaled toward the boardwalk.

"You're fast," Christine said as she rolled up beside her.

Nelson turned and smiled. "Want to race?"

Christine smiled despite herself. Fillingham had obviously been challenging her to a bike race during their patrols.

"As fun as that sounds, we're nearing the Martin house. We need to show up with dignity. They don't think much of Island police right now."

The wooden boardwalk arced slightly to the left, and Christine saw a group of people ahead. The protesters were hooked arm-in-arm around the front and side of the house.

Christine biked over and hurriedly placed her bike on the empty lot beside the Martins'. Nelson and Fillingham did the same.

Approximately thirty people, Christine estimated. They wore hats and carried knapsacks. Half had binoculars or cameras slung around their necks. The birders. Or the Toronto Ornithological Society.

Christine approached the group. "Toronto Police. PW Lane. What is happening here?"

A man in a short-sleeved green shirt stepped forward. Mr. Applegate. "Toronto Island is an important bird sanctuary—a key nesting place for many species in their annual migration cycle. We are advocating for a chemical-free habitat. And we vehemently disagree with the construction of a massive community development."

Christine nodded. "Have you made your concerns known to Toronto and Metro Council?"

The birders nearby nodded. "We have. In several letters. And a petition."

Fillingham said, "The Martins have made a complaint about this gathering. We are going inside to discuss this with them and will instruct you when we return. Be prepared to disperse."

"We have the right to peaceful assembly," Mr. Applegate said.

"In front of City Hall," he said. "Or the Parks and Recreation facilities. Not a private residence."

Mrs. Applegate spoke from beside her husband. "We are not on their property. We are on the boardwalk and the lot next store."

Christine turned to Nelson. "Stay here. We'll be back in a few minutes." Before she sent the birders on their way, she wanted to talk with the Martins and check in with Sergeant Bard.

Fillingham had wandered away from the front gate. He pointed to the newsprint posted on the side fence.

"What does it say?" Christine asked. At first it looked like posters, but on closer inspection, it was the front page of a newspaper taped to the pine boards. She recognized the article. It was the *National Post* column: "Killing an Island, One Duck at a Time." There was a copy at the station. The reporter asserted that the local government, including the superintendent, commissioner, Metro Hall and the mayor were collectively making Toronto Island uninhabitable for residents, with an eye to building a new housing development.

She sighed. "This must be why the Martins wanted the evidence bags. Vandalism."

They returned to the front gate. The protesters moved so the officers could enter the yard.

"I'll be damned!" he exclaimed.

The yard looked like an open garbage dump. Bottles, tins and containers of liquids, waxes, creams and solids were littered around the yard. Christine squatted to read the labels: soap, bleach, laundry detergent, shampoo, spray starch, laundry soap, dish detergent, vinegar, insecticide, paint thinner, paint, window cleaner, jewelry cleaner, toothpaste, mouthwash, glue and oven cleaner. There must be over three hundred containers spread over the yard.

"People are throwing their cleaning products in the yard," Christine observed. "No wonder the Martins called us."

Fillingham surveyed the pockmarked lawn. "Is it from the Parks and Recreation garage?"

Christine straightened. "I don't think so. There's a gardening and vehicle products, but most items are from kitchens and bathroom cupboards."

"We should call Sarge," he said.

She nodded.

"But for now," he said, "let's go in and get yelled at." He rapped on the door.

Mrs. Martin led them into the sitting room, where Douglas Martin occupied the leather chair. Past the sitting room, Christine saw their two children sitting at the kitchen table with bowls of cereal. Matilda met Christine's glance. Her expression was guarded and anxious.

This situation mustn't be fun for the children. It must be terrifying to have your yard vandalized, fish and seaweed dumped on your front porch, people protesting outside your gate. If Matilda was worried that people disliked them before, Christine could imagine her feelings now.

No one should be harassed in their home, especially when there were children. The tormentors had crossed the line. She would ask the birders to leave. Take their concerns to Metro Hall or the Parks and Recreation sheds or the press meeting happening later that week. She would ask her sergeant to ban protest groups from gathering at the Martins' family home.

Mrs. Martin sat in the blue wingback chair. For a moment, Fillingham and Christine stood. When no one directed them to sit down, they shuffled over to the white couch and took a seat.

Christine took out her memo pad.

"Mr. and Mrs. Martin," Fillingham began. "I see several concerns here."

"You do, do you?" Mr. Martin said. He was in a cream linen suit and white shirt, no tie, like the men Christine had seen at RCYC.

Mrs. Martin crossed her legs in her mint-green shift, regarding the officers with tightly controlled emotion.

"Let's start with—" Fillingham began.

Mr. Martin spoke over him. "For the last month, since we moved to Toronto Island, which is expected of the superintendent of Parks and Recreation, we've been subjected to harassment and intimidation." His expression was openly hostile. "After reporting these offenses to Island police and notifying senior officers of the highest rank," he raised his two hands in the air, "nothing! No suspects apprehended. No arrests. Just more harassment, as you see today." His hands clasped together.

Fillingham said, "Sir, it's challenging to find witnesses to the earlier incidents of the garden theft or the seaweed. We conducted door-to-door interviews. No one saw anything suspicious."

Mr. Martin bristled. "Of course not, you ninny. You were interviewing the people who perpetrated the acts." He pointed his finger in the air. "It is not rocket science to conclude that these vexatious offenses have been perpetrated by Islanders, likely a Ward's Island resident. I can name a number of families off the top of my head: the Merriweathers, Owens, Conways, Brines, Hamiltons, Munros. There's your suspect list," he gestured to the officers, "since you're incapable of coming up with one yourselves."

Mrs. Martin leaned over to the side table, retrieved a menthol cigarette from a package and lit a cigarette. She squinted at the officers through a plume of smoke.

Fillingham looked over at Christine, his glance telling her to take over.

Christine began, "Mr. and Mrs. Martin—"

Mr. Martin said, "Should I bother to ask if police have leads regarding the break-in at the Parks and Recreation garage?"

Christine replied, "We haven't found the items yet. It doesn't look like they've been dumped on the Island."

"Tell that to the raging group outside," Mr. Martin said.

Fillingham said, "Forensics dusted for prints around the cupboards, but with so many staff coming and going, they won't find a match unless the perpetrator's fingerprints are in the system. The facility was unlocked, which means someone just needed to drive in, load up and leave. It would take ten to fifteen minutes."

"They wouldn't need to drive anything," Mr. Martin said. "Just pull up with a bloody bike and wagon. Any Islander could have done it."

"Or visitor," Christine said. She glanced over at Fillingham. They were getting nowhere.

Fillingham said, "Let's start with today's concerns, beginning with the group outside."

Mrs. Martin said, "Yes. It seems we are bird killers now." She took a long drag on her cigarette.

"And the containers on your lawn," Christine said. "I assume people have been throwing them onto your property?"

"Astute observation, PW." Mr. Martin's tone was sarcastic. "Can I write out a second suspect list for you? It looks like the first."

Mrs. Martin tapped her cigarette on the ashtray. "I cannot leave my house without being accosted by a protestor. My children can't play in the yard safely."

"Is it possible for the children to stay elsewhere?" Christine suggested. "At grandparents'? A cousin? Until things calm down." She glanced back over her shoulder at Matilda and Reginald.

Mr. Martin leaned forward in his chair, elbow on knees. "If the police were doing their jobs and not in cahoots with the residents, we would have arrests by now and none of this," he waved his arm in a circle, "would be happening."

"Until arrests are made, sir," Christine said, "do you think you and your family might be more comfortable somewhere else?"

"We are not going anywhere!" Mr. Martin sat back in his chair with a thump. His finger stabbed the air. "I will not have the likes of Gary Owen, the Merriweathers, the residents' association, Mark Fraser or those damn bird watchers run me off my property."

Fillingham said, "How about if your wife and children left for a week? You could hold down the fort."

Mrs. Martin reached out to touch her husband's forearm. "Douglas, we could go to the cottage."

He turned to her, her hand slipping from his arm. "I will not allow someone to scare my wife and children away. No one intimidates me or my family." Mr. Martin's chest was heaving with anger.

Mrs. Martin's lips pressed together, and she looked away.

Fillingham said, "I'll radio my sergeant to bring the camera from the station. We don't have to wait for the Identification team to ferry over. We'll take photographs of the dumped materials, and then they can be removed. That should expedite the cleanup of your lawn."

Mrs. Martin harrumphed.

Christine said, "And we'll remove the newspaper articles posted on your fence."

Mr. Martin turned to Christine. "There's more?"

"What do you mean?" Christine asked.

"I ripped them down last night," Mr. Martin said.

"We counted forty postings along the west fence," Christine said.

"Jesus!" Mr. Martin said. "Matilda! Reginald! Come here!"

Mrs. Martin sat up in her chair, quickly stubbing out her cigarette.

The two children slowly walked into the room, positioning themselves between the chairs and the couch near their mother. Matilda looked glumly at the officers and then her father. She was in a maroon-and-white polka dot dress. Reginald was in navy shorts and a short-sleeved white shirt.

Mr. Martin addressed his children. "That damn newspaper article has been glued to our fence again. Run out and take them down. They'll be a fifty-cent piece for whoever does the most."

"All right, Father." The boy sounded excited.

Matilda clasped her arms by the elbows. "Can't you do it?"

Mr. Martin frowned. "Matilda, you need thicker skin. Head out. The both of you."

"Are there people outside?" the girl asked.

Christine stood up. "Actually, sir, we need to photograph the fence for evidence. And we'll take the newsprint down. No need to involve a child."

"I'll get her to help you, then," he said.

"Mr. Martin," Christine said, "I'm not sure it's safe to have a child doing that in this environment." Matilda was only eleven and Reginald eight.

Mr. Martin cocked his head. "It's a good thing I didn't ask your opinion on how to parent my own children."

Christine tightened her hands into fists.

Fillingham stood up. "While we're waiting for the camera, we'll disband the bird watchers. PW Lane and I will stay until another officer relieves us."

Mr. Martin remained in his chair while his wife walked them to the front door. "Thank you," she said.

Christine nodded and the officers exited.

Sensing movement, the birders on the boardwalk started chanting, "Keep our water clean, for birds, nests and trees!"

Chapter 37

"All hands on deck today," Sergeant Bard said as he drove the three officers to the Centre Island police station.

"Who else is in for the press conference, sir?" Christine asked from the back seat beside Cadet Nelson. Fillingham sat in the passenger seat.

Bard replied, "Four of us for day shift. Four more officers will arrive for a split shift from noon to eight. Conference is at two."

Christine wondered if that was sufficient staff. Since the theft from the Parks and Recreation garage four days ago, the political reaction had spread like ripples in a pond. Families were protesting at City Hall, saying that the Island was toxic. The Toronto Ornithological Society had moved from the Martins' place to the ferry docks, picketing with signs saying *Protect the Island Bird Sanctuary* and *Save the Birds*. Operation Pollution staff handed out flyers to families heading to Centreville. Journalists hung around to interview residents and visitors, trying to get an angle on the story.

If there were more reporters, protesters and activists on Toronto Island, there were fewer visitors. Centreville and other attractions such as bike and boat rentals complained that attendance had plummeted since the duck deaths, the break-in at Parks and Recreation and the article in the *National Post* on "Killing an Island, One Duck at a Time."

And now it was coming to a head with a press conference initiated by Superintendent Martin and the Parks and Recreation department. Police expected Island residents past and present, reporters, photographers, environmental activists, wildlife groups and concerned citizens. Christine wondered if eight officers could contain it.

"Coffee's on," Fillingham said after they had arrived at the station.

The four officers sat at the small Formica table. Bard opened a file folder and examined a typed page with the title *Parks and Recreation Press Conference, August 11, 1969*, and below that, *Police Response*.

Things must be serious if her boss had typed up an action plan. Brass must be breathing down his neck, asking for a protocol to be set up beforehand.

Bard clicked a pen and looked at the paper. "Crowd control is important. We can't have speakers being hit with projectiles. I'll station two officers at the Ward's Island dock to check bags and pockets."

Fillingham put his coffee cup down. "You expecting weapons? More like rotten tomatoes and seaweed!"

Bard was not in a joking mood. If things went south, this would reflect on him. "I don't know how radical these groups are. But they'll be sitting cheek by jowl with families and children.

"And Islanders," Christine added. "I bet all six hundred residents will attend."

Nelson asked, "Where is everyone going to fit?"

"Ward's Island field," Bard said. "The Algonquin Community Centre is too small."

"So we are worried about crowd size and behavior when the superintendent speaks, correct?" Christine asked. She took a sip of coffee.

Bard grimaced. "There'll be a shouting match, no doubt. I don't want it to end in a brawl. Tempers are short. And I sure as hell don't want to be explaining why a scuffle happened on my watch. The chief is already up my ass."

Christine said, "We could put a few more officers at the ferry. Have them identify volatile parties. Greet attendees. Let them know we'll be watching. That the press conference will be civil."

Bard nodded. "The rest of us will patrol the Ward's Island field, greeting the Islanders. They're not trying to make trouble for us, but their emotions are riding high. Our presence should be a calming influence." He looked at the paper. "Once people have settled, we'll divide the field into sections for each officer to supervise."

Nelson held her mug in both hands. "What's the press conference about, sir? Is there an announcement?"

Bard said, "Haven't a sod of an idea. My guess is that Parks and Rec want to deal with the bad publicity around the break-in. Talk about how safe the water is. That people can feel secure visiting the Island. But if you ask me," he scratched the back of his head, "this meeting is fanning the flames. All the unhappy parties together in one room, so to speak." He shook his head. "I'll be happy if the superintendent says his peace, gets booed and heckled and everyone goes on their merry way."

Nelson asked, "Will it end like that, sir?"

"Not a hope in hell, Cadet," Bard said.

Sergeant Bard ordered them to patrol the Island, even though it was nine o'clock in the morning. Bard wanted officers to be visible, letting residents know that there would be a police presence today.

Bard would head in the Jeep to the Ward's Island ferry dock and station himself there. Fillingham would pedal to the Parks and Recreation facility at Hanlan's Point. The two female officers would patrol the residential communities. The policewomen would keep a watchful eye on the Martin home to ensure no one picketed or bothered them before the conference.

Bard patted the radio on his hip as he opened the door. "Keep in contact, constables. And keep your wits about you."

Chapter 38

"Wow," Christine said to the officers beside her. "It's busier than Gala Day."

Christine, Fillingham and Nelson had been patrolling the Ward's Island field since noon, greeting people, reminding them to follow the guidelines of peaceful assembly during the press conference.

"What *are* the guidelines?" Nelson had asked as she walked beside Christine and Fillingham.

"Don't strangle anyone," Fillingham suggested.

Christine added, "Hands to yourself."

Christine spotted a little terrier bounding toward them, tail wagging ferociously. "Look who's here for crowd control."

"No jumping up, Lifeguard." Nelson bent to pat the dog's silky head.

"The crowd's getting bigger," Fillingham said. "I'll head to the south side."

It was an hour before the press conference and three hundred people were assembled. Christine wondered how six hundred residents could fit on the field, as well as other attendees. They'd fill the field from the ferry docks on one end to Ward's Island beach on the other.

Continuing her patrol with Nelson and Lifeguard, Christine spotted Judith Purnell with her three children in tow. Already settled at the front by the podium were the Merriweathers, Owens, Conways, Hamiltons, Stines and other Ward Island families. Christine wondered if it was wise to have antagonistic attendees in front of the superintendent.

"Hey."

Christine turned at the familiar male voice. Karl stood, offering her a bouquet of miniature daisies.

"Are these from someone's garden?"

"No," he said. "From the meadow. That's legal, right?"

"As long as they're not from the Martins' yard, I'm good." She took them from him. "Although I'm not sure what to do with them."

Nelson said, "Put them on your hat brim."

Christine said, "Sergeant Bard might not like that. It's not a love-in."

Nelson reached for Christine's hat. "May I?"

Christine unpinned the hat from her hair and handed it over.

After a minute, Nelson returned the hat with the flowers braided on the brim. "The blooms are at the back. Sergeant Bard won't even notice."

Christine spotted another thick ribbon of people entering the field.

"You're busy," Karl said. "Can I see you after the press conference?"

She shook her head. "I'm working late. Probably a double shift."

"Another time." He smiled, deep blue eyes crinkling in his tanned face.

She felt her heart twinge and smiled back. "Sure."

Christine and Nelson walked amongst the crowd, letting Islanders pat Lifeguard, since many knew the terrier. Another boatload of people disembarked from the ferry. Men with cameras and zoom lenses walked with reporters toward the field a hundred feet from the dock. One photographer climbed the tall willow to take an aerial photograph of the crowd.

Christine glanced at her watch. Twenty minutes until press time. A line of people carrying signs passed her, the birding club with the Applegates in the lead. The birding group seemed larger now—fifty people. They continued along the field past the podium, lining up along the eastern boundary of the field, their signs like a row of sails.

"Mrs. Polotov." Christine waved as she spied the older woman arm-in-arm with Mrs. Buckley, two folding chairs slung over a shoulder. "Mrs. Buckley, I have someone who would love to say hi to you."

Nelson whistled for Lifeguard, who came running over, right to Mrs. Buckley for a scratch behind the ears.

The old woman leaned over to pet the dog.

"Mrs. Buckley," Christine said, "Lifeguard is looking for a place to stay. Someone to love her."

Mrs. Buckley looked up. "I haven't had a dog in a long time."

"We could supply you with food, a collar and leash," Christine said. "And she'd still have her day job as a police dog. She wouldn't be in your hair. Home for dinner and a bed."

Nelson added, "Like a boarding house."

Mrs. Buckley laughed. "I might be able to do that."

"Where are you two sitting?" Christine asked.

"We'll be by the back," Mrs. Polotov said, "near the elm tree. Away from the commotion. It'll be easier to head home from there."

The women said their goodbyes, and Christine greeted the next influx of people, saying hello to Sammy, a water taxi driver. Undoubtedly, he'd had less business lately. She hadn't expected to see ferry staff but wasn't surprised to see the managers of Chapel House restaurant and Centreville. Island businesses had been impacted by the hysteria around dead animals and tainted water.

So many people had a stake in this lovely Island, Christine thought. Businesses. Homeowners. Artists. Kayakers. Rowers.

Beach lovers. The amusement park staff. Residents. Mainlanders. Tourists. Even the police. Even herself. She had a stake in being here.

"Greetings, everybody. I'm Sergeant Bard from the Toronto Police Force." Christine's boss held a megaphone to his lips as he addressed the crowd by the community center. "New arrivals, make your way to the back of the field."

Christine stood halfway down the field's expanse, swooshing her arm in a circle to move people toward the baseball diamond. Nelson was twenty feet away, doing the same thing.

"Phil!" Christine said in surprise as she saw him enter the field.

Phil Merton stopped when he heard his name. He wore a baseball cap and sunglasses.

"I'm surprised to see you here," she said.

"It's a free world."

"Are you here to get your equipment? I spoke with your manager, and he confirmed that the equipment was yours. It's at the station. I called your number but couldn't get an answer."

"I shouldn't need the police's permission to take my property." He turned abruptly and disappeared into the crowd.

Christine frowned. She didn't understand Merton. He didn't like his fisheries management job, so he quit. He returned clandestinely to retrieve his equipment, then showed up today for a Parks and Recreation press conference.

"Please settle yourself," Bard said through the megaphone. "The meeting will begin in five minutes."

Christine and Nelson headed over to their boss.

"Sir," Christine said, "should Nelson and I funnel newcomers toward the baseball diamond when the press conference starts?"

"Yes, but stay near the front. I've stationed four officers from 52 Division at the back and south side. I'd prefer it if you, Nelson and Fillingham stayed near the community center. You know the players."

Christine surveyed the swath of people sitting near the front. The birders, including Mr. and Mrs. Applegate. Mark Fraser and ten other members of Operation Pollution in their yellow t-shirts. Gary Owen, Rachel Conway and her partner. The Merriweathers, Stines and Hamiltons. Christine nodded to one of the players from the Osoezes baseball team. The press had hunkered down near the community center, photographers with heavy cameras in their hands.

A rustle from the crowd. A line of people walked toward the community center from the south, like a funeral procession. Mr. Martin led the group, holding Matilda and Reginald by the hands. The children looked at the crowd, wide-eyed. Mrs. Martin walked behind the trio, her eyes glued to the back of her husband's black suit jacket. Behind her was the commissioner of Parks and Recreation, Harry Westmore. She wondered why Westmore hadn't taken the lead. Maybe because he wasn't the principal speaker; Martin was. The group that followed Westmore were Parks and Recreation staff dressed in their work clothes: gardening pants, overalls, canvas work shirts and protective hats. They had the deep tan of outdoor workers. Why had Martin rounded up his employees? They looked like they had been plucked from their shifts and brought to the press conference.

Mr. Martin paused at the front of the community center beside Sergeant Bard. He directed his staff to stand beside him in a line, facing the spectators like security guards. Except they didn't look menacing in their coveralls and canvas work pants, or like they wanted to be there.

Martin released his children's hands, and his wife pulled them to her side as she stood beside the commissioner. Matilda and her mother locked their gaze on Mr. Martin.

Up at the podium, Martin said, "Greetings," into the microphone. "Thank you for joining me here today."

A chorus of boos from the audience.

He paused and scanned the group with his green eyes, taking his time, as if to show he was not intimidated. "I'm Superintendent Douglas Martin. To your right is Commissioner Westmore. On behalf of the Toronto Parks and Recreation division of your municipal government, welcome to Toronto Island."

Another round of boos. Mrs. Martin looked at her husband. Reginald moved closer to his mom. Matilda glared at the crowd. The cameraman walked in front of the podium, filming, before positioning himself near the Parks and Recreation employees.

Martin continued. "I'm heartened to have so many people here today interested in the welfare of Toronto Island, our jewel of Toronto. A jewel in the rough but a diamond all the same."

"She's not for sale!" a male voice yelled out.

The commissioner looked over at Martin, but Martin plowed on confidently. "Toronto Island is a beautiful, city-run archipelago rich with beaches, restaurants, a maze, amusement park and acres of lawns for family picnicking. It's a wonderful, fun, safe place to spend a day, whether you're a mainlander, a resident or tourist from Sweden."

"Safe for who? The ducks?" a woman's voice called out.

Several people laughed. One man yelled, "Right on!"

"Safe for everyone," Mr. Martin said, "including the ducks. That's why I called this conference today. To remind people of the natural attractions of our Island and to clarify the situation with the ducks. First, and this has been widely reported, two ganders were killed by boys trying to steal eggs to sell for pocket money. Not ideal, but we were all young once. Who hasn't thrown a rock at a bird or two in our youth?"

The birdwatchers looked at each other in horror. "We haven't!" a woman yelled.

"Youthful shenanigans," Martin continued. "The boys have been admonished. It won't happen again."

"What about the Centreville ducks?" someone cried.

Martin looked solemn. "That's still under investigation."

A slender man with press credentials around his neck stood up and said, "I heard that the report is in. The stomach contents of the ducks contained alphachloralose."

The camera operator turned his lens on the journalist.

Martin frowned, looking over at the commissioner. Christine looked over at Sergeant Bard. This seemed to be news to everybody.

"I'm not sure where you are getting your information from..." Martin said.

"What's alphachloralose?" asked Gary Owen, standing up.

The reporter said, "It's an anesthetic used by vets."

"Doc Hapler," a voice called out. "Tell us about it."

A few more voices called for Rob, and the vet made his way to the front.

"I don't think we should allow—" Martin said.

Gary Owen handed Rob Hapler a megaphone. "Go ahead," Owen said.

"Okay. I'm Dr. Rob Hapler. A local vet. But I'm not a toxicology expert." He spoke into the megaphone. "Alphachloralose is an anesthetic used to put animals to sleep for non-surgical examinations. I've used it in my practice to check dogs for injuries and set broken legs."

Christine remembered how Lifeguard had staggered after she returned from Centreville, blinking vacantly. Alphachloralose made sense.

Mr. Applegate stood up. "Could it have killed the ducks?"

"In large enough quantities. It depresses breathing."

"Dr. Hapler," Mr. Martin said from the podium microphone, "let's focus the meeting on what we know. The facts. Not fallacies or whispers or leaks." The vet handed the megaphone back to Owen and sat down.

"We know chemicals were stolen from the Parks and Recreation garage," someone yelled.

"Yes, the break-in is a concern," Martin said. "New security protocols have been established. Let me remind you, the garage contained typical household products: engine oil, windshield wiper fluid, baking soda, nitrogen fertilizer that residents," he stabbed his pointer finger at the front rows, "have in your kitchen and sheds. In your unlocked sheds."

"Are you blaming Islanders?" Owen yelled.

"I'm saying that the Parks and Recreation theft is concerning. It's a crime and a violation. I encourage residents to lock their sheds, too. But the purpose was to discredit our division." His tone was amiable, his aplomb unshaken.

Gary Fraser stood up in his yellow Operation Pollution shirt. Owen handed him the megaphone. "Someone is killing animals with vet anesthetic. Insecticides and lawn chemicals have been stolen that can taint our waterways, pets and wildlife—and you don't think this is disturbing?"

"Let's keep the threat in proportion," Martin said. "I can't speak to the anesthetic, but household products are available to anyone at any time. We don't live in fear because of that. Their misuse is not usually a concern."

"It's a concern now," Rachel Conway yelled out.

Christine glanced over at Mrs. Martin. Her arms were around her children, her hands balled into fists. Reginald looked scared, but Matilda looked angry, her glance bouncing between her father and the crowd. Why had Mr. Martin brought his family to such an acrimonious event?

"Then I suggest you follow the practice of Parks and Recreation and lock your sheds," Martin said. "And monitor your neighbor."

Owen yelled, "What does that mean?"

Martin glared at Owen. "My front lawn was dumped with bottles of bleach and household cleaners."

"Are you blaming residents?" Owen asked.

"I'll leave you to your own conclusions," Martin said.

Gary Owen stepped forward until he was six feet from Martin. He turned to the crowd and lifted the megaphone. "Enough of this subterfuge. Superintendent Martin, admit that you," he turned to the commissioner, "and Metro Hall and the members of the Waterfront Improvement Committee are purposefully creating an environment of hysteria."

"Just the opposite," Martin responded. "The purpose of this meeting is to reduce people's concerns and encourage them to visit our lovely, safe island."

Owen continued, "An environment where people feel unsafe to live because you want to evict them and create a sleek, expensive waterfront community."

"That is not the case," Martin said.

"Will you personally profit from a new development on the Island?" Owen asked.

Martin shook his head. "The committee's plan is in the research phase. No contracts have been signed."

"For goodness' sake, Martin," Owen said, stepping so that he was in front of the podium, "be honest for once in your life." He wagged a finger in Martin's face. "Evicting Islanders will put coins in your pocket and the development will be a feather in your cap. Isn't that right, Superintendent?"

Christine scanned the people up front. Commissioner Westmore was frowning, arms crossed. Mrs. Martin had gathered both her children closer. The Parks and Recreation employees' eyes bugged as they watched the argument.

Martin moved out from the podium so he stood in front of Owen. "Back off," he said.

Owen lowered the megaphone, leaned in and screamed, "Admit it!"

In a spurt of movement, Matilda left her mother's side and threw herself around Gary Owen's waist. Owen fell to the ground, megaphone sailing through the air as he tumbled into the group of birders, their cries of alarm ringing the air.

What the heck! Christine moved toward the podium.

Owen scrambled to his feet and launched himself at Martin's waist, like a football player tackling a wide receiver. Martin fell directly backward, taking down a Parks and Recreation employee standing beside him.

Matilda jumped on Owen's back as he pancaked Douglas Martin. Owen got to his knees, sliding the girl off his back.

Martin stood up and grabbed Owen in a headlock.

"Help me, you idiots," Martin said to his shocked employees beside him.

Christine hurried toward the front, but there were a hundred bodies between her and the podium. Her radio squawked.

"10-18," Sergeant Bard's voice over the radio. "All officers to the front."

The crowd was on its feet. Christine was blocked by a phalanx of residents who had converged around Gary Owen, still in Martin's hold. Mr. Merriweather grabbed Martin by one arm while Judith Purnell pulled at the other arm, her mouth twisted with effort. A

Parks and Recreation employee knocked Merriweather away. Christine watched as Sergeant Bard grabbed the employee by the arm.

"Police, move!" Christine yelled as she shouldered her way through people. A circle of residents was joining the shoving match while the line of Parks and Recreation had converged around their boss. Turning to Nelson behind her, Christine instructed, "Hold on to my belt!" She felt the cadet grab her around the waist.

Around twenty people were shoving or hauling others to the ground, and more were joining. Bard shoved Mr. Stine to his knees. Christine got closer and spotted Mrs. Martin squatting, frantically pulling at someone who had fallen underneath people's feet.

Matilda.

Christine and Nelson reached Mrs. Martin and began shoving people away from the girl lying prone on the grass. Mrs. Martin darted in and lifted her daughter in her arms. Matilda clung to her mom.

"Get the boy," Christine commanded Nelson. "Take Mrs. Martin and the children away. I'll get the husband."

Christine watched as Nelson took Mrs. Martin by the elbow and grabbed Reginald, who was still standing by the podium. The four fled behind the community center.

From the back came the chant, "Hell, no! We won't go!" The press meeting had devolved into a protest about Island evictions.

The commissioner retreated up the stairs. Christine saw Rachel Conway follow him, blocking him from taking shelter inside.

Forty people pushed and shoved, a churning, moving animal. There were screams. One person had a bloody nose. The Parks and Recreation staff were fighting fiercely, fighting for their lives in a field full of six hundred residents who hated their boss.

"Cease and desist! Cease and desist," Sergeant Bard yelled over the megaphone.

Good thing Christine had been a wrestler; it helped her efficiently grab people and move them off each other. "Stop, or I'll arrest you right now," she said to the perpetrators. "Move away. Off the field. Onto the path." She had only one set of handcuffs, and she couldn't waste it on one person. She shoved someone toward the docks and moved on to the next scrapping pair. In her peripheral vision, she saw the other officers prying people off each other. One officer dragged someone away in cuffs, dumping him on the grass beside the community center.

Christine turned, looking for Owen and Douglas Martin, and her foot banged against something soft. Geez, a person had fallen. Christine bent over, grabbed the person underneath the armpits and hauled up with all her strength. The woman staggered to her feet, her face white with fear. Were there more people on the ground?

She looked over to her sergeant, frantic, and caught his glance. Pointing to the ground, she signaled people were getting trampled. She crouched lower, feeling the ground with her feet, searching for more people.

"This is Sergeant Bard," the megaphone voice blared. "Toronto Police. Everyone, disperse! Off the field! Anyone who remains will be arrested."

A few people stopped, but the central combatants continued pulling people off each other and launching themselves back into the fray. Christine grabbed a man by the shoulder. He turned, his fist shooting out, hitting her on the chin.

She fell to one knee, stars in front of her eyes. She heard a growl. Blinking, her vision clearing, she saw Lifeguard's jaw clamped around the man's wrist.

"Jesus! Ow!" the man said, shaking his arm. Lifeguard let go, hitting the ground, snarling. The man held his wrist to his chest and turned, disappearing into the crowd.

Christine tried to get up and was bumped back down. A flicker of fear. Holding her arms wide, she got to her feet, bracing herself against the surging people. She had to find Lifeguard too. The dog could get kicked to death under the crowd. And she had gotten no closer to Owen and Martin.

Bang! Bang! Bang!

Everyone froze at the gunshot, a tableau of grappling people.

Sergeant Bard's gun pointed at the sky. "I will shoot anyone who continues to fight," he said, holding the megaphone in his other hand. "Everyone stand up, hands in the air. Move off the field!"

People slowly moved from their frozen position, hands raised.

Bard said, "This is now an unlawful assembly. Everyone is commanded to disband. Residents, go home. I order you to remain in your houses until 6:00 p.m. tonight. Visitors, leave immediately on the ferry or you will be arrested and fined. Officers, have your guns ready. Anyone who disobeys this order will be arrested or shot."

Chapter 39

The eight officers spent the afternoon at Ward's Island's field, ensuring that parties had dispersed. Bard told the Parks and Recreation staff to go home for the day, despite the blustering protest of Douglas Martin.

Bard had not minced words. "Mr. Martin, go home to your family and stay inside. Better yet, head over to the mainland and stay there. I'll view any other action as contempt and have you arrested."

Residents had hurried to their homes, shaken not only by the fighting, but also by the gunshots. As Christine walked people off the field, windmilling her arms, addressing those she knew by name, she wondered how a fight between residents and the Parks and Recreation workers had happened. The locals disagreed with the superintendent's strategy to evict Island residents, but they had no beef with the employees who watered the gardens, mowed the lawns and removed the Island's garbage.

The journalists rushed to catch the first ferry back to the mainland so they could write their articles about the press conference riot for the next deadline. And check into the report about alphachloralose.

Sergeant Bard had phoned the chief of police, reassuring him that the situation was under control and that no new reinforcements were needed.

After people vacated the field, Bard sent officers to patrol the residential communities and the ferry docks for any lingering attendees.

One constable remained at the Martins'. When things seemed quiet, Bard told them they could expand their patrol to Centreville and Centre Island.

At five thirty, Christine and Nelson knocked on the doors of Ward's Island residents, including Rachel Conway and Mrs. Polotov, to let them know the curfew had ended. The two women would notify other residents in their phone tree. Christine was relieved to see Lifeguard in Mrs. Polotov's backyard. The dog had followed the Islander home from the press conference. The officers biked over to Algonquin Island and let homeowners know they could go about their normal activities, then headed back to the station for a dinner break.

Nelson, Fillingham and Christine sat around the kitchen table, exhausted. Sergeant Bard was out back with one of the 52 Division officers who was having a smoke. She hoped her boss stayed there the rest of the shift, tippling from the flask he kept in his jacket pocket.

Bard had been fuming after the press conference. He didn't know who to blame and yelled at any officer within sightline. He would be called into Internal Investigations tomorrow to account for the use of his firearm. And he would have to complete reams of paperwork.

If things remained calm on the Island, Bard and the officers from 52 Division would leave on the eight o'clock ferry. Christine, Fillingham and Nelson would stay until eleven.

Christine grabbed her dinner out of the fridge and sat at the table to have a bite. She had a cheese sandwich, carrots and an orange. Fillingham left to pick up a meal from Chapel House.

Nelson turned to Christine. "Want a glass of lemonade?"

"Sure. Where from?"

"I'll make some."

"With what?" Christine asked.

"I brought lemons and sugar," Nelson said.

"Once you make lemonade for everyone, you'll be doing it the rest of your time here," Christine warned.

Nelson shrugged. "I got seven brothers and sisters. I do this stuff all the time."

After a few minutes of vigorous lemon squeezing and stirring, Nelson poured Christine a glass, then headed out to the backyard with a pitcher to offer Bard and the other officers.

As Christine ate her sandwich, she flipped through a magazine, looking for the same font as the threatening note to the Martins. It soothed her to turn pages. She was still knotted up by the afternoon's fight, her stomach twisted with fear. She had thought someone was going to be trampled to death. It was hard to uncoil from that. She had never heard a gunshot outside of the rifle range. To add insult to injury, her jaw hurt where that man had clipped her. She saw it purpling in the bathroom mirror.

One Parks and Recreation employee told her that Martin had instructed them to protect him at all costs. Their jobs were on the line. This threat had probably contributed to the brawl.

Christine sighed as she reached for another magazine. This summer had been frustrating. The police had no leads, evidence, witnesses or arrests for any of the violations. Who had been harassing the Martins? One Islander? Different Islanders? Who wrote the note? A resident? An ecological protest group? Did Douglas Martin have political enemies?

And what was the point of the theft from the Parks and Recreation shed? Was someone trying to discredit Martin, or did they intend to dump the toxins on the Island or in the water? Christine didn't know how she felt about the journalist's statement that the ducks had died because of an overdose of anesthetic. Who would do that? And why?

The doorbells rang. Christine stood up to greet the visitor.

"Karl," she said, surprised. She went out into the waiting room.

"I've been trying to find you, but—"

"We've been busy herding people off the Island. Monitoring the residential areas."

"That was some conference," he said.

"Remind me not to sign up for the next one," she said.

"Everything under control?"

"For now. What's up?"

"The reporter said that the ducks were given alphachloralose."

Christine gestured for them to sit on the red leather benches. "You're familiar with it?"

He nodded. "I've heard of it. It's used for experiments and wildlife studies. Like when they need to tag animals, deer, birds, wolves."

"Someone was studying the ducks?"

"Could be," he said.

"So, they weren't trying to kill them. They were examining them for scientific purposes?"

"That's my guess. Except they didn't know what they were doing and used a large dose."

"If it was accidental," she said, "why doesn't the researcher come forward and say so?"

"It could have been unsanctioned. Maybe they didn't go through the regular channels," he said.

"Do you know organizations or research labs that use local animals? Who would we talk to about a current study of Island wildlife?"

"I'm not sure what organization to contact, but I have a name for you."

"Who?"

"Phil Merton."

After Karl left, Christine sat back at the kitchen table, dazed. Could Phil have accidentally killed the ducks? And poisoned Lifeguard? Phil, who had no connection to the Islanders or Parks and Recreation. Because he had a family to support, he was always picking up jobs to make ends meet, which was one reason it was taking him so long to finish his thesis paper. His part-time jobs had been in animal and research labs.

Karl said he wouldn't have connected Phil to the waterfowl, except that Phil had disappeared soon after the dead ducks were found in Centreville. And then he quit. And surprisingly showed up today for the press conference.

Christine took a long sip of lemonade. Was there enough evidence to bring Phil in for questioning? She should go out back and talk to Sergeant Bard, even if he was grumpy, and get his opinion.

As she stood up, she bumped the kitchen table with her hip, sending a pile of magazines to the floor. The *Maclean's* magazine fell open at an article about the prime minister, with *PIERRE ELLIOT TRUDEAU* in red block letters.

Christine stared at the bold headline. There! There it was! The red "E" and "T" in the headline. It was the same font, the same crimson color, the same shiny paper as the note that read, *YOURE NEXT.*

Christine grabbed the magazine and ran out the door! "Sergeant Bard!" she bellowed.

Chapter 40

Christine sat on the second-floor bench seat of the ferry, the wind pulling at her hair, the twinkling lights of the skyline like stars.

Nelson and Fillingham leaned over the railing ten feet away, chatting, Fillingham pointing out recognizable buildings on the waterfront.

What a day, Christine thought. It seemed to last forever, from the morning preparations for the press conference, to the free-for-all meeting, to the follow-up patrolling.

And there was the shocking information about Phil Merton. Sergeant Bard thought the link between the duck poisonings and Phil was tenuous. It was coincidental that Phil had quit after the waterfowl had been found, but he would forward Phil's name to the investigators and let them shake that tree. Bard's understated reaction had been discouraging. Karl had seemed so sure.

Additionally, Christine's discovery of the source article for the letters from the threatening note proved unfruitful.

"It's from a *Maclean's* magazine?" Fillingham said after he returned to the station with his dinner.

"Yes!" Christine said.

"Did it have the subscriber's name on the front?"

"No." She paused. "But let's see which Islanders have a subscription."

"Okay," Fillingham had said, unpacking the bag containing steak filet, baked potato and slaw.

"You don't seem enthused," she said.

"Anyone can buy that magazine from a newsstand."

"True," she said. "But the perpetrator likely grabbed a paper at hand."

He forked into the slaw. "Or someone else's."

"What do you mean?"

"You know the Islanders. They borrow stuff from each other. One person has a subscription, two others might read it. Or they place it in the Bridge Boutique."

The boutique was a covered shelf rack by the Algonquin Bridge where Islanders placed things they no longer needed, ranging from tools to clothing, books, plant pots, seedlings to house décor. It was a free store.

"Now," he said, "if we could find a *Maclean's* with the Trudeau article cut out and the subscriber's name on the front, then we have a lead."

So, her leads and conjectures had been shot down, first by Bard, then by Fillingham. The ferry bellowed as it neared the Bay Street docks. Wearily, Christine stood up. She couldn't wait to crawl into bed across from her sleeping sister. This had been a brutal sixteen-hour shift.

Nelson waved as she walked east along Queen's Quay toward her boarding house. Fillingham headed for his car in the parking lot. Unlatching her purse so she could easily access her billy, Christine walked up Bay Street. The sidewalk was sparsely populated. The businesses and offices in Toronto's financial district had long since closed.

A man stood in the middle of the sidewalk ahead, backlit by the streetlights, face in shadow.

Hawk.

She had forgotten about the medicine bag Fillingham found in her bike basket two days ago. It seemed like an eternity ago.

Her quick walk turned into a jog. Hawk walked toward her. Without thinking, she ran into his arms, feeling his broad chest, the pressure of his hands on her back, his unique smell. He felt so strong, so steady. An anchor.

She had thought she would never see him again. And he was here. Tears filled her eyes. Why couldn't she be with this man if she loved him?

He stepped away to look at her.

She smiled, blinking back the tears. His look was so tender that she had to look away.

She moved out of his embrace, wiping her cheek with the edge of her hand. In a shaky voice, she said, "Long day."

He frowned, one hand still touching her arm. "Everything okay?"

She said, "Lots going on at work."

"I read about the ducks. And the break-in."

"Wait until you read tomorrow's paper," she said.

His brows knitted. "What happened?" He scanned around for somewhere to sit. "Here." He pointed to a bench by Union Station.

They sat side by side.

"A shoving match between the residents and the Parks and Recreation staff, goaded by the superintendent."

"Anyone hurt?"

"A few bloody noses. We shut it down before people got trampled, thank goodness." She had to stop herself from touching her sore jaw.

He reached for her hand, and she allowed him to hold it. The man was married, she reminded herself. He belonged to Remi. He had a daughter.

She slid her hand away.

"I wanted to say goodbye." He paused. "I won't be back. At least for a long time."

She closed her eyes for a second, his words stabbing her. When he was in town, she could maintain the fantasy that one day they would be together. But he was married now. And had a family.

She pulled out the medicine bag so the necklace hung outside her blouse. "I didn't see anything in the news." She didn't know if he had taken Layla or met up with the girl.

He nodded. "I didn't either." He looked ahead at the street, the thrum of car tires a steady background noise. "Sometimes children run away from residential schools, even though their home is far away. A hundred miles. The school looks for these children. Some are never found."

She met his glance.

"And the school says nothing," he continued, "to the parents. To the newspapers. To the government. It's like the children are ghosts. Or garbage that the school is happy to be rid of."

Was that what happened here? Did Layla leave and the Crawfords remained silent?

She shook her head. She didn't need to know more. Leaning in, she examined his face, touching his cheek lightly with her hand, and kissed him one last time.

Standing up, she turned and fled west, trying to put as much distance between her and Hawk as she could. With each step, she shoved her love down, down, down, ramming it so low that she would never find it again.

Chapter 41

"This better be a quiet night," Christine said as she pushed open the door of the police station.

Christine had two days off after the press conference and had missed the surge of journalists, photographers and curiosity seekers who had swarmed the Island to satisfy their inquisitiveness about the ongoing Island issues. Interest was further piqued by the publication of the lab report confirming that the ducks' stomach contents and the pink substance found in Centreville were alphachloralose, as the reporter had divulged.

She hoped that an overnight shift would be calm with Islanders, Parks and Recreation staff, media and protesters tucked in their respective beds.

Fillingham followed Christine into the kitchen. As he made coffee, she pulled out her memo book.

"Got any new ideas?" he asked.

She shook her head. "Fresh out."

He placed a coffee in front of her, milky and sweet.

"Thank you," she said. They were trying to be civil. They didn't need to be friends to work together and try to solve Island crime. "Now that it's confirmed that the ducks overdosed on anesthetic, my guess is Phil Merton accidentally killed the ducks. But the investigators haven't been able to track him down. And likely a variety of residents harassed the Martins. Not sure we'll ever get to the bottom of the seaweed incident. And anyone could have pasted together the threatening note because everyone has access to *Maclean's*. And lots of people had motive to break into the Parks and Recreation garage."

Fillingham sat across from her. "So we're not closing any cases tonight?"

"I'm afraid not." She took another sip of her coffee. "Actually, I'm wrong. Nelson made an interesting point about the plant theft. Unless the item is written in the bill of sale, gardens do not necessarily come with the house. She said when farmers sold their homestead, they often dug up the lilac or rose bushes that had been there for fifty years and brought them to their next property."

"So," he said, "the garden theft is not robbery but merely a legal horticultural transfer."

She nodded. "I talked to two realtors. They would agree. It's not nice when gardens are removed, but it's not illegal."

The doorbells rang. Christine looked at her watch. Midnight. Both officers scraped their chairs back and went into the office. Sometimes a tourist dropped by to use the phone to call a water taxi.

"Judith," Christine said as she stood at the counter. "Is everything okay?"

The housekeeper nodded. Her brown hair was up in a loose pony-tail, and she was wearing cotton shorts and a t-shirt. "I forgot my keys here when I cleaned the station today."

"Are you locked out?" Fillingham asked.

Christine levered the counter up to let Judith into the office.

She went to a small box on a shelf. "They're not my house keys. They belong to a couple of my customers."

"You're not cleaning now, are you?" Fillingham asked.

Judith turned to them, keys in hand. "No. I have an early-morning job tomorrow. Kids are asleep. I wasn't. I thought I might as well get the keys now."

Judith looked like she could use more sleep. There were bags under her eyes, and her shoulders slouched in exhaustion.

"How are you doing, Judith?" Christine asked. She remembered watching her pull Martin away from Owen at the press conference, her lips drawn back in a snarl.

"I'm okay." She glanced at Fillingham, then at Christine. "As okay as any other Islander is these days."

"Challenging times," Fillingham said, nodding. "Do you want a drive home?"

She waved him off. "It's the only time I have to myself, my walks back home. It's peaceful. The kids are sleeping."

After the doorbells clanged behind the housekeeper, Christine said, "We should head out. Sarge wants us to do additional patrols of the communities, make sure nothing is happening under the cloak of night. I'll take Ward's and pedal by the Martins. You take Algonquin. Do you want to meet up in two hours at the Ward's Island ferry dock?"

Fillingham agreed, and they headed east together on their bikes from the station. They didn't say much, just enjoyed the breezy summer night, the quiet lapping of the water. The Island at midnight was a calm, peaceful place.

After they parted ways, she decided to check the community center and washrooms first. As she headed through the small enclave of Annex houses, she saw a flash of light in the dark sky to her right.

What was that? Had someone started an illegal fire on the beach?

She sped up, head cocked to spy telltale signs of smoke in the air. Turning sharply, she sped onto the boardwalk.

"FIRE!" a woman's voice screamed from ahead.

There. To her right. A lick of flames. It was coming from a house that faced onto Lake Ontario.

Pushing hard on the pedals, Christine biked swiftly past a row of houses.

Oh no! It was the Martins' house, tendrils of smoke coming from the back, barely discernible in the dim yellow of the boardwalk lights.

She threw her bike down on the adjacent lot and pawed at her radio on her belt. "Dispatch. This is PW Lane. 52-25. I have a 10-70. Fire. I repeat. 10-70. Sixty-eight Lakeshore Avenue."

"10-4. 52-25. Fire Services notified."

"Dispatch, this is PC Fillingham. 52-25. Responding to 10-70 call at 68 Lakeshore. Over."

Christine didn't wait to hear the rest. She ran around the outer fence. The back of the house was lit by sporadic licks of red and orange light.

She ran back to the front of the house. Two people were standing on the boardwalk in pajamas and robes. It was the Mackeys from next store: George, a firefighter, and his wife Alice.

"Where's the fire department?" George asked.

"They're on their way," Christine said. "Are the Martins inside?"

"We don't know," Alice said.

"George and Alice, can you knock on the doors of everyone in the next five houses?" Christine commanded, arm gesturing eastward. "Get everybody out. Find a common meeting point thirty feet away from the houses. Account for everyone. You know the drill."

"Let me know when fire gets here," George said. "I'll lend a hand."

As the Mackeys hurried to their neighbors, Christine flung open the Martins' gate and ran inside the front yard. She could feel the heat from the fire.

"Mr. Martin! Mrs. Martin!" she screamed. She ran to the front door and touched the wood with her palm. It was warm but not hot.

She banged on with a fist. "Fire! Everyone out! Come out the front door."

Her basic fire training at the police academy had taught her that opening a door or breaking a window allowed oxygen in, accelerating and spreading the fire. But what if the family was inside?

Fillingham appeared beside her. "George is going to spray the back of the Martins' house with his hose over the fence. He's going to wet his walls and roof too to prevent spread. Alice is getting people out of their homes."

Christine looked for a faucet along the front of the Martin house while Fillingham banged on the front door. Islanders drew water from the lake for their gardens, dishwashing and showering. Their drinking water came from the water treatment plant.

"I can't find a water tap. It must be in the backyard," she told Fillingham. "Should we go in?" She pointed to the door.

"If they're home, they're probably upstairs in bed." The two officers backed up, looking up at the second-floor window above the porch. It was open, blocked by an insect screen. It was big enough for an adult to go through.

"Haul me up to the porch roof," he said. "I'll check the second floor." He pulled out a handkerchief from his pockets and wrapped it around his nose and mouth.

"Let's wait for Fire Services," she said.

He shook his head. "At night, it's volunteers. It takes longer for everyone to gather. They might not be here for twenty minutes."

"Let's talk to George," she said.

Fillingham said, "He's busy trying to smother the fire. Let him do that. He knows what he's doing. Lean down," he commanded. "I'm going to sit on your shoulders, then I'll stand. Can you hold me?"

She nodded, fear clutching her throat. Fillingham. Mrs. Martin. The children. Every second ticked away.

She kneeled and with a grunt lifted Fillingham onto her shoulders. She staggered for a second, then righted herself. Quickly, she could feel him stand, his heels digging into her shoulders, then release as he sprang onto the porch roof.

She backed up to watch him. He jabbed at the screen with his elbow, tearing it, then disappeared into the room.

Christine ran out to the boardwalk. A group of thirty or more Islanders had gathered at a meeting place five houses down. A few other residents were spraying their houses, the water droplets illuminated in the light from the boardwalk lampposts.

"Anyone have a ladder?" Christine yelled.

"I do," a man said.

"Bring it!" she yelled.

Christine placed the ladder against the porch roof.

"Where's the firemen?" the neighbor with the ladder said.

"I don't know," she replied. She grabbed a tablecloth from the front porch table, wrapped it around her mouth and nose and climbed up the ladder. She crawled onto the porch roof, hoping it would take her weight.

Small trails of gray smoke were trickling out the open window.

Fillingham had to get out. Now. Smoke was toxic. It would kill you before the flames ever reached you.

"Fillingham!" she yelled. No response. She stepped through the window, immediately overcome, and began coughing. Sliding to the floor on her belly, she felt around.

Her elbow banged against something hard. She groped it. It was hard and rectangular. A bed leg. She touched the top of the bed, sliding her hand across its expanse. It felt like a double bed. Empty. This must be Mr. and Mrs. Martin's bedroom.

"Fillingham, get out!" she screamed. *Where was he?*

She could smell things burning: wood, fabric, plastic. And crackling sounds. She tried to breathe shallowly, only through her mouth. Trying to visualize the smoky room in her head, she slid away from the bed. Her right hand banged against something flat. Furniture. A clothes bureau. She felt the round handle knobs.

Pushing herself deeper into the room, she gave herself ten seconds before she would have to come out. She was coughing and coughing, every breath burning.

There. Something solid but soft. Someone's leg. She grabbed the leg and it moved, trying to wiggle away. Clamping a hand around the ankle, she dragged it backward with her toward the window, although she couldn't see now and was disorientated. She banged her foot against a wall, turning to feel behind her for the window ledge.

There! The window.

Christine crouched, perched on the windowsill, one hand on the person's ankle, the other grabbing the waist, and with a violent yank dragged the person up and out the window, onto the porch roof.

Fillingham!

He rolled from her grasp, the momentum taking him down the tiles and over the edge.

"Geoffrey!" she screamed.

She ran over to see him crouching on the grass, two men holding his elbows.

Thank goodness. The neighbors had caught him, or at least braced his fall. Coughing, she ran down the ladder.

"Did you see anyone?" she asked, crouching in front of him.

He slid down his handkerchief, sooty with smoke, as was the rest of his face. "I got as far as the door to the room. It was hot. I couldn't feel anyone in the room. They must have gone into the other bedroom or downstairs."

"The kids' room must be in the back," she said. With the fire. She thought of Matilda, the light in her eyes as they crossed the finish line of the three-legged race, of the bronze medal clutched in Reginald's hand.

A siren wailed. It was the fire engine. They were finally here, parked in the empty lot beside the Martins, flashing lights strobing the house with white and red light.

A fireman came into the front yard. It was Samuel Fairmont, the owner of Clergy House.

Fillingham stood up. "The front door is warm. We didn't want to risk opening it, so we entered the second floor from the porch roof. We didn't find anyone in the south bedroom. There's possibly two adults and two children in the house."

Fairmont barked orders to the team. They were volunteers but looked organized. Fire was the enemy on the Island with its wood houses, floating cottonwood and illegal fires.

"Any of the neighbors know if the Martins were home?" Fairmont asked.

Fillingham shook his head. "No one talks to them. George Mackey is the next-door neighbor. Grab him if you need more help."

"What can we do?" Christine asked Fairmont.

Fairmont said, "Let us tackle the Martins' house. The wind is southwesterly, so sparks could travel next door. Police need to get the houses vacated from here to Withrow Avenue. Allow one person from each household to stay behind to spray their house. The roof, but also the yard. Have people remove laundry lines, towels, outdoor wooden furniture, barbeques and other ignitables. Check in with me to see if the Annex houses behind need to be vacated as well."

For the next hour, Christine ensured people vacated the nine adjacent houses, matching a list of family members with the people in front of her. Rachel Conway took the children across the field where the bulk of Ward's Island houses were and assigned them to families who volunteered to host them for the night.

Before vacating, Christine let the adults retrieve personal items and documents. Passports, photo albums, money, and jewelry were thrown into suitcases and beach bags. Then she checked the inside of each house, closing windows and doors when she left. The owners could not return unless notified by the fire department or police. She suggested they join their children at the host families.

Then she checked in with Fillingham, who was spraying one of the neighboring houses. Two houses didn't have an outdoor water connection, so a line of people formed between the houses and the lake fifty feet away, and residents passed pails of water in a human chain to their yards so volunteers could soak the walls and roofs. Christine helped haul buckets for an hour, side by side with Gary Owen, water slopping on her uniform, the smell of smoke engrained in its wool fabric. As she passed the metal bucket of lake water, her head pulsed with the thought that the Martins were trapped in the fire.

She returned to the Martins' house to check in with the Fire Department. Two large-wattage lights lit the front and back yards, the arced water sprays caught in their light. A fireman was watering the front of the house, the hose draped like a snake across the yard.

"Did they find anybody? Was anybody home?" she yelled to him above the sound of the pulsing water.

He shrugged.

She found George Mackey in the back with the bulk of the volunteer firemen. He said the house was too dangerous to enter. The flames had diminished, but the core of the fire was hot, and the frame was unstable, the house collapsing in on itself.

Mr. and Mrs. Martin hadn't been in their bedroom. They could be out for the evening. Or visiting family on the mainland. But

Christine couldn't get the image of the family lying at the base of the stairs, parents curled protectively around their children's bodies.

Above the shouts and noise of spraying water, Christine heard the drone of an engine, at first loud, then lowering to a rumble as it neared.

She headed out to the boardwalk. "Fillingham!" she shouted. "Harbor police!" She could see the white stern light of the boat as it neared the line of Islanders lowering buckets into the lake.

The wooden boat got as near as it could to the shore without grinding the propeller into the ground. Three men were on board. The engine cut out. Fillingham and Christine waded into the water and held the bow of the boat as two men jumped into the shallow water.

"The volunteer fire chief is Samuel Fairmont," Fillingham explained. "You'll find him and another fireman, George Mackey, at the back of the house."

Two hours later, the Island volunteer fire department had been replaced by men from the Harbor Police and the full-time firefighters who had taxied over on Harbor Police boats.

Christine accompanied one of the Island firemen as he inspected the sodden walls and roofs of the neighboring houses, reassuring homeowners that no sparks or ignition sites had been detected.

At five o'clock in the morning, the gloom of the evening and the smoky air began to clear. The homeowners who had stayed behind to spray their houses were told that the danger was over and that they should find somewhere to bunk for the rest of the night. They would meet with the Fire Department at ten in the morning.

A fire crew would continue to spray and monitor the Martin house. No one would venture inside until later in the morning, when the house had cooled and the forensic fire team arrived.

Several homeowners stayed behind to guard their houses, grabbing a blanket and settling on the boardwalk or the beach in front of their homes.

At seven thirty, two police officers arrived at the Martin house in the patrol car to relieve Christine and Fillingham.

Christine and Fillingham biked silently back to the Centre Island police station, so exhausted they could barely stay on the path. Christine washed up in the bathroom as Fillingham made coffee. She stared at herself in the mirror. Her hat had come off, left somewhere, and her hair was a loose, tangled knot. Black grime was smeared her face, crossed with lines of sweat.

She stared at her hollow eyes in the mirror. Were the Martins dead? That question had pounded her brain all night long as she helped the residents. Would the forensic fire crew find their charred remains?

Had someone, an Islander, set fire to the house and killed the family?

She shook her head and smelled smoke. It was in her hair and her clothes and her skin.

Christine exited the washroom. "I need air," she told Fillingham and bolted outside. She headed to the station's back yard and sat on a picnic bench, staring across the lagoon as her chest heaved.

After a few minutes, she heard the screen door slam. She felt rather than saw Fillingham sit beside her. He nudged her elbow and held out a mug of milky, sweet coffee. Gratefully, she took it from him. Her body trembled, which was strange after being so hot, so sweaty all night long. She pressed both hands around her cup to stop them from shaking.

Dawn was pinking the sky, basking the farm in its glow, turning the wooden fence golden brown and the bales of hay a soft amber.

She gave a big shiver, and Fillingham moved closer so that their legs pressed together.

"When will we know?" she asked.

"The forensic team will investigate as soon as they deem it safe. Probably later today."

"I'll come back then," she said.

He said, "If the Martins were away, someone would have called them about the fire. Someone will know where they are. We'll hear from them soon. We can call the station for updates."

Christine took a sip of coffee, trying to get warm.

Fillingham said, "You threw me out of a second-floor window."

"You're welcome," she said and leaned her head on his shoulder.

Chapter 42

"No one was in the house," Fillingham said over the phone.

Christine grabbed blindly for the kitchen chair and sat down with a thud, receiver in hand.

"Lane? Christine? You still there?"

"Yes. I'm here." Her hand pressed above her heart. She was so relieved.

The fatigue from last night weighed heavy on her. Fillingham had dropped her off at her apartment at eight this morning, in time for her to see her siblings head out to camp, Wayne to baseball camp at Christie Pits and Donna to the community center camp. Phyllis had already left for her day shift at Records.

After a shower, Christine had slept four restless hours before rising to put the kettle on a few minutes ago. "I'm so glad the kids weren't in the house. That the Martins weren't there."

"Sarge said the family is in Detroit." He paused. "And there is evidence of an accelerant used at the back door. Looks like arson. Although I don't know if that's official."

She took a few seconds to absorb this information. "What's happening today?" She and Fillingham were scheduled for the afternoon shift.

"Let's meet an hour before shift," Fillingham said. "Sergeant Bard won't let us come in early. He wants us to be fresh and rested from last night. But we could have an ice cream in Centreville before work."

"You've been talking to Nelson," Christine said, smiling. Nelson often purchased a cone if they were patrolling the amusement park.

"She's going to meet us, too. Two o'clock."

Christine said goodbye and hurried to get ready. She would have to leave shortly to get the Centre Island ferry on time.

Nelson was sitting at a picnic table in the food area of Centreville, licking a double scoop, when Christine arrived.

"Chocolate and vanilla?" Christine asked.

Nelson's eyes widened. "Chocolate *fudge* and vanilla."

"I stand corrected," Christine said. She scanned the area.

"He's going to get fried chicken," Nelson said. She licked the top vanilla scoop. "So, the fire last night! Are you two heroes?"

"Why do you say that?" Christine asked.

"PC Fillingham said you went into the house to see if anyone was inside. You got everyone out of the neighboring houses and made sure they were sprayed down and kept safe." She sighed, shoulders lowering. "I wish I was there."

Christine regarded Nelson steadily from across the picnic table. "Honestly, Cadet Nelson, it was terrifying. We didn't know if the family was trapped inside. Or if other houses would catch fire. If people's homes and possessions would be destroyed."

Nelson look chastened.

"Everyone helped," Christine explained. "Residents took the evacuated families into their homes. Carried people's important possessions to safety. Sprayed down the homes. It's the neighbors who are the heroes."

Fillingham came over and placed a plastic basket of fried chicken and fries in front of each of them.

"Wow!" Nelson said. "Thank you!"

"You don't have to buy our food," Christine demurred.

He sat beside Nelson, across from Christine. "Did you eat anything before you left your place?"

"No."

"Did you bring lunch? Dinner?"

Normally, Christine brought a sandwich and an apple, or leftover spaghetti, but she had been rushed. "I have something."

"What? An apple?"

Christine grimaced as she nodded. He knew her too well.

Nelson said, "She's trying to say thank you."

Christine picked up the plastic fork. "Thank you, Fillingham."

They were quiet for a minute as they chewed, listening to the excited screams of the children on the rides, smelling the aromas of popcorn, pizza and fried food.

"You eat fast," he said as the cadet quickly finished her ice cream and picked up a chicken thigh.

"I have four brothers and three sisters. First come, first served."

"All right," Fillingham said, "let's chat about the newest addition to our crime list: the fire at 68 Lakeshore!"

"We're not really the investigators," Nelson said, "right? There are the investigators from 52 Division. And the forensic fire team."

"True," Fillingham said, wiping greasy fingers with a serviette, "but Island police usually do a better job."

"That's why you got commendations, right?" Nelson said, eyebrows raised. "You solved the case in Yorkville."

"Darn tooting," he replied.

"Do you think that the note, *YOURE NEXT,* is from the person who set the fire?" Christine asked.

"Could be," Fillingham said. "Doesn't have to be."

Nelson forked a French fry. "The fire is a different type of crime than the note. To light someone's home on fire with the people in it, that's pure hatred."

Christine said, "I don't believe an Islander would knowingly hurt the family, especially the children."

Nelson said, "Maybe they knew the house was empty. They checked first."

Christine nodded. "Who hates them enough to burn down their house?"

"Gary Owen?" Fillingham postulated.

"The Merriweathers?" Christine added.

Fillingham said, "The Applegates? The Toronto birding clubs?"

Christine added, "Judith Purnell," She thought for a moment. "She was the last person I saw before the fire." Come to think of it, Christine hadn't seen Judith at the fire. She wasn't helping with the families or hauling water. Did Judith snap after being fired by Martin, exhausted by trying to feed her family and being ostracized by the community?

Fillingham said, "And the families Douglas Martin threatened to cut their electricity: the Munros, Brines and Hamiltons."

Christine grimaced. "I still don't think it was an Islander. Judith and the Ward's Island families hate Martin. But they know the danger of fire. How easily it spreads on the Island. They wouldn't risk harming other people, even if they knew the Martin house was empty that night."

Nelson put her chicken thigh down. "How about the ecological groups? That guy Fraser from Operation Pollution has a temper."

Fillingham daubed his mouth with a serviette. "So, an outside group is your first suspect choice?"

Christine nodded, then looked at her watch. "We should head to the station."

The officers stood up. Nelson stretched, hands over her head. "I'm glad you guys kissed and made up."

Fillingham glanced over at Christine.

"What do you mean?" Christine said.

Nelson wagged her finger at Christine and Fillingham. "The two of you. You love each other again."

Christine shook her head at Nelson's silliness. "We're back on the same shift, that's all." She turned on her heel and walked away.

Chapter 43

"Stop," Christine said in a low voice to Fillingham biking ahead. "Get off your bike and get down."

The officers laid their bikes on the pathway in the shadow outside the circular lamplight. It was ten o'clock, the last hour of their afternoon shift. They were patrolling Centre Island, looking for visitors to urge onto the last ferry leaving at eleven.

Christine crab-walked over to her partner.

"What's going on?" he whispered.

"Someone's in the maze," she said. The maze was a recent addition to the Island, created with eight-foot-tall cedar trees, dead ends, false trails and two pathways to the center. Christine had visited it last summer with her siblings. Christine had wandered around the cedar paths, never finding the middle, despite Donna doing so with ease.

"Okay." Fillingham's tone was hesitant. Tourists and locals were often in the maze.

"They're carrying something," she said, leaning close to his ear.

"It's probably teenagers," he whispered back, "with a case of beer."

They waited, ears strained for youthful laughter and screams.

Christine pointed toward the back of the maze, and they jogged over, backs hunched, keeping to the shadows. They crouched against the ten-foot metal fence that surrounded the maze. The fence also wound inside the maze, positioned behind the cedars so that visitors didn't push their way through branches to take shortcuts.

"I don't hear anything," he said. "Teenagers are loud."

"I know," she said. "Run along the north side. I'll take the south. Meet at the entrance in five minutes."

She walked along the fence, peering into the maze, seeing nothing but trees and dark shadows in between. Swiveling the other way, she spotted a vehicle off to the side of the entrance. Not a vehicle...it was smaller than a car. A rented quadricycle? She moved closer, cedar branches poking her uniform.

A golf cart. Someone had driven it to the maze. Why? The only organizations with golf carts were yacht clubs, the Chapel House restaurant, the school, the filtration plant and the Parks and Recreation department. Why would staff be at the maze in the dark?

She heard a clanging sound inside the maze. She creeped closer to the entrance. For a second, she aimed her flashlight beam at the back of the golf cart. There were jugs, containers and bottles in the back compartment. Windshield wiper fluid? Car oil?

Was someone inside the maze with chemicals? Could the metallic clink be the sound of gasoline cans banging together? Was this the arsonist who burned down the Martins' house?

She ran to the front of the maze and spotted Fillingham along its far side. She squatted beside him.

"I think someone's inside with combustibles," she said. The cedar trees would go up in seconds. It might even light the grass and spread to the nearby washrooms. "There's a golf cart out front with containers."

"What? Did you see anyone?" he asked.

"I heard a metallic sound, two things clanking inside the maze."

"Let's go into the maze, quietly. If we announce 'police,' we'll spook him, and we'll go up in flames. I'll go in the right side. You go in the left. No flashlight. Let's surprise him."

She entered the maze through the left path, keeping to one side, her hands sliding along the soft needles of the cedars. It got darker the farther she went in. As she turned a corner, her shoe hit something. She got on one knee, barely able to make out the shape. A bottle of insecticide; she could make out the aphid on the front. A bottle of weed killer was beside it.

Were these the items stolen from the Parks and Recreation garage? Why were they here? Was the thief dumping them in the maze right now? Why?

Christine continued onward, barely able to see in front of her now, her palm touching the trees as if sliding along a wall.

A cough. Followed by a second cough. Was someone nearby?

"Toronto Police," Fillingham yelled suddenly from inside the maze. "Halt!"

"What's going on?" Christine called out.

She heard feet running. "I don't see anyone. Fillingham, where are you?"

Fillingham said, "He's run. I've gone the wrong way."

Christine lunged into the space between cedar trees and grabbed on to the fence. She scrabbled to the top, branches scratching as she scanned the maze. It was dark, but she could make out the lighter brown of the pathways. Clinging to the fence with one hand, she pulled her flashlight out of her purse.

The beam ricocheted around the trees. "I can't see anyone," she yelled. Her beam paused on a pair of large tins. Paint? More items from the garage theft. She caught a flash of someone moving and aimed her beam. It was Fillingham, returning to the entrance.

"I'm coming," she yelled, sliding quickly down the fence, wincing as a branch poked her face.

Flashlight on, she made her way back to the entrance, going in one dead end but finding her way to the front.

Fillingham stood at the entrance, head swiveling. "Did you see him?"

"No," she said. "I didn't see anyone. I found weed killer and insecticide."

Fillingham ran to look around one side of the maze. Christine ran over to look at the other. They met back at the front. "I found antifreeze and engine oil," he said.

"The golf cart is gone!" she said, pointing to the place where it had been parked.

"It's our guy! Get your bike!"

Did he mean the arsonist or the thief? They ran back down the path to the grassy area where they had left their bicycles.

"Where's he gone?" Fillingham said.

"Who has golf carts?" she asked him.

"Lots of places. What did it look like?"

"I don't know. It was a dark color. Had a canopy. A carrier compartment in the back."

"Any logo on it?" he asked.

"I couldn't tell," she answered. "Did you see someone? Is it a man? Tall? Short?"

He shook his head. "A blur in the dark. But taller rather than shorter. Probably a man."

They started biking.

"He coughed," Christine said.

"What?" Fillingham looked at her.

"He coughed. Twice. It sounded like a man."

"From the way he coughed?"

She froze and stopped pedaling.

"What?" he demanded. "What are you thinking?"

"It's Mallory. Ollie Mallory. I recognize the cough."

Fillingham said, "Why would Mallory be placing paint tins in the maze?"

"I don't know," Christine replied. "But Parks and Rec use golf carts. He could be heading back to the garage."

"Let's go in behind the facility so he doesn't see us," he said. He turned his bike around and headed north.

They didn't talk as they sped along the trail bordering the inner harbor with its spectacular view of the Toronto skyline.

Was the suspect Mallory? Lots of people contracted summer colds and coughs. Why had Christine instantly thought of him? She remembered his wan complexion, thin shoulders, uneven gait. He seemed sick. His deep cough sounded like a lung infection.

Why would he be dumping garden chemicals? Christine thought, echoing her partner's question. Did he take them from the garage—his own workplace?

She kept an ear out for the sound of the golf cart, but she only heard the whirr of their bike tires, the crunch of gravel and the occasional chirp of birds settling for the night. The wind whipped her face lightly, cooling her because her heart was racing, her thoughts swirling. Was Mallory the thief? The arsonist? Was he dumping chemicals in the maze or trying to set it on fire? Did he hate his boss? Was this what this was all about? Animosity toward Douglas Martin?

They reached the north fence that bordered the back of the Parks and Recreation facility. Fillingham was ahead. He put a finger to his lips, gesturing for quiet. They gently laid their bikes on the ground. The fence was shorter than the one in the maze, and Christine and Fillingham climbed over it easily, or as easily as she could in a skirt.

Crouching, they jogged toward the larger buildings, including the garage that had been vandalized.

The driveway was lit by two lights, one on a telegraph pole near the front gate and the other affixed to the front of the large garage. Staying in the shadows, the two officers slid along the building walls, getting closer to the gate.

Fillingham's arm stuck out straight to halt her. "I see a golf cart. Parked in front of the garage."

Christine leaned out from behind Fillingham to look.

"Is that it?" he asked.

"It could be," she said.

"So he's left."

"Or inside. Or somewhere on the premises," she said.

"He knows we're on to him. He'd want to get out of here. Except that he wouldn't take the ferry home. Staff would recognize him."

"As would a water taxi driver," she said. She added, "He could walk to Centre Island, where there are more visitors...try to get lost in the crowd. We could check there," she said.

"If this is planned, he may have a boat to take him back to the mainland. Let's follow the lagoon, see if we can spot him by Hanlan's Bay."

They jogged down the driveway to the front gate and followed the road that led to the water filtration plant.

"He can't have left a boat here," Christine said. The filtration plant was bordered by a cement wall, bare of docking rings.

"Let's check north," he said, "where the American boats are moored. Lots of places to keep a watercraft. We'll have to run around Trout Pond then make our way back to the lagoon."

He sprinted ahead of her, and she let him go, trying to keep him in her sights. She wasn't a fast runner, but she was steady. They rounded Trout Lake. Fillingham darted across the grass, disappearing behind a trio of tall evergreens. She caught up with him at the water's edge, chest heaving with exertion.

"I think I see him," he said, pointing to a gray smudge coming out from behind Hanlan's Island in the middle of the bay. "He's in a kayak." He clamped a hand on her shoulder. "Follow him. Run along the inside of the bay. See if he goes into Blockhouse Bay toward the city."

"Where are you going?"

"I'm going to find us a boat. Stop at the washrooms and look for me by the water. If you don't see me, then wait by the ferries, east side."

Fillingham took off. Christine jogged beside the water's edge, trying to keep the kayak in sight. It was so low to the water that in the dark it seemed part of the water, like a mirage.

She wondered if the person could see her, crouching along the shoreline, in and out of the shadows, keeping pace. Was that person even their suspect? It could be an Islander out for a night paddle.

The kayaker glided in and out of darkness, melding with the inky black of the bay. The night was dark, moonless, with the occasional light from a marina, boat or roadway lamp. A couple of times she lost sight of the paddler, then spotted the gray blur moving north along the flat water.

When she got parallel to the washrooms, she stopped and kneeled by the side of the lagoon. "Fillingham," she called, her voice low so it wouldn't carry over the water. Voices could be heard from the

Toronto Island Yacht Club, patrons having a drink on the front deck of the clubhouse.

The kayaker continued through Blockhouse Bay toward the Inner Harbor. He must be docking on the mainland. The person wasn't an Islander, then. They were escaping back to their city home to sleep. She could see that the paddler wore a dark sweatshirt and cap, the face in shadow.

She called Fillingham's name one more time, then headed north toward the Hanlan's Point ferry dock, trying to keep hidden from the kayaker behind a thick grove of trees.

As she neared the dock, she wondered what to do if she didn't see Fillingham. The kayaker was steadily paddling through the narrow bay into the Inner Harbor, the nose of the kayak pointing toward the cargo docks. She went to the water's edge, crouching as she called her partner's name, then standing tall to scan the bay for him, praying that the kayaker didn't turn around. Something soft brushed her leg, and she leaped away.

"Lifeguard," she whispered. The dog came over, tail wagging, licking her outstretched hand.

"Hey girl," she said softly, "you need to go back. Go home. To the station. To Mrs. Buckley's. Home!" She placed the dog away from her and gestured with her arms. "Shoo."

The dog sat down beside her.

"I'm here." Fillingham's voice.

She kneeled at the water's edge. "Where?" she asked. Below her was dark, inky water.

"To your right."

She walked south toward Fillingham's voice and spotted him in a rowboat.

"Is that a dog?" he said, voice low.

"It's Lifeguard. She must have followed me here."

"Let's pray she doesn't bark," he said. "Get parallel to me, then jump in."

"You're three feet below me. How do I jump in without tipping the boat?"

"Carefully."

She sat on the concrete edge, legs overhanging the water.

"I'll put my weight in the back behind the second seat," Fillingham instructed. "Dangle your legs and try to see if you can sit or fall on the middle of the front seat. Keep your weight in the center of the boat.

"For goodness' sakes."

"Hurry. The kayak's out of view." He continued, "I'm moving to the back. The oars are out of your way."

She wasn't a skilled boater or swimmer. And probably not adept at leaping into a boat, either.

"Hurry!" he hissed.

She called out, "One, two, three," then dropped into the boat.

She landed a bit off center, half on and off the front bench. Fillingham dived to the other side to keep the rowboat from capsizing. She clutched the bench to stabilize. Fillingham grabbed the oars, and she maneuvered herself into a sitting position.

"Look forward. Navigate for me. I face backward when I row." The boat pushed forward as he stabbed the oars into the water.

A splash beside them.

Christine turned. "Was that a fish?" It must have been big.

"Geez, it's the damn dog," he said.

"Lifeguard!" she said, her voice too loud. Did the dog know how to swim?

"She's following us," he said.

Christine twisted in her seat to see a shape thrashing in the water behind them. "Pick her up. She's going to drown. She'll follow us to the city."

Fillingham scooped the dog out of the water with a few choice words.

"I'll take her. Row!" she said as she grabbed the soaked dog and plopped her between her legs. "Head toward two o'clock. That's where I last saw him." They needed to get out of Blockhouse Bay into the Harbor where the city lights would help them spot the boater.

After a minute of frenetic rowing, their bow nudged into the Inner Harbor. "There. I see him. One o'clock," she said. She could feel the boat turn slightly right.

"Where's he going?" he asked, panting between each heave of the oars.

"The shipping docks, west of the ferry docks," she hazarded.

They didn't talk for a few minutes, Fillingham focusing on rowing. Christine watched the eggbeater motion of the kayaker's oars, her hands around Lifeguard. The dog had shaken the water off her fur and was sitting contently in the bow between Christine's knees.

"We're closing the gap," she said. The kayaker had stopped paddling several times as if exhausted, arched back bent low over the kayak.

He wasn't well, Christine thought again. It must be Mallory.

"Get as close as we can, then I'll call out to him," she said.

They were twenty feet behind the kayaker, halfway between the Island and the mainland.

"Mallory!" Christine called. "It's PW Lane. Toronto Police. Stop the boat." She clicked on her flashlight, first illuminating the officers in the boat, and then aiming the beam at the kayak.

The paddler had jumped when Christine yelled, jerking to look over his shoulder at them. He stabbed his paddle into the water, pushing hard for a minute. Immediately, Fillingham started rowing.

After a minute, the rowboat was catching up. The kayaker looked back over his shoulder.

It was Mallory. Christine recognized the grizzled, unshaven face, the sallow complexion, the thin frame.

Mallory stopped paddling. "Stop!" he shouted. "Stop where you are!"

Fillingham paused rowing, angling the boat sideways so he could see Mallory.

"Don't come any closer," Mallory yelled, "or I'll jump in. I can't swim." He coughed, a long chain of hacks.

"Okay, Mr. Mallory. No problem," Christine said as they floated fifteen feet away from the kayak. "We just want to talk."

Mallory's hands clutched the paddle.

"Mr. Mallory," Lane began. "Tell us about tonight."

The watercraft floated parallel to each other, their bows facing the city.

"We saw you in the maze," she said. "You left behind cans of paint and weed killer."

Mallory's lips pressed together tightly.

"Were you going to set the maze on fire?" Fillingham asked. He had turned around in his seat to face the kayak.

"Of course not," Mallory protested, arms jerking the paddle toward him.

"Then why leave the liquids in the maze?" she said. "That's not safe for others."

"That's right!" Mallory responded. "They aren't safe."

"What do mean?" Fillingham asked.

Mallory looked away from the officers and stared ahead at the downtown buildings. "I'm dying." Another string of coughing.

Christine glanced back at Fillingham.

"I don't understand," Christine said. The dog jumped over her seat and went to Fillingham.

"The fertilizer, insecticides, weed killers, engine oil," Mallory said. "I've been breathing their fumes for forty years as a Parks and Rec employee. Do you hear my lungs? They're done."

"You think your lungs have been damaged by these chemicals?" Fillingham asked.

Mallory nodded. "And the rest of me. I'm peeing blood, for God's sake."

"Have you seen a doctor?" Fillingham asked.

"Too late," the older man said. "They can't help. The cancer's everywhere. I got a couple of months. Tops."

They sat in silence, the water gently rocking their boats in the soft night breeze.

Christine motioned for Fillingham to paddle them closer so she could see Mallory's face. They pulled up beside the kayak. "Mr. Mallory, why put the chemicals in the maze?"

She could see Mallory now, his sweaty face bathed in the city's light, the hollowed-out eyes, the prominent cheekbones.

"I wasn't trying to hurt anyone. I want people to know that they make you sick," Mallory explained. "That the stuff in mechanic's garages, gardening centers, farms, in every Parks and Recreation facility is killing people. From the inside out." He coughed again. "I thought with more attention, from the newspapers, from the anti-pollution groups, the birders, it would force Parks and Recreation to change. To think about what they do and what they use."

"Did you inform your supervisor of your concerns?" Christine asked. They were side by side with Mallory's boat. Fillingham had one oar touching the kayak to keep them together.

Mallory snorted. "Sure I did. Filled out forms. Talked to my bosses. They said they'd review my concerns. Nothing ever happened." He shook his head. "I know why they won't do anything. It costs money to figure out what's safe and what's not. Plus, the department gets a huge discount on bulk orders of insecticides and weed killers. They won't bite the hand that feeds them."

"Did you call a newspaper or complain to the government?" asked Fillingham.

"I called a reporter once." Mallory said. "They said they would have to use my name in the article. I needed to keep my job. So I hung up."

"Mr. Mallory, did you add anesthetic to bread and leave it out for the ducks to eat?" she asked.

"No!" He shook his head vehemently. "I don't want to hurt anything. Anyone. I want to warn people. Other workers. That the sprays and oils can harm you. Can give you lungs like me."

Fillingham asserted, "You stole the chemicals from the Parks and Recreation garage."

Mallory gave a curt nod.

"Did you light Mr. Martin's house on fire?" she asked.

"God, no!" Mallory answered. "I don't like the man. He cares only about himself. Politics and power. But I wouldn't burn down his house."

"Did you threaten the Martins in any way?" Fillingham asked. "Harass them? Dump rotting fish in their yard? Or seaweed?"

Mallory shook his head emphatically. After a few seconds, he asked, "What happens now?"

Christine looked back at Fillingham. The officers would take Mallory to the Centre Island station. They'd call in a request to have him picked up by a patrol car city side and taken to 52 Division to be charged.

As if reading her mind, Mallory said, "I'll go back and clear out the maze. Take the containers out. No one will be the wiser."

"We have to take you in for the theft," Christine said.

"I...I can't go to jail." He coughed. "I got two, three months left. Let me walk away. I won't come back to the Island, I swear. I'll leave town, head to my brother's out east. I don't want to die, coughing myself to death in a jail cell."

"I wish we could do that," Christine said.

"You can leave," Mallory said, his tone frantic. "Let me paddle away. They'll be no more chemical thefts. No more dumping. Islanders are safe. People won't be scared anymore."

Christine's emotions tumbled together, regret and shame at arresting a dying man, uncertainty about what to do, and fear of getting caught if they let him go.

The rowboat jerked, and Christine could feel the boat angle starboard. She turned to look at her partner. He was rowing them back toward the Island.

"You can blame it on me," Fillingham said.

Christine swiveled in her seat so she was facing the kayak. Mallory was looking at them, blinking as if he couldn't believe his vision. Then he snapped into action, plunging the paddle in the water at a break-neck speed like two windmills heading him north toward freedom.

Chapter 45

"Sorry," Fillingham said as he rowed toward Hanlan's Point Island.

"It's okay," Christine said as she gave a last look at the fleeing Mallory. "It's probably the right thing to do." She slid around in her seat to navigate them to the Island, the dog behind her in the cockpit.

"No, I don't mean about that."

The dog placed her head on Christine's seat, and Christine stroked it.

"I'm sorry for being mad," he said.

Her breath caught. The night had been long. Emotional. The adrenaline was still flowing. She wasn't sure she was ready for this conversation. Their backs faced each other, but she didn't turn around.

"I understand that the real issue was between Julie and me," he said. "It wasn't up to you to tell me about what was bothering Julie. She needed to talk to me. To trust me."

They rowed for a few minutes until the bow entered Blockhouse Bay. Christine stared at the sky above the Island, the faint curtain of twinkling stars, like small diamonds.

"But that's not why I stayed mad." He stopped rowing.

Christine looked over her shoulder. He had turned toward the Island, his blonde hair plastered flat with water and sweat, his eyes a shadowy blue.

Slowly, she swiveled to face him on the bench. The boat floated, rocking gently.

"I realized something undercover." He kept the oar blades in the water. "And it made me mad. So I took it out on you."

Christine's brows knitted in puzzlement.

The boat drifted away from the lights of the Island Yacht Club on Mugg's Island. Fillingham's face was partially in shadow. "I've been a jerk, to you, to people you care about. Hawk. Karl. Because I realized I loved you."

Christine froze, her hands gripping the dog.

"For one minute," he continued, "I thought it might work. I knew we were good together. At least at work. And that we cared. We had each other's backs."

Christine's mouth opened to say something.

Fillingham looked at the water as he swirled the oars in gentle figure eights. "In Yorkville, something relaxed in you. You allowed yourself to have fun. To be fun. To enjoy. And I couldn't get enough. I couldn't wait to come into work and be with you."

They moved into a circle of light from a large boat moored in the bay.

She gazed into Fillingham's eyes. *He loves me.*

He broke eye contact first. "But I knew you couldn't do it. I knew you wouldn't do it. Be with me."

Christine stared at him.

"I think you love me," he continued, "in your way. But for you, that wouldn't be enough."

"What do you mean?" she croaked.

He sighed. "You'd have to meet my family. Talk about trusts and bonds and the wonder of being a Fillingham. They'd ask you what business your dad was in and if your family owned real estate."

He slowly turned his back to her and started rowing. "I don't care about that stuff. If I did, I wouldn't be a police officer. I have my grandfather's inheritance, which makes it easier not to care. But you...." he rowed a few more strokes, "you couldn't hack it. Conversations about art collections, the five types of forks, what private schools our children should attend. The way my older sister would look at you. A policewoman, of all things. And even if we were all-in, even if we loved each other, you'd bail. You'd think you weren't good enough. That you didn't fit." He sighed, pausing his strokes. "And so I asked myself, why start it up? So I didn't. And that made me mad."

They were in the channel, heading toward Lighthouse Pond. "I took it out on you," he said. "Became jealous. Acted like an ass. I'm sorry."

Her body was stiff, frozen with incredulity. He loved her. He thought she loved him. But he concluded they couldn't be together without saying one word to her. As if her opinion didn't matter. As if she had no say or power or influence. Like she was a patsy.

She didn't know whether to scream or cry or punch Fillingham in the face. "Let me off." She turned to face the Island.

Without speaking, he rowed toward the small beach by the lighthouse. When she heard the scratch of sand underneath the hull, she jumped out into the shallow water, soaking her leather shoes, and ran up the beach to the trail, Lifeguard trotting behind her.

Chapter 46

The next day was a short shift turnover for Christine where her schedule switched from afternoons to days. She had come home last night at twelve thirty and was up again at five thirty.

She stood on the second floor of the ferry beside Nelson, hoping the fresh morning breeze would rouse her. Nelson was counting the goslings of the Canada geese trailing beside the boat. Fillingham was not on their shift, thank goodness. He had asked for the day off a while ago. Rumor was he had an interview with the Harbor Police.

Today would give her time and space to consider Fillingham's remarks of last night. That he had loved her and she had loved him but they were over before they had begun.

The partners had said little during the last hour of work last night. They were late; their shift had already ended, and they hadn't signed off with Dispatch. They had missed the last ferry to the mainland. Neither had they picked up Pilkington, who was on the overnight shift. The constable would have to make his own way to the police station from the ferry docks, a twenty-minute walk.

After they retrieved their bikes from the fence by the Parks and Recreation facility, Christine headed to the station. Fillingham would clean up the maze.

Lifeguard kept trotting near her bike wheels, so Christine placed her in the front basket. As she dropped the dog into the plastic carrier, she nuzzled the terrier's head with her own. "I'm going to kill Geoffrey," she whispered into the dog's ear.

Lifeguard licked her hand.

"He loves me," Christine added, looking into the dog's choco-late-brown eyes, the news an electrical jolt to her heart.

When Christine walked into the Centre Island station, Pilkington was sitting in the kitchen, miffed the patrol car hadn't been at the dock to pick him up. After murmuring her apologies, Christine called a water taxi and headed to the dock. She had no idea when Fillingham made it home.

So, today, sleepy, muddled, conflicted, she stared at the green tree line as the ferry approached Centre Island, trying to soothe herself. Things were looking up at work. At least one incident had been resolved. Mallory had confessed to the theft. Not that they would tell anyone. And Christine would check today if the investigators had tracked down Phil Merton.

That left the torching of the Martin house. It had to be an Islander, she thought. But when she remembered how the neighbors had worked through the night to save the houses, including the Martins', it seemed improbable again.

Nelson and Christine organized the office for the first hour, sweeping the floor, updating the logbook, making a few calls. She found the number for 52 Division and made a call to the team investigating the arson.

After introducing herself, she asked, "Can I speak to Investigator Allen?"

The desk duty officer said, "He's not in. Investigator Fenwick is here."

The weasel-eyed, mean one. Christine had met him last summer. She gritted her teeth. "Yes, can I speak with him?"

After a minute, a gruff voice said, "Investigator Fenwick. Who's this?"

"This is PW Lane, Toronto Island Police. I understand you are investigating the arson at 68 Lakeshore."

"Who are you?" he asked.

"PW Lane. Toronto Island police."

"The pain in the ass one?"

"I'm not sure—"

"The tall one."

"Yes."

"What do you want?"

"I want to help with the arson investigation. Give you names of people to interview."

"I have my list," Fenwick said.

"Is Judith Purnell on there? She's a local. How about Ron and Carol Merriweather? They used to live in the home. And Mark Fraser from Operation Pollution. It's a long shot, but the Applegates from the Toronto Ornithological Society. And to be sure, check Gary Owen."

"Are you deaf? I don't need your help. I'm a fuckin' investigator. Not some rube in a skirt biking along the waterways like Mary Poppins."

Her fist clenched.

Nelson looked over at her from her perch at the other desk.

"Sir," Christine said, "local police have information because we patrol here. We know the community. Can we work together?"

"Not in my lifetime." He hung up.

Christine looked at the receiver, which was emitting a dial tone, and placed it back in its base.

Nelson said, "Is this when we solve crimes ourselves?"

Christine gave a wry chuckle. "Yes. Exactly."

The two women were heading out for bike patrol when the phone rang.

It was Sergeant Bard. "You're to meet the Martins at two o'clock at the King Edward Hotel on King Street," he told Christine. "PC Fillingham will meet you there."

"What for, sir?" she asked.

"They want to thank you for trying to save their home. They heard you went inside the house, at grave risk to yourself."

"I don't need a personal thank-you, sir. It's part of our job."

"I didn't ask for your opinion, PW," Bard said. "This is a top-down request. Meet them in the lounge at 14:00 hours. Make sure you're tidied up."

What did that mean? Had her sergeant realized she was wearing her old, slightly stained jacket, since the uniform worn during the fire had so much smoke damage, she had to toss it in the garbage?

"Yes, sir," she managed.

She appreciated that the Martins wanted to thank the police for their efforts on the night of the fire, but the whole Ward's Island community had pitched in. She would make sure that the Martins knew this. Everyone tried to put their house fire out.

Christine headed out on the earlier ferry to give her time to reach the tony King Edward Hotel. As she stood pressed against the railing, inhaling the lake smell from the thrashing engines, she thought about her partner's confession. On the one hand, she was inflamed by his presumption, by the one-sided way he had dealt with their relationship. He had never told her he wanted to be with her. She had no chance to respond. And that was enraging.

The engines throttled down as the ferry approached the dock. Was Fillingham right? Would their relationship have ended in acrimony, suffocated by her insecurity? She had been ridiculed all her life because of her height, unfashionable clothes and poverty. Was her perspective so skewed that she couldn't survive his Forest Hill family? Christine wasn't sure.

As she disembarked, she pushed her thoughts of Fillingham to the back of her mind. If she hustled, she could catch the next streetcar and arrive at the King Edward Hotel early to tuck stray hairs into her chignon and wipe the travel dust from her shoes.

It was a majestic place, Christine thought as she crossed the hotel foyer to the washrooms. She'd only been inside the hotel a few times and never had a room here. It was posh, with a history of serving kings and Hollywood elite.

After she tidied up, she spotted the Martin family sitting around a stone fireplace in the lounge, an overhead fan whirring gently from the towering ceilings. Fillingham was already there, standing beside Mr. Martin.

Mr. and Mrs. Martin sat on a carved wood settee upholstered in burgundy velvet. Matilda and Reginald shared an oversized wing-back chair set at ninety degrees to the settee. Matilda looked at Christine with wide brown eyes as she clutched a mustard-colored teddy bear. Reginald was holding a toy car.

Mr. Martin stood up when he saw Christine and indicated the couch across from them. Christine and Fillingham sat down.

Mrs. Martin looked at the officers with a small smile. She must be happy to be off the Island, even under such terrible circumstances.

Mr. Martin looked surprisingly placid. Christine hadn't been sure if he would respond to the arson as an affront to his ego or as evidence of the lunacy of the people opposing him. She guessed by his calm demeanor that it was the latter.

Christine held her hands in her lap, waiting for the Martins to speak. She hoped the meeting would be brief. If she left shortly, she could meet her siblings after school and take them to the candy store as a special treat. She had seen little of Donna and Wayne this summer, especially with so many afternoon shifts.

Mrs. Martin laid a manicured hand lightly on her husband's knee.

"The two of you were on duty the night of the fire," Mr. Martin said, "and helped to minimize its spread."

Fillingham said, "Scores of people sprayed down homes, removed valuables from houses and hosted families for the night. The Ward's Island residents should receive your thanks."

He coughed. "Nevertheless, I understand you worked alongside the firemen. You have our thanks."

"You're welcome," Christine and Fillingham said in unison.

Mrs. Martin crossed her legs. Today, she was wearing a white skirt with a matching short-sleeved tunic. "I was told you went inside the house to rescue our family, at great risk to yourselves. We are deeply grateful for this heroism."

Fillingham responded, "The best news was that the house was empty and your family safe." He spoke to the Martins about the forensic fire team's analysis. There hadn't been an electrical short or a pan left on the stovetop. The source of the fire had been the back door. The house had ignited rapidly. He began reviewing the points in the forensic report that led to the conclusion of arson.

Christine looked over at the children as her partner spoke about the fire. The girl was staring at them, unsmiling, arms tucked around the teddy bear. Reginald stood up to drive his toy car along the top of the wingback chair. His behavior reminded Christine of Wayne when he was younger. Her brother had loved his cars, trucks and army of plastic soldiers. Reginald rolled the car along Matilda's shoulder, and she swatted him away.

Christine stared at Matilda, who quickly grabbed the teddy bear again. Her right hand was taped with gauze, from the palm around to the top of the hand, bandaged like you do for burns.

Christine stared at the girl, their brown eyes meeting.

It was you.

Christine blinked.

Mrs. Martin looked at Christine, then at Matilda, frowning.

"Mr. Martin," Christine said when Fillingham had finished speaking, "where were you the night of the fire?"

Fillingham looked over at her questioningly. They knew the Martins were in Detroit that night.

Mr. Martin said, "We had gone out of town, thank goodness."

"Where?" Christine asked.

He frowned. "Detroit. I had a meeting and thought the family could use a few days of holiday."

"Your family was with you?" Christine asked.

Mrs. Martin interrupted. "What does it matter? We're safe and sound. Thank you again, PW Lane and PC Fillingham, for your efforts. We won't take any more of your time." She stood up.

"Mr. Martin," Christine continued, "were both your children in Detroit with you?"

His brow furrowed. "Yes. Well, no. Matilda had a girl scout sleepover. Why?"

Christine's head turned to Matilda, who shrank into the ornate blue and silver fabric of the chair.

"Matilda," Christine said, "what happened to your hand?"

Mrs. Martin leaped in front of the chair, blocking Christine's view of her daughter. "Don't answer her!" she yelled.

Mr. Martin stood, lines creasing his forehead. "Barbara!"

Fillingham looked at Christine, eyes widening in comprehension.

"Matilda," Christine said, leaning sideways to make eye contact with the girl, "did you burn your hand? It's okay to tell me the truth. I won't get mad."

Mrs. Martin turned to her daughter. "Shut up, Matilda. Don't say a word! Not one word!"

Mr. Martin roared, "Somebody tell me what the hell is going on!"

Mrs. Martin held out a placating hand to her husband. "Nothing is going on here, Douglas. The officers were leaving."

Christine said, "We have a few questions for Matilda."

"She's not talking to you," Mrs. Martin said. "I forbid it. She's eleven. A minor. I don't give permission."

"Permission to say what?" Mr. Martin demanded, his green eyes bright with rage.

Matilda jumped out of the chair, teddy bear tumbling to the carpet. "I did it!" she screamed, her bandaged hand smacking her chest. "*I* did it. I wrote the note. I wanted us to leave. I hate it there. I hate the kids. The adults. The house. Toronto Island. *I* set the fire." She was crying, two ribbons of tears trailing down her cheeks.

Mr. Martin's jaw hung open, as if he could only absorb part of his daughter's rant. Reginald clutched the back of the chair, toy car in hand, his gaze bouncing from his sister to his father to his mother.

"*I* set the fire," Matilda repeated, "with cottonwood. And I'm glad. We don't have to live there anymore with everyone hating us. Calling us names. Saying we're terrible people. I'm glad the house is burned to the ground. Glad! Glad! Glad!" she shrieked.

They stood frozen as Matilda ran across the hotel foyer and disappeared through the elaborate bronze doors.

Chapter 47

It had taken a while to find Matilda after she ran out of the King Edward Hotel. Christine had yelled for the parents to head west on King Street while she and Fillingham ran east, her partner searching the north side and Christine the south.

Christine had found the girl hiding behind the trash bins of the hotel, curled up against the brick wall, hands over her face.

Christine sat beside her on the pavement, back against the wall.

"Are you going to arrest me?" Matilda sniffed, sliding her hands away from her tear-streaked face, her right hand bandaged.

"No," said Christine.

Matilda's back straightened. "Why not?"

Christine regarded her. "I can't. You're eleven years old. The *Juvenile Delinquent Act* applies to children twelve to seventeen."

Matilda's eyes widened as if unable to believe it.

They sat for a few minutes as the girl's sniffling lessened.

"Tell me about it," Christine said.

Matilda's eyes darted to the police officer. "I...I didn't like it on the Island."

That was an understatement, Christine thought.

"I tried to tell them. My mom. My dad."

"Is that why you made the note?"

Matilda nodded. "I thought it would scare them. Make them leave right away." She swallowed. "But it didn't."

Christine waited.

"And...and...at the press conference, I could see how everyone hated us. Hated my dad. I fell down. I got stepped on. And still my father wouldn't leave."

"Were you on the Brownie trip?"

She nodded. "I pretended to go. My parents dropped me off. At the last minute, I told my Brownie leader I was homesick. My family had already gone to Detroit, but they didn't know that. So I hid until nighttime."

"How did you burn your hand?"

"I had gathered the cottonwood seeds, a whole bunch, in a garbage bag and hid it in the trees. Then I stuffed it behind the screen door and lit it. I...I didn't know it would light so fast. It went in up in a second, all the way to the top." Matilda shuddered at the memory.

"That must have been scary," Christine commented.

"It hurt."

"What happened next?"

"I met my parents at the city ferry docks the next day before they came to get me on the Island. I told them I burned my hand while making a fire for our Brownie roast."

After a few moments, Christine said, "The police will want you to talk to someone, for your family to talk to a social worker or counselor. What you did was extremely dangerous."

"I know," Matilda said, her voice small. "Do you...do you talk to someone?"

Christine said, "I'm lucky to have friends. One of them used to be a social worker, so she's a good listener." She turned to face Matilda. "Bad things happened when I was younger. I felt stuck too. But things change. You get older. There are more options. Things get better."

After a few minutes, Matilda agreed to return to her parents. Christine and Fillingham escorted the family to 52 Division. The officers waited while investigators spoke with the family. No charges were laid, and they were released.

Chapter 48

"As soon as you returned to Island patrol, everything hit the fan," Julie remarked to Christine. The four policewomen, Sarah, Gail, Julie and Christine, were sitting around an oval patio table, eating cake. Pink and blue balloons and streamers arced around the back door and along the wooden fence on both sides of the backyard. Beside Sarah was a pyramid of opened baby presents: pacifiers, blankets, change table, stroller, diapers, onesies, bibs and pajamas.

The women were at the Jack and Jill baby shower for Sarah, hosted by Sarah's parents, Geraldine and Joe Fletcher. The Fletchers had a long backyard, perfect for a Sunday barbeque and outdoor games. A ping-pong table had been hauled out of the garage onto the grass, and four men were playing doubles, loudly protesting points. Three small children kicked balls into a soccer net at the bottom of the yard, supervised by two dads holding beer bottles. On the right, a horseshoe game had been set up on the grass with two metal pegs hammered into the lawn thirty feet apart.

Beside the policewomen were neighbors who had known Sarah growing up. Sarah's social worker colleagues sat around a card table. Ken had invited his police buddies, several with families in tow, and Fillingham.

Fillingham. Yesterday at the Centre Island station, he had told her he was heading over to Mrs. Buckleys' with dog food and a dog bed.

The older Islander had agreed to share custody of Lifeguard with the Island police.

"You're a nice guy," she had told him.

He had stopped in the station waiting room, dog food in one arm, dog bed under the other. "You're just noticing that now?"

"No. I noticed a long time ago."

They paused.

"Are we good?" he asked.

She nodded. "I'm not a coward."

"I didn't think you were," he responded.

"I don't want to feel bad about who I am. My job. My family. Where I live. I don't want to be around people who think I'm wrong." She exhaled. "I'm not wrong."

"I know that," he said. And that was that.

Christine had told her friends before the baby shower that she and Fillingham had made up. They were back as partners. She would act like Fillingham had never mentioned loving her or the obstacles that kept them apart. It was too confusing. And maddening. And sad. If she could wipe that conversation from her mind, she could continue as his partner and friend. And that's why she could be okay that he was here today at the shower.

Christine swallowed her forkful of cake before responding to Julie's comment that trouble seemed to find her. "I didn't cause a duck overdose, chemical theft or arson."

Julie shrugged and then took a sip of Champagne from a fluted glass.

Sarah smiled, hand on the slight bump of her pregnancy. She was dressed in a yellow smock dress, and she looked tanned and happy, surrounded by friends, colleagues and family. "You do seem to sniff out crime."

"You must have seen the newspaper article about the PhD student, Phil Merton," Christine said. "He and another scientist were charged with researching without a permit, causing death to wildlife and possession of an illegal substance."

Gail said, "I heard no charges would be laid in the arson." Her gray eyes looked questioningly at Christine.

"It's confidential," Christine began.

"Ooh," Julie leaned forward. "Pray tell."

"It was a child. Under twelve. No charges can be laid."

"An Island kid?" Julie asked.

Christine paused, then nodded. Matilda had been an Island kid, at least for a month or two.

Sarah looked concerned. "Are they getting the child counseling? That type of behavior is a cry for help."

Christine nodded. She had asked Mrs. Martin if she could drop by and see Matilda next week. The three of them were going to meet at a bakery near the hotel.

"Wow," Julie said as they discussed the arson case, "kids these days. When I was young, my tantrum involved pulling the head off my Barbie doll. Not igniting a house."

Julie turned to Gail. "I bet you blew up a few things in the navy."

Gail snorted a laugh. "I wish. I was land-bound—the medic for sailors going on or off the vessels. Only boys were allowed to play with the ship's big guns."

"Speaking of kids," Sarah said, "I did like the new cadet on Toronto Island. What's her first name?"

Christine said, "Olivia. Olivia Nelson." She smiled. "The girl gets in a bit of trouble, but she's smart. And the Islanders love her."

"I heard someone else loves her too," said Julie, eyes wide as she looked at Christine. The three other women burst into laughter.

"How do you know about that?" Christine asked. She could feel herself blushing. Who else knew Nelson had said they were a couple? Had Nelson confessed to Fillingham?

Gail said, "Nothing wrong with a different kind of love."

Christine said, "And you wonder why my romantic life is in the toilet."

Sarah said, "What happened to Karl?"

Christine shrugged, "He's still around."

Sarah placed a hand on Christine's wrist. "Oh, did you hear that the union and police board are meeting about our request to return to work after pregnancy?"

"That's great," Christine said. She looked at Sarah's bump. "They better talk quickly. You've got what, five months left?"

Sarah smiled. "Due date is February 1st."

"That's 1970!" Julie added. "Can you believe we'll be in a new decade?"

"Christine!" It was Fillingham, waving her over. "Be my partner in horseshoes." He turned to Ken, standing beside him. "She was a high school javelin champion. Got an arm on her."

Ken turned to the table of women. "Gail, Julie, Sarah, anyone dare take on the crack Island duo with me?"

Gail stood up. "I'm in."

"Javelin city finalist," Christine corrected Fillingham. "I'm only a champion at ax-throwing."

He raised his eyebrows skeptically. "Debatable."

"You two go," said Sarah to her friends, arms sweeping upward.

"Lane throws hard," Fillingham said to the crowd around the horseshoe pit. "You better back up."

"I'm likely to ring *you* around the neck," Christine said to a chorus of laughter. Maybe things could be okay between them. Not the same. But okay.

Fillingham handed her a red metal horseshoe. "We're a team, right, Lane?"

Christine took the horseshoe. "We're something," she muttered and followed her partner to the horseshoe pit.

The Christine Lane Mystery Series Books 1-5

Each book in the series is a standalone mystery. Readers can choose to read in chronological order or out of sequence. Ebooks are sold at all the regular online retailers and also via Dianne Scott's website at diannescottauthor.com. Print versions available on Amazon.

**Book 1: *Final Look*
In an island full of intrigue, the best kept secret is a killer's identity.**

Policewoman Christine Lane felt the humiliation like a slap. Transferred to this sleepy island station, she could almost hear her career screeching to a halt.

During a violent protest on the island, a resident is found dead and Christine is hurt. Her boss threatens to sack her for incompetence and she vows to maintain a low profile.

When the homicide leads dry up, Christine is shocked when investigators move on to their next case. She secretly gathers information on suspects, digging up local dirt. When Christine is ambushed, she knows she is closing in on the perpetrator. Can she flush out the murderer before she is shut down for good?

Book 2: *Missing*
A missing student. A dead-end investigation. Can a police officer uncover the truth before the child is lost forever?

When a ten-year old boy goes missing from the Toronto Island school, Policewoman Christine Lane and her partner search every corner of the Island. Three months pass without sign of the boy and Christine assumes he ran away. Or is there something more sinister going on in this idyllic island community?

Book 3: *Lost and Found*
A drug-ridden Village. A missing daughter. An undercover cop way over her head.

Policewoman Christine Lane was accustomed to the easygoing pace of Toronto Island patrol. Then Lane and her officer friends are handed a risky undercover assignment: stamp out the illegal drug trade poisoning the hippie neighborhood of Yorkville Village in downtown Toronto.

Not only is Christine inexperienced in dealing with gangs, bikers and drug dealers, but she's assigned a secret mission to find a missing Village teen. Immersed in subterfuge, Christine desperately searches for the girl while trying to ascertain the heroin pipeline. Can she rescue the teen and expose the drug kingpin before her cover is blown?

Book 4: *Sabotage*
A community in fear. A government in chaos. A saboteur on the loose. Can a police officer hunt down the felon before deeds turn deadly?

Police Woman Christine Lane is content to return to Toronto Island patrol with its idyllic beaches teeming with tourists and friendly locals. When a gaggle of ducks is found poisoned, Lane searches for the perpetrator. Was it a prank by teenagers? Is the lagoon water tainted? Was it a scare tactic to force residents off the island so a lucrative new development could be built?

When an island house is set aflame, Lane worries about the next act of sabotage. Can she untangle the knot of conspiracies before someone gets killed?

Book 5: *Taken*
Publication date: June 2025

Christine Lane's investigation into an old crime on Toronto Island uncovers secrets and scandals from the past. As Christine is stonewalled in her search for answers, she realizes that danger lies closer to home. Can she put a cold case to rest and keep her family safe?

Get Your Free Short Story!

FREE PREQUEL SHORT STORY!

Receive a free short story about Christine Lane and her friends when you sign up for my monthly newsletter where I chat about my books, writing process(lots of coffee!) and other things I am enjoying. Check out my newsletter at my wesbite at diannescottauthor.com

LEAVE A REVIEW

If you enjoyed reading this Christine Lane mystery, I invite you to leave a comment or review at your favorite bookseller. Reviews guide readers to my books and help me expand my audience, so they are much appreciated.

Acknowledgments

I would like to acknowledge the people who support, cheerlead and act as resources for my writing. First, thank you to my writers' group, Leanne Lieberman, Elsie Sze, Ania Szado and Roz Spafford, for your crucial feedback on my manuscript. Your thoughtful comments and ongoing friendship keep me writing the Christine Lane Mystery series.

Thank you to former police officers Kay Burford and Donna Brown for allowing me to ask so many questions. To my extended family, my mother, siblings, in-laws, nieces and nephews, I appreciate your interest in my books. And to my coffee klatch friends who hear regularly about my writing process, thank you for listening. And, of course, I thank my family, Michael, Claire and Matthew, for supporting my creative endeavors.

About the Author

Dianne Scott lives a short ferry ride from Toronto Island, which is the setting of her mystery novels. She is the award-winning author of the Christine Lane Mystery series. The first book, *Final Look*, was a #1 Amazon bestseller, Kobo Emerging Writers Award nominee and winner of the Crime Writers of Canada Arthur Ellis Award. The second book, *Missing*, was a Finalist for the CWC Excellence in Writing Award. *Lost and Found* and *Sabotage* are the third and fourth books in the series.

When Dianne is not writing, she is walking Toronto's neighborhoods, coffee klatching with friends and cuddling her Bichon Poodle. She also teaches literacy skills and is working on her Erne in pickleball. For more information about Dianne, visit her website at diannescottauthor.com

9 781738 262700